Hoping Since Forever

KILTIE JACKSON

Also by Kiltie Jackson...

The Lovestyle Series

A Rock 'n' Roll Lovestyle
An Artisan Lovestyle
An Incidental Lovestyle
A Timeless Lovestyle

The Since Forever Series

Waiting Since Forever
Hoping Since Forever

Standalones

A Snowflake in December
The Prosecco Pact
Love is on the Air

The Bay Series

The Bay of Lost Souls

**Available on Amazon in ebook, Paperback
And Kindle Unlimited.**

DEDICATION

This story is wholeheartedly dedicated to the REAL Sally Edwards who runs the home-based rescue, The ARC – The Ashmore Rescue for Cats.

This amazing woman sees, and deals with, the results of animal cruelty every single day which continually brings her great heartache yet she never turns away from any cat who needs her help.

I could never do what she does and I remain humbled by her, and everyone who works in animal rescue, for the pain they endure daily by trying to help the creatures who don't have a voice of their own.

Thank you.
xxx

ACKNOWLEDGEMENTS

Here we are, once again - another book has been sent out into the world and I have the following wonderful people to thank for making it so:

John Hudspith - my awesome editor who takes each manuscript and turns it into something worth reading.

Berni Stevens - the amazing lady who keeps on producing the most beautiful covers that still take my breath away. This one was no exception.

Mark Fearn - my truly lovely beta-reader who still drops everything when I send him my latest manuscript for his perusal and whose honest feedback means so much.

Zoé-Lee O'Farrell - the most wonderful blog tour organiser who everything into ensuring each blog tours is better than the last and I am eternally grateful to her for all that she does.

All the wonderful bloggers who take the time to read, write up their reviews and share their thoughts on their blogs, on Amazon and across social media. I cannot thank you enough – your efforts are hugely appreciated.

Kym Wood – my best friend 'since forever' and who has always been there for me through so much.

Sue Baker – this gorgeous woman gives so much support to authors and is tireless in producing fantastic Publication Day parties. Thank you. xx

To the members of my FB group, Kiltie Jackson's Books, Bits and Bobs– thank you for all the encouragement you give, for sharing my books to the world and for helping me to laugh on the dark days.

The following wonderful Facebook groups – The Fiction Café, Chick-Lit & Prosecco, TBC – Reviewer Group, especially Helen Boyce who co-ordinates it so beautifully, The Friendly Book Community who live up to their name in every way, Riveting Reads and Vintage Vibes which is so much fun, and Jenny Colgan and More Great Books. These groups share, promote and support all of us authors in these ventures and this one appreciates them greatly.

My family who still insist on reading everything I write.

The Moggy Posse - my bunch of fabulous, furry, feline friends.

Mr Mogs – for just being you. Love you to the end of eternity… and a day!

Till the next time.

xx

ONE

'Oh, that's nice!'

Sally Edwards touched the screen on her tablet to expand the picture she was looking at.

'Hey, Herbert, what do you think of this?'

She tilted the device to show the cat who was curled up tighter than a cinnamon roll by her side and whose interest in deep-turquoise, roll-top baths with pewter claw feet was non-existent.

'Hmm, I'm guessing it's not your thing,' she chuckled, as a wave of happiness flowed over her. Six months and two weeks ago, they wouldn't have been her thing either. For a start off, you would never be able to get one in the door of their tiny, two-bed semi-detached house, never mind fit it in the bathroom which was so small they joked it had a wall-to-wall carpet tile!

Everything had changed, however, on the day she'd had a sudden desire for chocolate. A desire which could not be quashed and had resulted in a quick run down to the little newsagents next to the office where, on impulse, she asked them to throw in a lucky dip for the Euromillions lottery that night. As she was so rarely ever *"In it to win it"*, the ticket was shoved into her purse and forgotten about by the time she was back at her desk.

Sally glanced away from the stylish bathroom to check the time in the corner of the screen. Three o'clock. Her husband, Steve, would just about be signing the paperwork on his new car.

He'd asked her if she'd like to join him but she'd declined. This special moment was all his to savour and enjoy. He'd grown up watching the James Bond movies with his dad and like most boys, he'd dreamt of owning an Aston Martin ever since. Now his dream was coming true and she couldn't be happier for him.

Her mind slipped back to when they'd realised they were the lucky winners of the £137million jackpot. It was a week after the draw and they happened to catch an article on the news talking about how the winner hadn't yet come forward to claim their prize and that the winning ticket had been purchased in their town. Sally, suddenly remembering her impulsive purchase, had rushed off to find her purse and the lottery ticket lurking within and, after checking the numbers three times, had sat in a state of quiet shock for a long moment before asking Steve to take a look. In an instant, everything they'd only ever dreamed of had become a reality.

'Not today, Herbie Baby, but soon. Very, very soon.'

She bookmarked the link of the house she'd been admiring and shut down the device.

'Coming with me to make the lasagne, sweetie? There'll be mince…'

But her big marmalade fluff-ball simply pulled his paw tighter over his snout and let out a little huff.

'Yeah, you say that now. I give it fifteen minutes till you're under my feet, trying to cadge a bit!'

She gave his head a gentle rub and headed towards her itsy-bitsy kitchen where she began to prepare their meal for tonight. The plan was that Steve would collect his car, come home to pick her up and while the lasagne was baking in the oven, take her out for a spin.

She let out a quiet curse at the jar of spice that fell out of the cupboard when she opened it. She enjoyed cooking but the kitchen simply wasn't big enough to accommodate all the ingredients she liked to keep to hand which meant all the cupboards were stuffed to overflowing.

Not for long though, she thought, with a smile, not for long.

Like most people, she and Steve had had the "If we won the lottery" discussion and they'd agreed that should they ever be the recipients of "a big one", they'd keep it to themselves for six months. No one would be told – not even their families – for they didn't want the press all over them nor did they want fake friends crawling out of the woodwork looking for handouts. After a time, they'd tell those closest to them that they'd recently had a lucky windfall and lead them to think the value now residing in their bank account was considerably less.

As she sprinkled the herbs into her mince, Sally thought over how difficult it had been to keep their secret and act as though nothing had changed for them. Steve had been champing at the bit to get his car and she'd been driving herself daft viewing all the property websites, looking for their new home. But they'd managed to be patient and were now rewarding themselves for sticking to their plan.

It didn't take long for the lasagne to be created and she popped it inside the microwave, out of Herbert's way, until Steve arrived home when it would be transferred to the oven to cook. Another glance at the clock told her it was almost quarter past four. Steve would be home any moment so she ran up the stairs to change her top and give her hair a quick brush. After all, one didn't want to have one's first drive in an Aston Martin looking like some kind of street urchin!

An hour later, Sally found herself pacing up and down the lounge. Steve should have been home by now. The dealership was only ten miles away and even with weekend traffic, it shouldn't take this long to get home.

The afternoon sun was streaming in the window and glinted on the glass of their wedding photograph. Three years they'd been married; three wonderful years. From the first time she'd met him, in a pub in

Lichfield, Steve had made her laugh. And he'd carried on making her laugh ever since. With his sticky-up, bright ginger hair, big blue eyes that always seemed to be twinkling and a wide mouth that never stopped smiling, he had the ability to make everyone around him feel happier just by being in his orbit. He gave out happy vibes and everyone benefitted.

She picked up the photograph and ran her fingers softly over his face.

'I love you,' she whispered.

She held it in her hands for a few more seconds and then replaced it on the mantlepiece next to the clock which had added a further thirty minutes to her waiting time.

'Oh, for goodness' sake, Steve, where are you?'

She picked up her mobile and swiped through until his number came up. After a brief hesitation, because she didn't like phoning him when she knew he was driving, she hit the call button.

"Hi, you've reached Stevie Eeeeeeeeeeeeee, leave me a message and if it's a good one, I'll call ya back!"

Despite her ire, she smiled. The sound of his voice did that to her. She left a message asking him where he was and to call her if he could.

She plonked herself back down on the sofa next to Herbert who, having just eaten his own dinner, was going through his bathing ritual. He turned his back on her, expressing his disgust that he'd been fed some slop out of a sachet and not the homemade lasagne he'd seen being prepared.

She picked up her tablet again, this time with the intention of checking for traffic delays on the route home from Derby, when there was a knock at the door.

'And about time too, wouldn't you say, Herbs? And so typical of your daddy to make a big show of the event by knocking the door. D'ya wanna bet I'll get hit with a "Tah-da!" when I open it?'

The door knocker went again just as she was putting the key in the lock.

'Okay, okay, I'm here… hold onto your six-hundred and seventy-one horsepowers!'

Yeah, she even knew the horsepower of the new family baby. Steve had gone on about it long enough and some of the info had clearly sunk in.

'What took you so long— oh!'

It wasn't Steve standing on the doorstep.

'Mrs Edwards? Mrs Stephen Edwards?'

She looked at the two police officers in front of her and felt a sudden kick of fear in her stomach. The blood in her veins turned to ice and she had to grip the door to hold her upright.

'Yes,' she managed to squeeze out from her now tightly constricted throat.

'May we come in?'

TWO

"In a quarter of a mile, turn right."

Sally glanced at the GPS display to the left of the steering wheel and checked the turning. She shook her head. It didn't look right at all.

"Now turn right."

She did as the electronic voice dictated but knew instinctively that something had gone horribly wrong.

"In 150 yards, you will reach your destination."

As her little car hobbled and bumped down the overgrown, pot-holed lane, the air inside turned blue as every cuss word known to man was uttered.

"You have reached your destination."

'I don't bloody think so, love!' Sally growled, cringing as she rumbled over an unseen cattlegrid, the weeds under and around it so high, it was hidden from view.

'Oh, for the love of…'

An old wooden gate, hanging on by half a hinge, leant drunkenly over the grass verge, making the already narrow lane even narrower. Sally held her breath as she eased Frida the Focus through the gap.

By the breadth of a cat's whisker, she made it and peered ahead, trying to spot a place where she could turn around and work out where the directions had gone wrong. Finding Lower Ditchley shouldn't have been this hard.

The lane swung round to the right and there, in front of her, loomed a house. A dark, decrepit, hovel of a house.

She drove closer and seeing there was enough space to do a U-turn, she parked up, letting the engine idle while she pulled the address details out of her handbag.

'Oh, you dozy mare! Maybe putting in the CORRECT postcode might help!'

Where she should have put a "G", she'd accidentally tapped the "T" above it, hence her now sitting in the middle of nowhere.

She retyped the details and waited for the GPS to work out the new coordinates, looking at the house in front of her as she did so.

The old, moss-covered roof was patchy and dipped in the middle. The paintwork was peeling and some of the upper-half render had also come away, exposing the brick underneath. There was a raised porch which looked like it wrapped around the left-hand side of the building but it was difficult to be sure as nature had claimed back the land it once owned and vast bushes were growing up the sides of the house.

The large windows, which she always felt were the eyes into the soul of a home, were dirty and bleak despite their beautiful bay design. Beyond the panes, she could just about make out lace net curtains which hung at odd angles and only served to enhance the desolation the building emanated.

Her curiosity now piqued, she switched off the engine, stepped out of the car and made her way gingerly up the wooden steps, taking care to keep to the edge where there was less chance of her going through the rotting wood, while wondering if anyone still lived here although the vibe she was picking up said no, as there's a type of stillness that comes when no other humans are around and this was the sensation she was feeling.

Testing each board as she went along, she came to the vast front door. It was a solid piece of wood adorned with old-fashioned cast-ironwork. She tried the handle and was disappointed to find it locked. Glass panels were fitted on either side but they were too dirty to see through. She bent down, pushed open the solid, black letterbox with the word "Letters" engraved upon it and peeked through the aperture. Unfortunately, the exercise was pointless in satisfying her curiosity as little was revealed within the dark hallway inside.

'I wonder if I'll be able to see in through the windows…' she muttered, walking over to the large bay on her right.

Sally took a tissue from her pocket and with a little bit of spit, cleared a hole in the grime. She used her hands to create a shield around her eyes and tried to see into the room on the other side. With some difficulty, she was able to make out what appeared to be a large room with a beamed ceiling, wooden floor, and wallpaper hanging off the wall.

Just as she was about to wipe the window again, her mobile started ringing in her pocket, splitting the air with its shrill tone and making Sally jump. She quickly pulled it out and answered it.

'Hi Karen, sorry, I'm going to be a little late. I put the wrong postcode in the GPS and I'm now in the middle of nowhere. I'm just about to turn around and should be with you in about ten minutes or so.'

Surprised at her reluctance to leave, she made her way back to the car, turned and began the bumpy drive back to the main road.

As she squeezed past the wonky gate for the second time, Sally noticed an old wooden sign which had fallen over into the long grass. She got out of the car for a closer look and could just about make out the faded, painted words.

Bramblebush Farm.

'Ohhhhhh, *so* good! I needed that, it's blooming freezing out there.'

Sally took a large sip of the mocha coffee which had just been placed in front of her. She'd been looking forward to this lunch as she hadn't seen Karen for ages – the downside of her best mate having moved to London when she got married.

'Happy birthday, how does it feel to be forty?'

'Absolutely no different to how it felt being thirty-nine!'

'Have you got any plans for this evening?'

'Goodness, no! I want this day to pass without any fuss. Seeing you is the only celebration I need.'

Karen leant over to squeeze her hand.

'And in true Sally style, you did it by getting lost! Where did you end up?' she asked as she got to work on her lunch of quiche and salad.

'Some old farm about fifteen minutes from here. Although, if the driveway was in better nick, it would only be ten minutes!'

'Did you see someone to give you directions?'

'No, it was totally deserted. I made the satnav do the work.'

'Deserted, eh? Are you sure? We've all seen the horror movies of innocent young girls arriving at deserted old farmhouses only to end up being kidnapped by the monster in the basement, never to be seen again.'

Karen waggled her eyebrows and Sally laughed before taking a bite of her cheese and ham toastie.

'Thankfully, I don't watch those kinds of movies otherwise I may not have been so keen to get out of Frida and have a nosy.'

'You didn't!'

'I did!'

'You're a better woman than me then, Sally Edwards!'

'There was something about it, Karen. It didn't feel

scary. It felt more… sad, I suppose. It felt… unloved.'

'Oh, away with you. Houses don't give off feelings.'

'I dunno… some do. This one definitely did.'

'You always were the fanciful sort. Anyway, how are things? How're you doing?'

'I'm okay, thanks.'

'Are you still working in the supermarket, stacking shelves?'

'No.'

'No? You've moved on?'

Sally gave a small smile at Karen's hopeful tone.

'Yeah. I now work on the tills!'

'Oh, Sally! Why? Don't you think it's time you went back to doing what you used to do best?'

'What? Being someone's PA? Being bossed about, bawled out when *they* make mistakes, and getting run ragged sorting out their crap? Thanks, but no thanks.'

'But you're so good at organising things. My hen night is the stuff of legend thanks to you. You deserve better than working in a supermarket.'

Sally felt herself bristle at this comment.

'Karen, there is nothing wrong with working in a supermarket! It's an honest job with honest pay and I won't have anyone looking down on me or anyone else who works in that environment.'

'I didn't mean it like that. I simply meant you have skills which you're not utilising and that's a waste.'

'I like it. It gets me out of the house, no one asks questions, no one showers me with pity and as long as I'm pleasant to the customers, no one bothers me.'

'But Sal, it's been three years since Steve… you

know—'

'Died, Karen. He died! You can say it, I'm not going to turn into a blubbering lump lying prostrate across the table.'

'I…' Karen stopped and looked at her.

'I'm sorry, Karen. I'm just tired of people still walking on eggshells around me. Yes, I was pretty much a zombie for those twelve months afterwards but everyone knows that's when it's hardest – you have to deal with all the "firsts" – the first birthday without him, the first anniversaries, the first Christmas. Mind you, having to deal with the court case didn't help; it felt like I had to hold on tight to myself until it was over and I could give in to the grief. In all honesty, it delayed much of the pain so the "seconds" weren't any better but I knew I'd already coped once and I could do so again. I'm now onto the "thirds" and trying to find my way forwards and move on but people don't seem willing to let me despite regularly telling me it's what I need to do.'

'I'm sorry. I'm a shit mate.' Karen put her hand on top of Sally's and gave it a squeeze.

'You're anything but a shit mate. You're the only person I feel safe saying all that to – if I'd spoken so openly to anyone else, they'd be stomping out of here in a right huff. And, talking of here, how did you find this place? I love it!'

Sally looked around the beautiful Victorian tearoom with its glorious cast-iron beams and sunny conservatory. She'd had to walk through a rather pretty bookshop to reach it and had noticed some stairs leading up to an antiques place above. A room she fully intended to have a look around before she left.

'My mum told me about it. She joined Gran on one of her coach trips last month and this was one of the locations they stopped off at. When we agreed to meet today somewhere between London and Birmingham, this place immediately came to mind.'

'I like it. It has a lovely relaxing ambience.'

'Sod the ambience; did you see the three-tiered chocolate cake when we placed our order? I'm having some of that, even if I have to jog back to London to work off the calories.'

'In that case, I may have to join you but you can beggar off if you think I'm jogging anywhere! You're on your own with that one.'

When the waitress came to clear their table, they were giggling like the schoolgirls they'd been when they'd first met.

THREE

'Hey, Dad, I've brought you a coffee.'

'Aw, thanks, Flora.'

Matt O'Brien looked up as Flora placed his favourite mug in front of him.

'Whatcha doing?'

He looked down at the design in front of him.

'Just being a little creative. What do you think?'

He pushed the garden design he'd been working on across the desk.

Flora studied it for a moment before smiling as she handed it back.

'I like it. The colours look great and the paved path meandering through is a lovely touch. It takes you to the flowers, allowing you to appreciate them up close.'

'That was my thinking too. I'm glad my little artist agrees with me.'

'Graphic designer, Dad, not an artist.'

'You started off as an artist, graphics is just your speciality.'

'I suppose. So, is this design for a specific job? You haven't mentioned anything.'

Matt let out a sigh. 'No, I was just messing about.'

Flora frowned at him but didn't say anything, clearly waiting for him to continue.

'With Robbie being tied up on that big renovation job over the other side of Oxford, I'm stuck here picking up all the small jobs. Which is absolutely fine – I'm not objecting to the work, not by a long chalk – but I'd really love a project I could get my teeth into. I miss the challenge and the thrill that comes with turning a beast of a building into a thing of beauty.'

Flora nodded. 'I understand. Say, tell you what, since we're talking about things of beauty, why don't we walk over to The Cabookeria for some cake and coffee. The rain has stopped and if we wrap up well, we'll stay nice and warm.'

'Taking me back to where this all began?'

'For sure. And the fact that I really want a large slice of Sam's fabulous carrot cake which I happen to know she makes on Fridays.'

'Honestly, I don't know how you stay so slim!'

'Uncle Craig says I get it from my mum.'

'Yeah, he's probably right there. You are the spit of her after all.'

'Dad, don't you wish you'd re-married?'

'Flora, please, let's not go there again. Come on, coffee and cake. If we dally too long, there may be none left.'

'Oh, good point. I'll just go and change into my

boots. I'll see you at the front door in two minutes.'

She ran out of the room and Matt smiled at her energy. His glance fell back down to the sketch in front of him and as he stood and began rolling it up, he looked at the photograph of Flora's mother which stood on the side of the desk. Also called Flora – apparently it was a family tradition that the first girl born was named Flora – she was her daughter's double. The only difference was their hair. In the photograph, Flora had deep, dark auburn waves which fell and swung around her waist. Her daughter, however, had recently lopped off her own long locks and was currently sporting an Audrey Hepburn pixie look. It suited her delicate features but he missed seeing the beautiful waves that reminded him so much of the woman he'd loved and lost.

A short time later, they were walking through the bookshop to the tearoom when Matt stepped back to allow two women coming out to pass by him. They smiled their thanks before walking up the stairs to the antiques shop above.

He stood for a moment, watching them as they disappeared from view. One of the women had seemed familiar but he couldn't put his finger on who or how and his brow wrinkled up as he stood, trying to force his brain to make the connection.

'You okay there, Matt?'

He turned and smiled at Jenny, standing behind the

counter of the bookshop.

'Yes, thanks. Just… you know when you see someone and you're sure you know them but can't figure out how?'

'Yes, I do.'

'Just having one of those moments.'

'Then I hope you work it out soon because I usually find those kinds of things persist in playing on your mind until you do.'

'Hmmm, I hope so too.'

He glanced up at the ceiling, hearing the footsteps overhead, but unless she walked around tapping out her name in Morse code, he didn't think he'd be solving the puzzle of the woman's identity anytime soon.

FOUR

Sally pulled onto her driveway, switched off the car engine and sat for a moment, looking at the front of her house through the raindrops sliding down the windscreen. The move she'd been planning with Steve hadn't gone ahead and she was still in the same pokey semi-detached new build, on a characterless estate in the Midlands.

She looked across to her neighbour's house – a mirror image of her own, just like every house in their little cul-de-sac. They'd been marketed as starter homes and she and Steve had been thrilled with their new purchase the day they'd moved in, even though they'd known it was only a stepping stone. They'd already begun discussing their move up the property ladder before the lottery win; the only thing the extra bucks had changed was the chance to climb a few more rungs.

She picked up her handbag and let out a little sigh

as she got out of the car. After locking it and going inside, she pondered why this was going through her head now. She no longer wanted to leave this house – her memories of Steve were here and while the place wasn't a mausoleum for him, she didn't feel she was quite ready to leave him behind.

'Hey, Herbie-baby, how's my little smoochy man?'

She picked up the cat and revelled in the vibrations of his warm, purring body against her chest.

'Would you like some yummies for your tummy, baby boy? Come on then, let's get you fed.'

She carried the cat through to the kitchen, putting him back down on the floor while she sorted out his meal. She flicked on the kettle and after pouring some hot water over his food and mashing it up, she made herself a cup of tea and stood looking out the window into the postage stamp garden while Herbert slurped up his meal behind her.

An unsettled sensation kept sliding around her chest and stomach and Sally tried to figure out what had brought it on.

After unlocking the patio doors and sliding them open for Herbie to have a runabout in the wet, cat-proofed garden – the only upside to it being so small – she wandered through to the lounge, dropped down onto the sofa and picked up her tablet. She stared at the blank screen for a few minutes while she sipped her tea, then, placing her mug on the coffee table, booted up the device and after logging in, typed "Bramblebush Farm, Ditchley" into the internet search bar.

Much to her disappointment, very little came back in the results. A few websites provided the address and some others had very old articles regarding cattle sales. The latter clearly dated back to when it was still a working farm.

She clicked over onto the images but all she found there were a couple of ordnance survey map pictures and about a thousand images of bramble bushes!

A little humph of frustration slipped from her lips and her fingers tapped her thigh while she sat thinking.

'Ah, I know…'

Her index finger flew across the screen and thirty seconds later she let out a small exclamation.

'Hah! Gotcha!'

She expanded the aerial satellite picture as much as it would allow. It wasn't ideal but it was the best she could get to be able to explore further.

Sally turned the tablet round until she got her bearings.

'Right,' she murmured, 'this is the main farmhouse where I was standing this morning.'

She pulled her finger down the screen, moving the image and letting her see what lay behind the main building. Judging by the expanse of roof, the farmhouse went back further than she'd expected. Beyond it were three more rooftops, one along each side creating a sheltered square in the centre. The two side buildings were narrow in comparison to the one directly opposite the farmhouse. She suspected it may be a kind of hay barn, or something along those lines while the side buildings could be cattle stalls perhaps... Her knowledge of farming was decidedly limited and she certainly had no intention of expanding on it now. She was just being nosy. The old, desolate building had piqued her interest. She'd said to Karen that she'd picked up a feeling of sadness from the farmhouse but she now realised that it wasn't sadness she'd sensed.

It was loneliness.

And that was something she had become rather well versed in!

"In a quarter of a mile, turn right."

Sally followed the satnav instructions once again but this time it was taking her where she wanted to go. Back to Bramblebush Farm.

She'd finally acknowledged this morning, after a night of dreaming about it, that the farmhouse had found its way under her skin. Her sleep had been erratic and she'd only drifted off properly as the sun was coming up which meant she'd overslept and was sitting at the small dining table, sipping her first coffee of the day, after ten o'clock! Herbert had been less than impressed and it had taken a handful of dry treats to mollify him.

When Steve had died, she'd moved their wedding photograph from the lounge and brought it into the kitchen where she seemed to spend more time than was probably considered normal talking to it.

She would tell Steve about her day, relaying some

of the things either his or her family had said or done and, more often than not, tell him how much she missed him. In the early days though, most of her comments had contained the words "selfish", "bastard", "bloody car" and "how dare you die on me". She'd moved on from those now although there were still occasions when she felt it necessary to repeat them.

This morning, however, she had asked his opinion on something quite different, knowing as she did so, that it would have made him smile.

The night they'd first met, Steve had been trying to squeeze past her in a crowded pub. He'd apologised for being so close and personal with her and when she'd smiled at him, saying it was okay, he'd stopped in his tracks, returned her smile, and then asked, 'What would you do, in an ideal world, if money, life and people weren't a consideration.' She'd thought it over for a moment before giving her tongue-in-cheek reply, 'I'd have a small Bed & Breakfast with a cat rescue attached.'

He'd looked at her for a few seconds before giving her the widest grin and asking, 'Will you marry me?' They'd gone on to spend the rest of the night talking and he'd later told her it was probably the best reply he'd ever had to the question and definitely the most unusual. He'd also asked her how the setup would work and she'd said simply, 'The profits from the B&B would go towards the upkeep of the rescue although, in this ideal world, there would be no stray cats needing to be rescued in which case, I'd have a small but highly exclusive B&B.'

Their conversation had come back to her through the night as she lay awake in her bed and for the first time since her husband's death, she'd felt a small tingle of excitement.

Over her coffee, she'd told his photograph about the farmhouse, how she'd sensed its loneliness and reminded him of their long-ago conversation.

'What do I do, Steve? We both know I need to force myself forward. Like it or not, Karen was right in what she said – sitting at a supermarket cash desk is not where I should be. I just don't want to go back to where she thinks I belong. I now have the means to follow that old dream from when I was young but am I strong enough to do it alone? Can I follow this through without you by my side?'

She paused in her musings, almost as though listening to him speak.

'Yes, I know I was a strong, independent woman before you came along and quite capable of looking after myself but being with someone changes you. You become used to sharing your decisions, having someone to give you their opinion and reining you in when you go too far. Or pushing you on when you have no faith in yourself. I'm in a different place now and it's scary. I don't know what to do. Help me…'

Sally hadn't expected an answer to come and she wasn't disappointed. What she did get, however, was an overwhelming urge to revisit the old farmhouse, which is why, two and a half hours later, her Focus was bouncing back up the pot-holed lane with a set of garden shears, some extra thick gardening gloves and a pair of sturdy boots rolling about in her boot.

FIVE

'Good morning, my beautiful daughter, how are you today?'

Matt walked into the kitchen to find Flora already sitting at the table. He dropped a kiss on her head as he walked past and chuckled when she rapidly turned over her phone so he couldn't see the screen.

'Oh, err… morning, Dad. I didn't hear you get up.'

'You must have been quite engrossed in your phone to have missed hearing the boiler go when I was having my shower.'

'Ah, I was out in the garden doing a spot of yoga and communing with the elements.'

'And how are our elements today?'

'Cold!'

He grinned as he replied, 'Well, now that I've had my weather report, how about sharing your intentions for the day.'

'I'm visiting a new client in Oxford just after

lunch.'

'On a Saturday?'

'Yeah. The lady in question works full-time but has a sideline in homemade soaps and lotions which she's trying to develop and hopefully grow into a proper business. She needs a company logo designed and has invited me over to see her range of products. She thinks this will give me a feel of what she's trying to achieve and I can create accordingly.'

'I hope you're charging double-time with it being a Saturday.'

Flora laughed. 'Don't be silly, Dad. I'm developing my client list – I can't afford to be a diva just yet.'

'One day, eh! What about this evening – am I cooking for one or two?'

'Ben's away this weekend but I was going to pop in and visit Uncle Craig and Essie on the way home. They've returned from their road-trip around Ireland and I want to catch up with how it was.'

'Oh, right!'

'Daaaaaaaaad! Behave!'

'What? I didn't say anything…'

'You didn't have to – your voice gave you away. Look, when are you going to get over yourself and realise that Uncle Craig is still part of our family? It's not just you and me. You almost never visit him or Grandpa Archie.'

'You know how I feel.'

He ignored his daughter's sigh as he turned away and refilled the kettle.

To avoid souring the day, he changed the subject,

'Where's Ben this weekend?'

'Down Bournemouth way. They've been asked to play at a wedding.'

'It's a bit of a trek, is it not?'

'Apparently the groom is friends with the drummer's brother.'

'Fair enough. I suppose a gig is a gig when it comes to these things.'

'That's how they're looking at it. So, how come you're stopping in tonight? No hot date?'

'Well, you know how it is. I've had that Kylie woman on the blower again, begging me to show her the finer points of the village but I just had to tell her, Ms Minogue, I appreciate you're a lovely lady an' all but you really need to accept that we're just not meant to be together.'

'I hope you let her down gently…'

'I did what had to be done.'

'It's a tough life!'

'Sure is!'

Matt put his coffee mug on the table as they both laughed at their absurd conversation.

'Since the little blonde bombshell is off the cards, any other offers worth considering?'

'Well, I'm sorting out Hilda Brown's garden wall later…'

'Senior or junior?'

'Senior.'

'Nope! Don't fancy your chances there. She's only got eyes for Fred the butcher.'

'Then it's definitely a meal for one tonight.'

'Again!'

Matt said nothing and took a slug of his coffee. He really hoped the conversation wasn't heading down the same old path previous ones had taken a number of times over the last year.

'Dad, you need to find someone.'

'No, I don't.'

'Yes, you do. I'm not going to be living here forever and I don't want you to be all on your own. You might end up marrying some atrocious old bitch like Uncle Craig did and that would never do.'

'Flo, if I'm not interested in meeting anyone while you're here, it's highly unlikely I'll want to meet someone when you're not.'

'You say that now but loneliness is a funny thing.'

'I'm not lonely, Flora. Now will you please leave this be.'

'Sorry, Daddy dearest, no can do.' She waved her phone at him. 'I've just set up an account for you with an online dating site and I'll be monitoring the responses.'

'You've done WHAT?'

'It's okay, it's a respectable one – I checked it all out first.'

'Flora, no! Take it down. I am not interested in dating.'

'Dad, it's been over twenty years since Mum died – how many women have you dated in that time?'

Matt was too angry to answer.

'Exactly! None! It's not healthy. You're a good-looking bloke, even if it does feel weird saying that about my father, and I want to see you with someone who is worthy of you.'

'And I've told you I don't want— wait! Hang on a minute… Are you planning to move out?'

He felt his blood run cold at the thought. Okay, Flora was now in her twenties and she'd been away to college followed by a house-sitting stint for her Uncle Craig for a few months but she'd always come home. Her bedroom had still been waiting for her. This, on the other hand, would be a very different type of "moving out" and he certainly wasn't ready for that.

'No, Dad, I'm not. Well, not yet. But Ben and I have talked about it. It may not be happening tomorrow but it's going to happen one day and that day may not be as far away as you think.'

She pushed her seat back, got up and placed her mug and plate in the dishwasher. As she walked past him, Flora returned the kiss on the top of his head that he'd given her earlier.

'I'll see you later, Dad. Have a good day and please, think on what I've said.'

She walked out, leaving him gripping his coffee mug tightly in both hands. The thought of trying to meet someone new turned his stomach. There had only ever been three women in his life – the schoolboy crush which had gone nowhere as the girl had moved away before he'd plucked up the courage to ask her out. Flora, his wife, whom he'd met when he'd just turned nineteen. Even though she'd been several years older than him, it had been love at first sight for them both. And then, his little Flora. After her mother's death, he'd focused everything he had on ensuring she grew up knowing she was very much loved.

No, trying to find a new woman to fit into his life

was never going to happen, no matter how hard Flora pushed for it.

SIX

Sally sat in Frida, in front of the farmhouse, and looked at it through the windscreen. The grey overhead clouds didn't help to bathe the building in any glory. Yes, she could still sense the loneliness she'd picked up before but there was more to it than that. Something else was in the mix but… what?

She stared at the house, wondering what it was she was feeling until, suddenly, it hit her.

Neglect!

Unloved, lonely, and neglected – that's what was emanating from it. She glanced in the rearview mirror and saw her own unloved, lonely, and neglected face looking back. She gave a small start at this sudden realisation and sat up straighter in her seat. The sun visor above the steering wheel was slowly lowered and she slid back the little cover to expose the mirror. For the first time since Steve's death, she looked at herself in the mirror. As in, *really* looked at herself, not a quick glance to check she was tidy for work but a proper, hard look and noticed her own appearance after three years of neglect. Her medium brown hair was scraped back in a low ponytail, her fringe – courtesy of the kitchen scissors – sat straight across her eyebrows. The warm, honey-coloured highlights which had accentuated her sharp, shoulder-length bob had long disappeared as she'd trimmed the ends that now reached halfway down her back.

Her clear, soft green eyes took in the pale, pasty complexion that was no longer adorned with a plethora of beautifying products but which now only ever saw soap, water, and moisturiser. There wasn't even a hint of concealer to hide the dark shadows which gave away her inability to have a decent night's sleep.

In this wake-up moment of self-realisation, Sally saw the shadow of herself that she had become. She glanced over at the house. They were both shadows of their former selves and somewhere, deep in her chest, she felt her heart turn itself back on. It was only the smallest of flickers but for someone who'd been emotionally dormant as long as she had, it was enough. It was the first sign of life her soul had felt after she'd locked away all the pain and hurt brought on by Steve's death and she could feel herself grappling to hold onto it, trying to breathe life into it in the same way you would try to coax the smallest of flames in the fireplace as you encourage it to grow into something bigger.

'Well, sitting here isn't going to do it, girl,' she muttered to her reflection. With a deep intake of breath, she opened the car door, stepped out and gathered up the garden shears and gloves she'd brought along before walking across to stand on the few, visible, cobbled rows of a pathway that disappeared beneath the thick thorny bush she was now glaring at as she prepared herself to do battle with it.

She tightened the scrunchie holding her hair back, pulled on a sweatshirt with a hood for added protection and donned the pair of thick garden gloves although now that she was face to face with the solid curtain of green wilderness, she was beginning to think chainmail might have been a better option.

'Right, buster, here goes. You are the only thing standing between me and that footpath and I refuse to be beaten.'

She launched herself at the bush and began to sever the branches closest to her. Slowly but surely, she made headway through the greenery, her shears cutting at everything around her. Finally, she'd made enough of a tunnel which enabled her to pass through the thicket without sustaining any grievous bodily harm.

She kicked the stems she'd trimmed off underneath the bush and followed the cobbled path along the side of the house, through a gate and down a flight of moss-coated, stone steps. She passed some low-level windows along the side but their coverings had stayed in-situ and there was no chance of seeing in.

To her right, she glimpsed some wooden fencing which had toppled over. Sally stopped for a closer look and saw what she thought may have been either a little cottage-type garden or, perhaps, a herb garden. It was also very overgrown but some lavender could be seen on the far side and she spotted one or two cobbled areas which could be pathways.

She turned back and continued along the side of the farmhouse until she came to a second gate – one which had once been white but now had just a few flakes of paint left on it. She leant over, undid the latch, and walked into the courtyard she'd seen in the aerial shots.

This close, she could see the cobbles underfoot but the weeds and grasses had grown up between them and they added to the air of neglect.

She turned to look at the rear of the farmhouse and was momentarily surprised to see it was on three levels at the back. She'd been expecting two, in keeping with the front. This explained why the rooftop went further back on the overhead images.

The lower ground-level windows had wooden shutters over them and when she gave them a tug, they remained firmly closed. She bent over sideways and looked up from the underside where she was able to see they were bolted from the inside. The door, less ornate than the main one at the front, was also locked.

Sally slowly spun around to face the yard and surveyed the outbuildings before making her way over to the first building on her left which, looking at the split doors along the front, had probably once been stables. She walked along the front of it, trying each door as she passed until, much to her surprise, one of the upper partitions swung open. She stuck her head over and saw the old wooden stalls still standing in position. The smell of hay and leather loitered in the air.

She pushed the half-door closed again and walked over to the barn which was, in comparison, massive!

Two five-bar gates stretched diagonally across the gap between the stables and the barn with a small kissing gate to the side. Next to the kissing gate was a flight of stone steps leading up to a peeling, green painted, wooden door which she thought may lead to a hayloft. A hefty padlock held the gates firmly together but as she could see the grass-filled ruts on the other side, she guessed this was the route the tractors would have taken out to the farmland beyond.

The barn was also securely locked up and she couldn't find a gap anywhere for a cheeky peek inside.

The third and final building turned out to be old workshops. None of the doors were locked and some of the benches held old, rusted pieces of small machinery and hand tools. The last one had become a storage unit for old crap – broken chairs, a mottled fridge with its door open, old wooden buckets and other odds and sods.

Sally turned away and walked into the middle of the yard where she stood looking at the upper floors of the farmhouse. Suddenly, as she raised her eyes to look at the upper storey windows, the clouds parted and the pale afternoon sun lit up the back of the house, bathing it in a bright yellow light which instantly made it look welcoming and peaceful.

'Oh baby,' she whispered, 'you are beautiful.'

As she stood on the weed-filled cobbles, she felt a

sense of peace wash over her, almost as though the house was reaching out to embrace her, wrapping its arms around her and telling her that everything was going to be okay.

In the still, soothing atmosphere, with the birds chirruping around her and the trees quietly whispering in the gentle breeze, the non-stop tumbling in her stomach, which had first materialised when she'd opened the door to find the police on her doorstep, slipped away. The eternal clattering of the recriminating thoughts in her head had ceased and her mind was finally quiet for the first time since Steve had died.

SEVEN

Back in the car, Sally eased her way over the potholes towards the main road. Her last words to the house had sounded like a corny line from an Arnie movie – "I'll be back" – but hers had been spoken softly and with love.

The problem she had now was finding and obtaining more information on the property. She could always go home and start with making an application to the Land Registry – she wasn't sure how to go about it but hey, that's what the internet was for. If you can learn how to plumb in a bath online, there will definitely be something to help you find out about unoccupied, derelict properties.

Or alternatively, she thought, as she sat at the T-junction, she could go into the village and see if anyone there could help her.

Her decision made, she flicked the indicator from signalling left to signalling right and had just started to pull out when something caught the corner of her eye. She stamped hard on the brakes, stalling Frida in the process, and peered closer into the shrubbery. It looked like a wooden post had fallen over and caught itself on the fencing.

A minute later, she was bent double across the fence, trying to yank the broken end of the pole away from the clutches of the long grass which had grown over it. Two minutes later, she'd clambered over the fence with the garden shears in hand and soon victory was hers. Just as she'd hoped, she was now proudly holding the details of the estate agent who was selling the farm.

Sally climbed out of the field, deposited the shears back in the boot and grabbed her phone from her bag along with a handful of wipes to rub away the dirt which was caked over the phone number.

"You have reached the office of Hedges and Burnett Estate Agents. Our hours are 9 till 5, Monday to Friday, and 8.30 to 12 on Saturdays. We are closed on Sundays. Please leave a message and we will call you back. Thank you."

'Damn and blast it!'

She kicked the tyre on the car in annoyance before looking up and down the road to see if anyone was around. Satisfied the road was still clear, she climbed back into the field and dragged the broken signpost further down the lane towards some overgrown hedging and pushed it underneath as far as it would go before messing up the grass to hide her tracks. It was, she acknowledged to herself, highly unlikely that anyone else would come sniffing around just when she had found the property, but why take the chance?

She got back into the car, took out some more wipes to clean her hands, pulled a brush through her hair and took off the stained sweatshirt. Now that she no longer looked like she'd spent the morning fighting her way through a jungle, she turned out onto the main road and drove towards Lower Ditchley.

Flora O'Brien slipped past the queue in the bakery and stepped through the entry into the tearoom. She'd had a shitty day so far and now her favourite table by the window was lending its services to four women doing their best hyena impressions. They looked pretty settled in so were unlikely to be vacating it anytime soon. Her grey mood grew a little darker as she sat at a table by the wall.

'Hey, Flora, what can I get you?'

'Hi, Saffy, a large Americano and an even larger slice of cake with a bucket of cream.'

'Sure thing. Any particular cake?'

'Whatever you have left will do.'

'Coming right up.'

The young girl flashed her a bright sunny smile and Flora couldn't help but respond. It took the edge off her glum demeanour but she was still riled up inside. Her conversation with her dad had started it off this morning. She'd been trying to push him back into the world of dating for two or three years now but the stubborn git kept digging his heels in. It was almost as if he'd buried his heart with her mother and had no interest in trying to meet anyone else. Then, when she'd reached Oxford and met her new client, the woman had been more indecisive than a six-year-old in a sweet shop. Flora had sketched out a number of logo options but nothing seemed to hit the spot. After several hours, she'd left the client to "take some time to mull things over and we'll talk again in a few days" but had a strong feeling her time had been wasted. If the woman couldn't make a simple decision on something like this, Flora didn't fancy her chances when it came to the other major business dilemmas she was going to face in the future.

'Hey, what's with the grumpy chops there, girl?'

Flora looked up to see Sam Doherty, the owner of the tearoom and the wife of her dad's business partner, holding a tray which contained her cake and coffee.

'Hi, Sam, thank you for this.'

'I had one slice of carrot cake left over from yesterday, figured you'd like it. Saffy mentioned you looked a bit stormy. What's up?'

'Bad Dad and bad client – in that order.'

'Wanna talk about it?'

'Only if you promise not to mention it to Robbie. I don't think Dad would be happy if he thought I'd been blabbing my troubles around the village.'

'Your secrets are safe with me.' Sam slid into the seat opposite. 'So, what's your dad been up to, then?'

'Nothing! And that's the problem. I want him to meet a nice lady to spend his time with. It's been too long since my mum died.'

'Most kids prefer their single parents to stay single. You're going against the grain here, why?'

'I just…' she sighed. 'I just… I feel guilty whenever I go out with Ben and leave him home alone. And I feel guilty when I see my friends, knowing he's sitting at home waiting for me.'

'I think that's a little dramatic, Flora, he's not exactly behaving like a hermit. He's on the village darts team and he meets us in the pub a couple of times a week.'

'I know. But that's all he does. He recently did an online landscape gardening course, telling me it was to add an extra dimension to the business so they can provide an all-round service. And that makes perfect sense. However, because he has nothing else in his life, he completed the course in half the assigned timescale!'

'I understand, and I think it's lovely that you're so concerned but it's your dad's life and only he can make the decision to take the next step.'

Flora took a bite of her cake, chewed, and then swallowed before speaking again.

'I've signed him up to a dating website…'

'You never have!'

She looked across at Sam, her face stretched in disbelief.

'Yes, I have!'

'Bloody hell, Flora! Have you told him?'

'I might have mentioned it this morning…'

Sam chuckled. 'Oh, Flora, I wish I'd been a fly on the wall when you broke that one to him. His face must have been a picture.'

'I don't think he quite believed me although he did tell me to get rid of it.'

'And have you?'

'Have I heck as like! I'll monitor it for a few days and see what bites. If there are any takers who I think are good enough for him, I'll try and get him to agree to a date.' She let out a small sigh. 'It feels like I've been hoping since forever for him to meet someone. It would have been nice to grow up with a mother, even an evil step one…'

'Well, good luck with it all.'

'I can be rather stubborn, Sam.'

'Yes, and so can your dad. Where do you think you got it from?'

Sam stood and pushed in her chair.

'Right, I need to get back to it. This is the lull before the storm. The next coach is due in half an hour so I need to get the prep done in the kitchen. See you later.'

'See you, Sam, and thanks for listening.'

Sam squeezed her shoulder.

'Hey, anytime kiddo, anytime.'

Flora finished her snack and after paying, made her way out through the bookshop, nodding to Jenny as she walked by.

She muttered her thanks to the woman who waited for her to come out the door before entering herself and walked over to her car, hoping her Uncle Craig could put her in a better frame of mind.

EIGHT

Sally waited until the young girl with the fabulous auburn pixie cut came out of the bookshop before walking in herself. She'd parked up in the small car park at the bottom of the village green and had wandered around, getting a feel for the place, before making her way back to the bookshop and tearoom she'd visited with Karen yesterday.

She slowly walked around, looking along the bookshelves, hoping to find something that covered the local history of the village and surrounding areas but all she was seeing was romance novels. Not that she had a problem with those but they weren't what she was after right now.

'Can I help you? Is there anything in particular that you're looking for?'

She turned to walk over to the counter and the lady with the nice, smiling face.

'Hi, I'm erm... I'm looking for a book, or books,

about the local area. Something which covers the history perhaps.'

'I see. Well, my primary stock is romance novels and thrillers but I do hold a small selection of local history pamphlets. They're just over there by the door, on that stand.'

Sally followed the pointing finger and saw a small wooden stand that she'd walked right past when she came in. It held leaflets for various activities in the surrounding areas along with some a bit further afield. Nestled in among them were some pamphlets, not more than half-a-dozen pages thick.

She pulled two out and had a flick through them – there didn't seem to be much substance to either one and she couldn't see anything about the farm.

'Is this all there is?' she asked, walking back towards the counter.

'I'm afraid so. If you're looking for something more in-depth, you may need to head into Oxford and look at the libraries there but I suspect if there was anything of note, our local authors,' she nodded at the pamphlets, 'would have included it.'

'I suppose…'

Sally took her purse out of her handbag.

'I'll take these anyway, I might find a mention of what I'm looking for.'

'May I ask what your point of interest is?'

'Bramblebush Farm.'

'Hmm, I can't say I know of it. Mind you, I've only lived here four years, there's probably quite a few outlying farmers I've yet to meet. I could ask around for you, if you like?'

'Thank you, that's a very kind offer but there's no need. It was just more of a passing curiosity.'

'Well, tell you what, take our card and if you change your mind, give me a call. I'm Jenny. Jenny Rowland.'

'That's a kind offer, Jenny, thank you. I'm Sally. Now, I'll just pay for these and get out of your way.'

'Ah, there's no charge for those. They're just little freebies for any tourists who are interested.'

'Oh, right, thank you.'

Sally put the items in her bag, picked up the business card Jenny had passed to her and with a smile and a wave, said goodbye.

The sun blinded her for a moment when she stepped back outside and while her eyes adjusted, she heard the gentle thwack of leather on willow, alerting her to a cricket match taking place at the top end of the village green. She thought of the date and realised it wasn't long now till the first game of the season. She wasn't a huge cricket fan but Steve had been. She turned to see the players, not yet in their whites which suggested this was a practise session, and the sight of them made her smile. There was something so quintessentially English about cricket on the village green that she loved. It lent a lovely, soothing ambience to the village and the added attraction of the duck pond only served to enhance it.

As she walked back to the car, Sally let the feel of the village soak in and she knew then that this was a place where she wanted to live.

It was Monday morning and Sally felt like a cat on a hot tin roof. She couldn't sit still and kept fidgeting at her cash desk.

'Girl, did you mix up your talcum powder with itching powder this morning? You ain't sat at peace since you got here.'

'I'm sorry, Joyce. Just got a few things going around my head.'

'Going around your head? Honey, they is going around your ass, the way you're wriggling on it.'

She laughed as Joyce turned back to serve the customer walking towards her. Despite being Midlands born and bred, Joyce liked to deliver everything with an American twang and it certainly added colour to their conversations.

Sally wasn't joking when she said she had a few things on her mind. She did, in fact, have a *lot* of things on her mind! Since returning from Oxfordshire on Saturday, she'd trawled the internet, written out lists, trawled the internet some more and written out more lists.

She'd done everything from checking out how many B&Bs were in the area (seven but none within a ten-mile radius), builders (four potentials and one who was actually based in the village which was handy), qualifications for the B&B (no legal requirements but several licences would need to be applied for) and a million other things besides.

There was so much to be considered. What age was

the farmhouse and was it listed? Would she be allowed to make alterations to it? How much work would it need? How many rooms did it have? She'd been more than a little pissed off when she'd gone onto the estate agent's website only to find the farm wasn't listed anywhere. How could she be expected to draw up plans if she didn't have all the information she required?

Everything would be moot, however, if she couldn't purchase the farm. And by now, her heart was firmly set on it. She'd phoned the estate agent in her break to arrange a viewing this afternoon and to say the woman she'd spoken with had been surprised by her request was an understatement!

'I'm sorry, did you say you wanted a viewing of Bramblebush Farm?'

'Yes, please.'

'Bramblebush Farm?'

'Yes, that's correct. This afternoon if possible.'

'Oh! Erm… one minute please…'

The minute had grown into five by the time Sally was taken off hold.

'I apologise for the delay. The file had been misplaced. Would you like the details over the phone?'

'Could you email them to me, please. I only have a fifteen-minute break.'

'Of course, I'm happy to do that. Once you've looked them over, you can call back if you would still like a viewing.'

'I've already told you I want to view the property this afternoon if you can fit that in.'

'What? You don't want to read the property details first?'

'Well, I could have done that if it had been listed on your website but since it's not, I'm going to have to go in blind as it were! Now, can you arrange a viewing for later today or not?'

'Err, yes… yes, I can. Would 3pm be suitable?'

'Perfect. Thank you. My name is Sally Edwards.'

After providing the agent with her email address and mobile number, she hung up and gave a little squeal of delight which echoed around the empty staff canteen. Her shift finished at twelve noon. Just under two-and-a-half hours until she was out of here and on her way. A frisson of excitement ran through her and for the first time since she'd taken this job, she really wished she wasn't there.

NINE

'I know, Frida, I know! It's this horrible bumpy road again. I'm sorry. I promise it'll be one of the first things I have sorted out, baby.'

Sally was fully aware her car was an inanimate object but she loved it and didn't like to treat it mean. And she felt very mean for dragging it up this track for the third time in four days.

As she drove round the bend that brought the farmhouse into view, her heart swelled at the sight of it. She no longer saw the peeling paint or the patchy render, the tatty woodwork, the dirty windows, and the overgrowth around it; she only saw how it would look once some much-needed TLC had been bestowed upon it.

She parked further over to the side to allow space for the agent's car when she turned up. There hadn't been time to see if the information had been emailed across as requested before she'd left home to get here so Sally pulled her mobile out to have a look while she waited.

'Bugger!'

The phone signal was weak and not strong enough for her to access the internet and her emails.

'Ah well, looks like I'm having a little wander again.'

Frida's door had only just been closed when the sound of a car approaching came up the lane. A blue Mini appeared a moment later and a woman not much older than herself, if looks were anything to go by, got out.

'Sally?'

'Hi, that's me,' she smiled, as she walked over.

'Fiona Parkridge, nice to meet you.'

They shook hands and Sally was pleased to receive one that was nice and firm. She laid a lot of stock on a person's handshake and was happy with the vibe she'd picked up from this one.

Fiona looked around her. 'I've never been to this property. In fact, until you called this morning, I didn't even know it was on our books. How on earth did you come to hear of it?'

'I found it on Friday. A serendipitous accident when putting a postcode into the satnav. I came back for a second look on Saturday and that's when I came across your seller's board with the phone number.'

'I see. Well, after we spoke, I asked around the office but no one could provide me with any information other than what was in the file and I can tell you, it was slim pickings in there. Eventually I phoned Mr Burnett Snr, who is now retired, and he was able to fill me in. It was a working farm until just over twenty-five years ago when the farmer, Mr Altshott, retired. His two sons had no desire to follow in their father's footsteps but he couldn't bring himself to sell up and move out as the farm had been in his family for many generations. Unfortunately, the declining profit in farming over the years meant he had to sell off most of the land to neighbouring farmers in order to clear his debts and have some funds to live off. When he died, there were family arguments over what remained of the property. One son wanted to sell, the other wanted to flatten the house and redevelop the area with some kind of posh estate. His plan was thwarted when his brother investigated the lease of the property and found all sorts of covenants which prevented that. Out of spite, the brother who'd wanted to develop it refused to sell so it sat empty and decaying until they finally came to an agreement about fourteen years ago.'

'How much land does the property come with?'

'Forty-five acres.'

'With the growing trend for, and recent interest, in smallholdings, I'd have thought that was a good size for someone looking to get back to being one with nature. Surely a place like this would have been snapped up? Why hasn't it sold?'

'You mean apart from the obvious case of not knowing we had it on our books?' Fiona grinned. 'Land around here has always come at a cost. The brothers set a price and refused to budge on it. They felt a premium location should have a premium price which put it out of the price-range for people looking to make that kind of move.' Fiona gave a little giggle. 'Mr Burnett became rather heated as he was relaying this to me. Apparently, when he tried to talk sense into the brothers and suggested they reduce the price, they were less than polite, used certain language in a tone Mr Burnett felt was unnecessary which led him to take the decision not to put any effort into trying to sell the property. After all, why should he waste his time giving viewings to people who were never going to buy it. He hid the file away and whenever the Altshotts asked how it was going, he simply told them there had been no interest. As time went on, they stopped asking and he forgot about it.'

'I see. I suppose I should ask the price before we go any further.'

'Ah, now you see, that's where you're in luck. What was waaaaaay out of the ballpark all those years ago, would now be considered quite reasonable by today's prices. Although,' Fiona looked up at the house, 'what you gain in the purchase you may lose out in the refurbishment!'

She proceeded to state the value and when Sally heard the asking price for the farm, she couldn't help but exclaim in surprise.

'But… that's almost the same price I paid for my tiny little house in Burton!'

'Like I said, you're in luck.' She gave Sally a small wink. 'Now, shall we head inside and see what other surprises this holds in store.'

'I can't wait.'

Fiona handed her a torch from the boot of her car and took a second one for herself.

'It's unlikely the power is still on but even if it is, I don't fancy touching any light switches until it's all been checked out.'

Sally nodded in agreement as they walked up the wooden steps to the main door.

'You should see the size of the key for this. It almost needs its own handbag!'

Fiona held up a solid cast-iron key – the sort you'd expect to see locking up the gates at the Tower of London.

'Wow, that's a beauty.'

'Isn't it just. Let's just hope the damn lock hasn't seized up.'

She put the key in the lock and with the use of both hands, managed to turn it.

'Phew, I was beginning to worry a bit there.'

'I had every faith in you, Fiona.'

'Glad one of us did. Right, here goes.'

She pushed the door and with an almighty creak, it slowly swung open.

TEN

The two women stepped inside and the daylight tried to follow them but gave up within a few feet of the threshold.

They switched on the torches and flicked them around the dark, wood-panelled hallway with a stunning black and white tiled floor. Well, it would be stunning once it had been swept, washed and polished.

Sally turned to her right and came face-to-face with a large double doorway. She pushed one of the doors open and walked into the room she'd viewed through the window a few days earlier.

She came to a stop in the middle and slowly spun round, casting her eyes over the walls, the dirty wooden floor, and the beautiful beamed ceiling. The latter had a large brown stain above a long side window – a window whose view was blocked by greenery from the bushes outside.

The wall opposite the front-facing bay window also contained a pair of double doors but these were sliding doors and when she opened them, they led into a second room which was almost the same size as the first although this one had two sets of French windows to the side. She could just about see the small, cast-iron Juliet balconies but pretty much most of the external view was obscured by the bushes outside.

'Well, these rooms are a good size. And with there being no furniture to clutter them, you get a great feel for the dimensions.'

'Yes,' Sally agreed, 'they're pretty decent.'

They exited through the single door of the second room back into the hallway and walked across to the room to the left of the main door which also had double doors leading into it. It was a mirror image of the room opposite although, this time, the front room had the French windows.

As Sally looked about, taking in the sorry state of the décor, she was already planning out her B&B. The first pair of rooms would be perfect for the lounge and dining area. The two rooms she was now standing in could be converted into a wheelchair-friendly bedroom and bathroom. The double-doors between the two rooms were perfect and meant little in the way of structural renovation would be required.

As much as possible, it was her wish to retain the greater part of the original farmhouse. She never understood those people who bought beautiful old buildings "for their amazing history" and then proceeded to rip out the innards and turn them into empty, modern shells.

'This is a bit upmarket for your standard old farmhouse, is it not?'

Fiona came back to stand beside her.

'If the farm has been in the family for generations, it's possible they were gentlemen farmers at one time. You know, the kind you see in those historical dramas where they "have a man" in charge of everything.'

'I suppose that could be likely.'

They made their way back into the hallway and stepped past the rather more-glamorous-than-expected staircase, going towards the back of the house where a corridor ran from left to right with several doors along one side. When these were opened and inspected, they revealed a downstairs bathroom, some walk-in cupboards, a staircase leading downwards and finally, a large kitchen.

'Oh, my days! Would you look at the size of this!'

Sally walked in and knew then that, come hell or high water, she was buying this house.

In itself, the kitchen wasn't exceptional – but it had the potential to be! A deep, old butler's sink was positioned under a large window which gave a perfect view over the yard outside towards the barn. Despite the dirt caked on the glass, some weak daylight rays were managing to filter through, picking out the terracotta tiled floor, the solid wooden worktop along one wall and an old cooking range in the chimney area.

Already Sally was envisioning the room with new shiny fitted units, a large marble-covered island, and the range all cleaned up and ready to cook up the eggs and bacon in the morning. In fact, with this much cooking space, she might even be tempted to offer afternoon teas with homemade cakes.

In the far corner was a large pantry which could be transformed into a wash room to accommodate the industrial washing machine and dryer she would require.

'Upstairs or downstairs next?'

'I think down and then up,' Sally smiled.

The concrete stairs led down to the lower ground floor that Sally had been surprised to find when she'd been trespassing on Saturday. She hadn't given much thought on what to expect but animal stalls hadn't been high on the list. The space was greater than anticipated and went the length of the house although not the depth. That explained the external steps she'd come across – the house must have been built on a hill.

'Ah, now my guess for this place is that it dates back a couple of hundred years when they used to bring animals indoors in the bad weather and over the winter. What do you think?'

'I'm thinking, Fiona, that you could be right.'

'Upstairs now?'

'If you think they're safe, let's go for it.'

'And there you have it. What do you think?'

They were perched on an old bench inside the barn, the large doors flung open to let the afternoon sunlight in.

'Honestly, Fiona, I really like it.'

Sally was, in fact, already deeply in love with the

property but she knew better than to let on to the estate agent how she felt.

'Is that like it enough to put in an offer?'

She grinned at the hope in Fiona's voice. If she could sell this, there would be a tasty bit of commission in it for her.

'I know how I want this place to work for me so I need to get a builder to come out and go through what I can and cannot do.'

'A perfectly sensible plan. I can email you a list of builders that we deal with. They're on our recommended list so no need to worry about any cowboys.'

'Thank you, I'd really appreciate that. I've already collated some names myself so I'll cross-reference with your list and maybe whittle it down to two or three.'

'I'll get that done as soon as I return to the office.'

'Thank you. Now, I suppose I'd better let you get back to work.'

They were walking back around to the front of the house and their cars when Fiona asked what Sally's intentions were for the property.

'I'd rather not say just yet. I'm not superstitious but I'd prefer to wait until everything is in motion first.'

'Okay. Well, when you decide if you want to go ahead and make an offer, you have my number.'

'I do indeed.'

Fiona checked the front door was secure before saying goodbye and setting off in her car, leaving Sally to lean against Frida's bonnet and stare at the house.

The upstairs rooms had again been perfectly situated for two further bedrooms with en suites to be created along with airing cupboards and rooms which could be converted to offices.

Oh, yes, this house had much to offer and was ticking all her boxes.

'Do you want me to look after you?' she whispered into the stillness of the afternoon. 'Shall I bring you back to the beauty you once were? Can we work together on healing each other?'

A gentle breeze blew, making the trees above her and the bushes around her all whisper their answer.

'Yes!'

She pulled her phone from her pocket, tapped in the mobile number on Fiona's business card and waited for her to answer.

'Good afternoon, Fiona Parkridge…'

'Fiona, it's Sally. I want to put in an offer!'

ELEVEN

The phone in her father's study began ringing just as Flora was coming out of the kitchen with a fresh mug of coffee in her hand.

She was about to walk past when she recalled her father telling her he was doing a plastering job over in Upper Ditchley today.

She quickly changed direction and managed to pick up the handset before it clicked over to the answer-machine. Her dad usually diverted it to his mobile when he was out but he'd clearly forgotten.

'Good afternoon, Doherty & O'Brien, how may I help you?'

She listened to the voice on the other end for a moment before walking around the desk to look at the diary which was kept in one of the drawers.

'I'm just checking Mr O'Brien's availability, if you could bear with me, please.'

It took Flora a few seconds to get to the right page

– how many times had she told her dad to use the blooming marker ribbon? – and note the jobs he had booked in.

'You say you're looking for an appraisal on an old property which may require extensive renovation work, is that correct?'

When the caller confirmed this to be the case, Flora checked the diary to work out which job this could be fitted around. Given the comments over the weekend, this sounded like it was exactly the project her dad needed.

'Mr O'Brien could be available on Thursday afternoon, just after 3pm if that suits you? It does? Great.'

She grabbed a pen from the pot on the desk.

'If I can just take your name, mobile number and the address of the property, I'll get you in the diary.'

When she'd recorded the details and hung up the phone, Flora looked at the address she'd written down. Bramblebush Farm? She'd never heard of that one.

'Hey, Dad, I'm in the kitchen.'

Flora, hearing her dad come in the front door, gave the pot on the hob a stir before turning to switch on the kettle.

'Evening, love, something smells nice.'

'I made that sausage and mushroom casserole you like but instead of spuds, I'm making rice. I also picked up some pitta breads – just for a change.'

'Sounds good. Have I got time for a shower?'

'Yup! I'm just putting the rice on now so you've got about twenty-five minutes.'

Her dad gave her a weary smile and headed off upstairs.

As soon as he was out of the room, Flora's own smile slipped off her face. Her dad was tired from manning the business at this end while Robbie dealt with the bigger renovation in Oxford. The problem with the smaller jobs was that the equipment was being loaded in and out of the van every day. On bigger projects, the heavy items could often be left in situ until the work was finished but the incidental jobs were usually completed on the same day.

She thought of the appointment she'd made for Thursday – all being well, it may turn out to be something halfway decent.

Her dad walked back into the kitchen just as she was placing the bowls of rice and casserole on the table.

'Here you go, you look like you could do with one of these.'

Flora passed over a chilled bottle of beer and opened a cider for herself. She took the rack of warm pitta breads from the oven, put them beside the rice and casserole and sat across from her dad.

They loaded up their plates and ate in silence for the first few minutes.

'How was it today? Did the new window frames go in okay?'

Matt took a drink before replying.

'Of course they didn't! Despite all the careful measuring, each frame still had to be altered to fit. The downside of working with very old buildings, as you know, is that most replacement items need tweaking before you get a perfect finished product.'

'I'll bet they looked good though, when they were done.'

'Yes,' Matt smiled at her, 'they did. Seeing the end result is what makes this job exciting, no matter how back-breaking it can be at times.'

'Well, just in case you forget to check, I've booked you in to do an appraisal on Thursday afternoon.'

'Oh, Flora, I was hoping to have an early finish that day…'

'I'm sorry but I think this has the potential to be a big job. Some woman wants you to give her an appraisal on Bramblebush Farm.'

'Bramblebush Farm?'

'Yeah. I've never heard of it, have you?'

'The name is vaguely familiar.'

'Do you know where it is?'

'I think it's to the north of the village but I can't say for sure.'

'The lady I spoke with is looking at buying it and wants an expert eye to appraise it, tell her if she can do the alterations she has in mind and a ballpark on the cost.'

'That could be a big job, right enough.'

Flora gave a small smile.

'Exactly! It could be! Which is why your early finish on Thursday has been cancelled. Sally… something, I can't recall her surname, will meet you there at 3pm.'

Matt's head shot up to look at her.

'Sally?'

'Err, yes… why? Do you know her?'

'No, no, I don't believe so.'

Flora waited for her father to expand on his comment and when he didn't, she continued, 'Okay. So, anyway, the postcode is in the diary and she said it'll take you right to the door if you use GPS.'

'Great. Thank you.'

'You're welcome. Now, since I did the cooking, I'll leave you to clear up. The soap woman in Oxford has finally got her act together and I need to finish off her logo for the morning so I'm going upstairs to do that.'

She stood and walked behind her dad to plant a kiss on his head as she passed by on her way out the door. Flora heard him let out a yawn as she stepped into the hallway and she stopped to look back at him, her concern lying heavy on her heart.

His shoulders had dropped and his head was drooping forward, almost touching the beer bottle clasped in front of him.

She held in a sigh and quietly made her way upstairs to her little box-room study, all the while hoping that this farm job would be the project her dad was looking for.

TWELVE

Matt cursed as his truck bounced along the country lane. He was late for his appointment at the farmhouse and tardiness was something he deplored. He would have been on time if Mrs Jenkins hadn't insisted he have a cup of tea and a homemade scone before he left. He knew his older client didn't get many visitors and hadn't the heart to refuse. He'd tried to call the mobile number Flora had jotted down but it had gone straight to voicemail.

He followed the lane round and pulled up beside the two cars already parked there. He'd just jumped down out of the cab when he heard voices and turned to see two women walking round from the side of the house. One was Fiona Parkridge whom he knew well through her working at the estate agents and the other… was the woman he'd seen in the bookshop!

The woman he now knew was called Sally Edwards.

Before he could gather himself together, Fiona was walking towards him.

'Hey, Matt, you're here. Great. This is Sally Edwards, Sally, meet Matt O'Brien, one of the best builders this side of Oxford.'

A little burst of irritation flared up in Matt when Sally made a point of looking at her watch before shaking his outstretched hand. Her lack of a smile annoyed him even more.

'Pleased to meet you, Sally, I'm sorry I'm late.' He looked at Fiona. 'I had a job over at Mrs Jenkins'.'

'Ah! I see.'

Fiona turned to Sally. 'Mrs Jenkins is one of the older residents in the village. She doesn't have any family close by so all visitors are treated to a cup of tea and a homemade scone – even if they don't want or have the space for one. She gets a bit lonely which makes it difficult to refuse.'

Sally turned to look at him with a stern look on her face.

'So, you're late because you were keeping an old lady company. Is that right?'

'Err, yes, it is!'

Much to his surprise, the stern demeanour was instantly dropped and a large smile lit up her face.

'Well, that is a more than acceptable reason for being behind schedule. Good for you.'

She turned back to Fiona.

'We'd better get on here, since you have another appointment to get to.'

'Actually, Sally, I'm going to leave you in Matt's capable hands. I need to go now otherwise I'll be late too. Matt,' she held out the keys to him, 'can I leave these with you to drop back into the office tomorrow morning?'

'Sure, no problem, Fiona.'

'Sally, let me know how you feel once you've had your walk round with Matt. Mr Altshott needs to understand that the amount of work required here will impact the price offered. I can't believe he's now decided to up the asking price after you offered the full value it was on for. Unbelievable!'

'He's probably taken advice from someone who's given him the current value on a fully-working house, not something ramshackle and weed-infested.'

'Most likely. Anyway, I'll wait to hear from you.'

She got in her car, did a speedy three-point-turn and with a quick wave, bounced out the gate and disappeared around the bend, leaving Matt and Sally standing in silence behind her.

For a brief second, neither of them spoke and then Matt said, 'Okay, shall we get on?'

'Yes, let's.'

'Before we begin, do you want to give me a quick brief on what you're thinking of doing, any concerns you may have noticed when you first viewed the house and any other plans which you feel may be relevant?'

As Sally informed him of her desire to make the house into a B&B with her cat rescue attached, Matt watched her face and listened carefully. He thought her voice held a Midlands lilt but it was very slight. Her hair was darker than he remembered but her eyes were the same clear pale green that occasionally popped up in his mind's eye. He was now quite sure that this was Sally Baxter – his first schoolboy crush!

'So, what do you think?'

Sally's question pulled his head back to the here and now.

'Oh, err, yes, yes… I think we can do that…'

She looked at him as if he'd grown two heads and he realised he hadn't taken in most of what she'd said. He'd got the bit about the B&B and cat rescue but after that… goodness only knew what she'd said. He was going to have to wing it for it a bit!

'I think the best thing here is to get inside and work our way down from the top. I have my trusty notebook to log everything we discuss. After you…'

He stepped back to let her lead the way.

'Well, this is a nice big hallway and the door is good and sturdy – would you be looking at keeping it?'

'Yes.' Sally smiled at him. 'I want to keep as much of the original elements as possible.'

'Not one for stripping everything out and replacing with fully modern gear, then?'

He grinned at her exaggerated shudder.

'Hell, no! Not my thing at all.'

'That is music to my ears. I prefer restoration over renovation. Now let's see what the roof is like…'

They set off up the stairs and Sally waited on the landing while Matt inspected the attic space.

'Well, that was actually much better than I expected,' he said, as he pushed the ladder and loft hatch back up. 'There are a number of beams that could do with being replaced which is why you can see the roof sagging from the outside, the liner is worn in a few spots and I suspect some of the tiles may be loose which could be bad news if the wind was blowing the wrong way but all in all, not too much to worry about.'

'Hmm, that may be about to change.'

Sally led him into the bedroom which was situated above the room she'd mentally designated the lounge. The reason for the large brown patch on the ceiling below was immediately clear – a branch from one of the trees at the side of the house had pushed through the window, breaking the glass, and was letting in water every time it rained.

'Ah! Would I be right in thinking this bit of greenery is not to your liking?'

'I personally don't mind it but I think if I'm going to offer a water bed, the customers would prefer it to be the plastic-encased variety.'

'Some folks are very boring.'

'I know but the customer is always right so best to stick to what they're happiest with.'

Matt smiled as he made another note in his book.

'So, tell me how you want this room to work.'

'Through that wall is a second bedroom. When we go downstairs you will see that the two rooms under these are connected by two sliding doors. I'd like to do the same with these two rooms and the two across the hallway. The rooms here at the front, with the lovely bay windows will be the bedrooms and through the wall / sliding doors would be the bathrooms. They all have side windows so natural light would still get in. Also, this side window here,' Sally pointed to the corner of the room, 'would be changed to accommodate French windows that I would like to lead out onto a small cast-iron balcony with a spiral fire escape attached. Again, this would be replicated on the other side.'

'Good. I like how you're already thinking of the safety precautions you'll need to put in place. All too often folks get carried away with what they want to do and then get upset when the plans need to be changed for safety purposes.'

'Since falling in love with this place, all I've done is research, research and then more research.'

'What made you choose a B&B with a cat rescue attached? Not the usual kind of pairing one comes across…'

'I was once asked what my dream would be if I could do anything I wanted and this came out of my mouth before I'd had the chance to think about it. Now, I find it's exactly what I want to do.'

'Fair enough. Let me look at the other two bedrooms but I don't see any problems with the alterations thus far.'

Satisfied that the rooms across the hall were a mirrored layout, Matt had a look at the other rooms on the floor. The house was laid out in a "T" shape with the vertical stroke of the "T" being the corridor leading to the front of the house and the horizontal going from side to side. The two large B&B bedrooms would be on either side of the vertical corridor, leaving Sally with several rooms running along the horizontal corridor, their windows facing out into the yard.

'You can see why the rooms at the front are for the guests. This is not the best view.'

'Yes, I agree.'

'I was thinking I could knock the rooms along this section together to make a small studio flat for myself and use the others in that section as an office and storage space.'

Matt took some measurements and made notes. Sally seemed to have a good eye and nothing she'd suggested so far was going to cause too much of a problem. He advised her on where she should place fire doors and was again pleased that she'd considered this and agreed with him.

Down on the ground floor, her plans for there also made perfect sense. His suggestion of an automatic opening facility on the door of the disabled bedroom, in the event of a lone traveller, was well received and she didn't flinch when he informed her that the French windows currently in the room weren't wide enough to accommodate a wheelchair and would need to be altered.

'I thought that might be the case,' was all she said when he mentioned it.

The tour of the kitchen and scullery area brought no surprises either and they spent a few minutes discussing a layout that would be practical for both cooking and serving in the dining room as she'd most likely be doing both herself.

'If you do find it too much, I'm sure there'll be someone in the village who'd be happy to help out,' he informed her.

'We'll see how it goes.'

Sally took him through the door that led down to the indoor byre underneath the house.

'I'm not sure what to do with this area. I was thinking about maybe opening it up, giving it a good clean and using it as a covered terrace – somewhere for the guests to sit if it's raining. I could put some bushes along there,' she pointed out towards the yard, 'to soften the view of the barn.'

Matt looked around him. The old stonework was visible and he couldn't help but admire its simple beauty. The interior walls had all been plastered over inside the house, but down here, it was showing in all its glory.

He slowly turned around and took in the higher-than-expected ceiling, the large barn doors in the middle and the windows on either side. He moved across to the nearest window, opened it and unbolted the shutters outside. With a resistant creak, he pushed them open and light filled the space around him. He walked along and did the same with the barn doors and the other window. With daylight creeping into every nook and cranny, Matt could clearly see the magnificent space in front of him and an idea began to fill his head.

'Sally,' he turned around again as he spoke, 'why don't you turn this area into your home space. You could have a kitchen over there and your bathroom over there,' he gestured towards the old sinks of which there was one in each corner of the room. 'You've already got plumbing down here plus some electrics,' he looked up at the single, bare fluorescent bulb above their heads, 'which is a good start. You could have this area open plan – replace the barn doors with big glass patio doors to let in a ton of light – and some stud walls popped in here, here and here to give you your bedroom space and bathroom. I wouldn't want to remove the cobbled flooring but it's not exactly practical so I'd suggest laying a wooden floor across the top with insulation underneath.'

'Do you think I could do that? Would planning allow it?'

'You won't need planning permission. You're not making any structural changes; you're not enlarging the building and all changes are internal.'

He watched Sally as she looked around the space, trying to visualise his suggestions. Her forehead was furrowed in concentration although a small smile sat on her lips, telling him she wasn't averse to the idea.

Finally, she turned towards him and the small smile had doubled in size. Once again, her face was bright with happiness.

'I love that idea. Oh wow, it would be glorious. I never even thought of that.' She gave him a gentle punch on the arm. 'I just knew you'd be the right bloke for the job.'

She grabbed his sleeve and began pulling him towards the doors which led out into the yard.

'Come, wait till you hear what else I have planned.'

As they stepped out into the sunlight, Matt looked down at the hand holding onto the sleeve of his jacket and for the first time in twenty years, since Flora had died, a little flame of warmth light up inside him.

THIRTEEN

Sally sat beside Matt, their bottoms perched on the side of an old stone water trough they'd found hidden in the long grass of the yard, looking towards the barn with the house behind them.

'This is one big job, Sally.'

'I know. But I'd really like you to take it on.'

She'd walked with Matt through the outbuildings, telling him what she wanted from the quarantine quarters in the old stables, the upper level of the barn to become a vet surgery and animal hospital while the ground-floor would be, mostly, an open plan area for the cats to mingle in but with a walled-off section to give nursing mums a safe area with their young kittens. Matt had been forthcoming with more great suggestions such as adding a run to the opposite side so the cats had more outdoor space and putting in high windows and skylights to make the hospital area bright and airy.

He hadn't once laughed at, or mocked, her ideas and treated each suggestion with total seriousness. They were currently discussing what to do with the third outbuilding – the one where the old work-sheds were located along with a room full of junk at the end nearest the main house.

'How do you plan to man your hospital?'

'Employ my own private vet and depending on how busy we are, maybe offer a service to the village. I've also done some research on that too and noted there's only one veterinary surgery covering quite a large area which suggests I could fulfil a need there.'

'Where would this vet live?'

'In the village?'

'Hmm, two problems with that – rental properties in the village are rarer than hens' teeth and on the odd occasion they do come up, the rent is extortionate. Your poor vet would probably use up all their wages putting a roof over their head.'

'Oh! I didn't realise that…'

'You could, however, turn those work rooms into on-site accommodation which comes with the job. The building would easily convert into a cottage of sorts. I suspect that, with such a sweetener thrown in, it would increase interest in the position.'

Sally thought this over. She hadn't given any consideration whatsoever as to where her vet would live – she'd been too busy thinking about how beneficial it would be to the rescue to have its own personal vet. She hadn't thought beyond that but Matt's suggestion had made her instantly see the advantages of having one on site.

'Planning permission?'

'Should be quite straightforward. There's an architect I work with – Charlie Rowland – who's good with this sort of thing. He could put together plans for the planning board.'

'Will I need him to draw up plans for my space too?' She pointed her thumb behind her at the byre.

'No, that one's very straightforward. I already know in my head how it's going to work.'

'Okay.'

They sat in silence again until Matt suddenly said, 'Have you thought about solar panels?'

'I'm sorry?'

'Solar panels. You have two fabulous roof spaces which are south facing. Put solar panels up there and they'll make you money. You won't pay for electricity again and you'll, most likely, earn some money back.'

'Seriously?'

'Yup! Between the two roofs, you'd make a nice little earner.'

'Are they heavy? The panels?'

'No. They'd be fine on the house but I'd need to put extra beams on the barn because the current ones are only strong enough for the tin roof. However, as you've already said you want that replaced with proper roof tiles, it's no extra work than we've already discussed.'

'Then yes, let's go with them. Anything that makes this place earn its keep works for me.'

She watched Matt as he wrote it in his book. She also looked at how many pages he'd written upon as they'd walked around. All this wasn't going to be cheap and while money definitely wasn't a problem – the lottery win had barely been touched since it had landed in the bank – trying to explain how this was being funded could be an issue if anyone asked. While it was nobody's business, that didn't stop folks speculating and being nosy.

'Also, while we're on the subject of electricity, it might be beneficial for you to put in a charging point for electric cars. They're continuing to grow in popularity so having one on site will give your business added appeal.'

'I can see that it would but how do I charge it back to the customer?'

'You install a pre-paid model. The clients do it all online so there's no cost to you apart from the price of leasing the charge point but you could easily recoup that as you set the tariff for the charge value.'

'How come you're so knowledgeable about them?'

'My business partner is working on a large renovation near Oxford and electric charge points were part of the remit. I had the task of researching them. I'm glad I did now.'

'Well, you've talked me into it. Add it to the list and, if possible, can you provide a cost for the work? All of it… off the top of your head, of course. I don't need an exact figure. Ball-park-ish will do.'

'Give me a second… this will be very rough though, so don't hold me to it.'

She waited while he skimmed through the pages and she smiled at his lips moving as he silently added up the costs.

Eventually he turned and presented her with a couple of figures, one for the house on its own and the other which included the outbuilding work. Figures that, once upon a time, would have seen her drop to the floor in a dead faint. Now she just smiled.

'Thank you. I can pass that onto Fiona tomorrow when she goes back to negotiating with the seller.'

'Do remember these are very rough. I will need to bring in contractors for some of the work so there's a good chance they'll increase.'

'That's okay. I understand. Does this mean you'll take the job?'

'I won't be able to start for another couple of months. Most of our men are tied up with the project in Oxford but it should be completed in about seven weeks if they stay on schedule.'

'Two months is good for me. By the time I get everything sorted out, I can't see me being ready before then. Always assuming the seller doesn't play silly sods for too long, of course.'

'Well, as soon as you know, you can let me know.'

'I will. Right then,' she stood up, 'I suppose we should get on before it grows any colder now that the sunlight has almost gone. Thank you so much for your time, input, and assistance.'

She stuck her hand out and Matt stood to shake it. As he let go, he seemed to hesitate, almost like he was about to say something, but then he just smiled and turned to walk back to the front of the house.

Following behind him, Sally wondered what he'd been thinking of saying before he changed his mind. Probably something to do with the house but given how much information she already had to digest, he'd most likely decided it would keep for another day.

'Are you leaving now?' he asked her, as he got into his truck.

'Shortly. I just want to have one more look around. Each time I come down here, I find it gets harder to leave.'

He smiled. 'I can understand that. Call me when you have news.'

'I will.'

She waved until he disappeared down the lane and as she stood alone on the gravel, Sally realised that she was looking forward to speaking with Matt again.

She turned to walk back towards the yard, wanting to check all the shutters and doors were closed before she left, and totally unaware of the happy smile playing on her lips.

FOURTEEN

Sally opened her work locker and fumbled inside her handbag for her phone. She was on tenterhooks waiting for Fiona to get back to her regarding her offer. It transpired that there was now only one Altshott brother and he'd been the one keen to sell the land for development. The estate agent had called her on Saturday morning to advise that he was still trying to play hardball and upping the price but she'd reminded him of the covenant on the land, that the new lord of the manor would definitely *not* lift it and given how run-down the property had become over the years, the cost required to renovate it would far exceed any value he hoped to make.

They were now playing the waiting game.

Sally was prepared to up her offer if she absolutely had to but she was keeping this to herself. While she may be able to afford to do so, it didn't mean she was prepared to throw her money at someone who was being greedy.

Just as her hand closed over her mobile, it began to vibrate and when she pulled it out, she saw Fiona's name on the screen. She hesitated for a couple of seconds while her nerves twanged in anticipation before drawing in a deep breath and swiping to answer the call.

'Hi, Fiona, how's things? Any news yet?'

'Hi, Sally, yes, there is. Mr Altshott just got off the phone... he's accepted your offer!'

Sally felt herself go lightheaded and dizzy and she had to quickly grab the door of her locker to help steady her.

'Hello, Sally? You there?'

'Err, yes, Fiona, yes. Sorry. Just letting the good news sink in for a moment.'

'It's great news. Apparently, he spoke with his family over the weekend and they told him to grab the offer because goodness only knows if they'd ever get another one. I'm guessing they saw the pound signs and didn't want the hassle of trying to offload an even more derelict property in later years. I also think you being a cash buyer swayed them.'

'Thank you, Fiona, for your effort, I really appreciate it.'

'Hey, all part of the service. So, now, if you can ask your solicitor to contact me, I will pass on the seller's information and we can get this ball rolling. Typically, now that he's accepted, Mr Altshott wants the sale to go through as quickly as possible.'

'Well, he's not the only one. Leave this with me, I'll see if I can get an appointment with my solicitor this afternoon. Thank you.'

Sally hung up and pulled out a chair from a nearby table and sat down heavily on it. This was it. Time to change lanes. She'd been crawling along on the hard shoulder since Steve's death, now she had to summon up the wherewithal to rejoin the motorway of life.

That night, while sitting on the sofa with Herbie by her side, Sally began to make, and check off, her latest to-do list. She'd read through the email Fiona had sent over with some pertinent issues relating to the sale which included needing to clear any change of use with the current lord of the manor for whom she'd also provided an email address for her to write to. Sally had already begun to compose a draft of her proposal for the property. As she had no intention of actually farming the land at any time, she hoped the landowner would be amenable to her intentions otherwise she'd just bought a large beautiful house in which she'd be rattling around on her own.

She'd also been to the bank and had gone through the authorisation required for a large cash transfer. All that was required now was to drop in on completion day and show them the paperwork from the solicitor who'd, fortunately, been able to squeeze her in with a late appointment. Given the circumstances, he'd agreed to expedite her case and had advised that unless anything untoward came up on the land searches – which could take approximately three to four weeks tops although he would make an enquiry about fast-tracking them – they could be all clear to exchange and complete within about six weeks. Less if the searches came back sooner. As there was no chain involved, she was happy to exchange and complete on the same day.

Satisfied with the number of ticks on her list, she placed the rapidly being filled A4 pad by her side and looked around the little sitting-room while pondering on what to do with her current home. The mortgage had been paid off after the lottery win so there was no need to sell, which was a blessing as she didn't think she could bring herself to sell it. Not yet anyway. The obvious solution would be to rent it out but she wasn't sure if she wanted strangers living in her home.

Sally let out a sigh at her quandary and lifted her hand to stroke Herbie, hoping the action would soothe her like it usually did.

'What do we do, Herbs, what do we do?'

The cat let out a small miaow before jumping down and walking over to sit in front of the glowing fireplace to groom himself.

'I guess I don't need to make a decision right away…'

She sat for a few minutes, staring at the flickering flames across from her, before picking up her mobile phone and swiping through and hitting the call button. As she'd known it would, the call went straight to voicemail.

"Hi, you've reached Stevie Eeeeeeeeeeeeeee, leave me a message and if it's a good one, I'll call ya back!"

Tears pricked her eyes as she hit "end" and redialled. She did this three times before finally placing the phone down on the coffee table, picking up her to-do list and adding a line along the bottom.

"Cancel Steve's mobile."

It was time to say her last goodbye.

FIFTEEN

Sally parked Frida in Lower Ditchley's little car park again. She'd managed to avoid the temptation to come down immediately after Fiona had delivered her good news but she found she couldn't keep away. Poor Frida was really clocking up the miles. However, now that she was going to be a permanent resident, Sally thought it would be worth getting to know the area better and maybe work on meeting some of her future almost-neighbours.

She walked up towards the bookshop as the lady in there, Jenny, had been friendly on her last visit and it might be a good place to start.

There were a few customers browsing around and waiting at the till when she walked in the door so she loitered close to the café entrance, checking it out until Jenny was free.

'Hi, can I help— Oh, you're the lady who was in recently, asking about Bramblebush Farm.'

'Hi, yes, I was. I'm Sally.' She put her hand tentatively over the counter.

'Lovely to see you again, Sally, I'm Jenny. Although you already knew that from my card.' Her grin was open and friendly as she gave Sally's hand a firm shake. 'Did you find out anything more about the farm?'

Sally gave a small shrug.

'A little but not much. There's next to nothing on the internet about it.'

'Well, I did some asking around and I was able to glean that it's called Bramblebush because the woodland on the property is full of bramble bushes. Original, eh? Anyway, a long time back, there was a village tradition that on the last week of the school holidays, the children in the village would go there to pick the berries. For every three pots picked, they got to keep one. They'd bring home their "wages" which would be made into pies, tarts, chutneys, and jam to be sold in the local markets over the winter season thus supplementing the household income in the leaner, colder months.'

'Wow! Really?'

'Apparently it stopped when the farmer retired about... twenty-odd years or so back?'

'Oh, that's a pity. I may have to look at reinstating that one.'

'I'm sorry?'

Sally looked at Jenny and said, 'I've bought the farm. Well... I'm in the process of doing so. And, apart from the estate agent, you're the first person I've told. Oh, no, second person. I had to get a builder to look at it.'

'Right, I see.' Jenny had a bemused look on her face at this information.

'I'm sorry. Didn't mean to blurt that all out. I'm still getting my head around it, if I'm being honest. It's been a bit of an impulse buy but I found the farmhouse and just fell in love with it. That probably sounds daft to you.'

She dropped her head, feeling more than a little embarrassed.

'Actually, *that* I understand all too well!'

The gentle tone of Jenny's voice brought her head right back up again.

'You do?'

'Oh, yes. This place did that to me.' Jenny swept her hand around, indicating her shop. 'I was waiting at the bus-stop across the road, loved the style of the building, saw it was for sale and now, here I am. So yes, I really do understand how it feels. Although, if I may say, you don't look like a farmer – are you looking for a career change?'

'Haha, no, I'm definitely not a farmer although, unless I hear back from the landowner, I may end up being one.'

'How so?'

Sally shared her hopeful intentions for the farm with Jenny and was surprised at the woman's response.

'Oh, that's a WONDERFUL thing to do. I don't think you'll have any problems getting the permission you're seeking but… hang on, give me a moment.'

Sally's surprise was enhanced even further when

Jenny picked up her mobile phone from beneath the counter and gave it a couple of swipes.

'Hi, Sukie, how are you? Everything good?'

She smiled widely at Sally as the voice in her ear answered her questions.

'Sukie, I know it's short notice but are you and Pete at home this afternoon? I have a lady here in the shop who's in the process of buying one of the local farms but she has other plans for it which she needs to clear with the lord of the manor.'

Jenny continued to smile at her as the voice in her ear responded.

'She has sent an email but has not had a response yet. However, she's just shared her plans with me and you *definitely* want to hear them. Trust me…'

Sally walked away to give Jenny some privacy as it felt all wrong to be listening to the conversation, especially when she was the subject of it.

When she heard Jenny end the call, she turned back to see the woman beaming in her direction.

'Well, that's that sorted. Sukie and Pete will be home just after four and have said they can meet with you then to discuss the change of use with you.'

'What? Just like that?'

'As the landowners, they live locally and are very hands-on, unlike some who run their investments remotely. For reasons which are not mine to divulge, I think you'll get a fair hearing.'

'Right. Well, err… thank you so much for setting that up, I really appreciate it. Once I get this resolved, I can move onto the next stage of the plans – sorting out my builder.'

'I have two cats, both of whom came from a rescue, so I'm more than happy to help you in any way I can. And if you're looking for a builder, I can recommend a local company who are good and honest. They helped to renovate this place.'

'I've been in discussion with a local gentleman, Matt O'Brien?'

'In which case, you've already met one of them. His partner, Robbie Doherty, is married to my business partner, Sam, who runs the tearoom there.'

'Oh my, is everyone related to everyone else around here?'

Jenny laughed along with her.

'Not quite but small villages are more like an extended family. We all know each other and we all look out for one another too. It can take a little getting used to but once you do, you won't want it any other way. Now,' Jenny looked at her watch, 'you've got a little under an hour till you meet Sukie and Pete so why don't you grab yourself a coffee and I'll draw you a little map on where to go. You could drive if you wish but, from here, it's only a ten-minute walk.'

'Then I'll walk, thank you.'

'No problem. That also means you can treat yourself to some of Sam's homemade cake which I highly recommend.'

Jenny gave her a conspiratorial wink before pulling a piece of paper from the printer and beginning to write on it.

SIXTEEN

Sally walked past the pretty little church with its cute pointy spire and through the kissing gate marked on the roughly drawn map in her hand. Just ahead, she could see a lovely house which Jenny had marked as being where she lived. As she walked past, Sally saw a tabby cat sound asleep on one windowsill and a ginger and white one on the other.

The sight of cats on windowsills always made her smile and this time was no exception although, if she was being honest, the sight of any animal made her smile. Unless they were in pain or being maltreated in which case her heart would twist with pain.

Steve used to tease her about being such a softy when it came to animals. Whenever adverts came on the television that had animals in them, he would quickly change the channel to avoid any potential upset. Even the Andrex puppy adverts were a no-go.

With thoughts of Steve in her head again, she

wondered once more what he would have made of what she was doing. Would he have said she was daft? Or would he have been right behind her, supporting her?

She let out a sigh. It was a question she'd never get the answer to so she had to stop thinking about it and just get on with doing the best she could on her own.

The path she was following went round a small bend and she stopped dead when she saw the manor house just up ahead.

'Holy shit!'

She glanced down at the map in her hand. Yup, this was absolutely her intended destination.

'Thanks for the warning, Jenny!' she said aloud, as she pulled her handbag up tighter onto her shoulder.

Three minutes later, she was standing in front of the large, solid wood doors and her finger was pressing the vintage ceramic and brass doorbell at the side.

'If a bloody butler answers this…' was muttered quietly under her breath.

She needn't have worried. The door opened and a woman not much older than herself stood in front of her. Wavy chestnut hair hung loosely past her shoulders, hazel-green eyes were shining a welcome that was matched by the smile on her lips. Her casual attire of jeans and a T-shirt helped Sally to relax a little.

'Hi, are you Sally?'

'Hi, err… yes, I am.'

'I'm Sukie Wallace, come on in. Please excuse the mess – the twins have been home all of half an hour and they've already made the place look like a bomb has dropped. I'll show you into the dining room before grabbing some coffees and my husband.'

Sally found herself being swept across the beautiful bright hallway and deposited in a room with a vast shining mahogany table. Even though the room was large – it needed to be to fit a table like that – the dark green walls and pale cream woodwork made it feel cosy and relaxing. She sank down onto a chair and tried to quell the nerves inside her. It was only now, where she was in the position for her dream to be rejected, that she realised just how deeply she'd come to desire it. Two weeks ago, she'd been merely existing and letting the world slip past her. Now, she was gearing herself up to fight for her future.

'Sorry about the wait, Sally, I had to drag my husband up from his studio. Sometimes, I swear, I think he's a bat or a vampire – only ever seen at night!'

Sally looked up and the smile on her face rapidly slipped away… standing in front of her was none other than the rock god that was Pete Wallace.

'Uh… err… urm…'

She tried to gulp down a breath into lungs which had frozen in shock. It was one thing seeing Pete Wallace on the television but when he was mere inches away, in all his golden-haired, emerald-green-eyed, razor-sharp cheek-boned, glory, it was something else altogether. The smattering of lines around his eyes and the peppering of grey on his temples did nothing to detract from the continuing handsomeness of this man.

'Jenny didn't tell you, did she?'

She looked at Sukie who was grinning back at her.

'Err… no!' she managed to squeak.

'I'm Pete, lovely to meet you. I can only apologise on my friend's behalf. I'm guessing she thought it best not to say too much.'

As her hand slipped into Pete's and he gave it a shake, she tried desperately to get her brain back into action.

'Argh, I'm really sorry about this. I'm not usually the star-struck type, you're just a surprise I wasn't expecting.'

'That's not a problem. We try to live a quiet life around here and the people in the village understand that so don't mention us too often.'

'Right. Of course. That's good.'

'Would you like tea or coffee, Sally? And while I pour, why don't you bring us up to speed on why you're here.'

'Err, yes, sure. Urm, coffee, please.'

As Sukie placed a mug of coffee in front of her and pushed the tray with the sugar and milk jug closer, Sally drew in a deep breath and began to explain about her purchase of the farm and how she wished to change it.

'A cat rescue? How wonderful.' Sukie's response gave her the courage to continue.

'As it happens, I'm hoping it'll be more than just a rescue. That was my initial intention but as I've done more research into the area, I would like to expand on that.'

'In what way?'

Sally looked at Pete as she answered his question.

'The barn has an upstairs hayloft which I would like to convert into a veterinary surgery that will be kitted out with fully up-to-date facilities. The ground-level area below would be for the rescue cats to run around and have some freedom. I don't want them to be cooped up in pens with little runs. The vet's main priority would be looking after the cats that come into the rescue but we'd also offer a service for small animals within a five-mile radius. There's only one vet that I could find, covering this area and they seem to be exceptionally busy. I tried to book an appointment and was told I'd have a two-week wait unless it was an emergency.'

'It is a problem we have here. I always have to book Tony and Adam's appointments at least a month ahead.'

'Tony and Adam?' Sally turned to Sukie.

'Yes, our two cats. They were rescue boys which is why I'm so thrilled with your proposition. Pete,' Sukie looked at her husband, 'what do you think?'

'I think it all sounds fabulous and from the point of the "change of use" I can't see it being a problem. I do have one concern though – do you honestly think a three-bedroom B&B will turn enough of a profit to fund what you're planning? Unless you're intending to charge a couple of hundred pounds a night, I suspect your outgoings will far outweigh your incomings. Or do you plan to register yourself as a charity?'

Sally hesitated before answering, giving herself a chance to think over what to say next. Could she share her secret with the Wallaces? After all, they were no strangers to a large bank balance and would also understand the need for privacy. She looked at the couple sitting across from her and the kind expressions on both their faces gave her the courage to take the plunge.

'The B&B is actually a smokescreen to prevent people asking too many questions. I have… err… funds to cover all the costs but I'd rather they weren't looked into too closely, so if I say the profits from the B&B fund the rescue, plus things like adoption fees, that'll be enough to keep folks at bay.'

'I have no wish to be rude, but may I ask more about your "funds"? If this is money obtained illegally…'

Sally saw the concern on Pete's face and quickly rushed to reassure him.

'Gosh! No! No! Nothing like that. I… err… we won big on the lottery three years ago. And I mean "big". Like £137 million big…'

'I see. You said "we" – is there someone else in this with you?'

'My husband died six months after we won, Sukie. We hadn't told anyone because we didn't want the publicity circus that goes with these things. After he died, I didn't want anything to do with the money, it felt… I don't know… tainted somehow, so it has just sat in the bank, gathering an obscene amount of interest – even in these restricted times – until I found Bramblebush Farm and now I want to put it to good use but still without the media interest.'

Sukie looked at Pete and they nodded together

before turning back to Sally.

'Now, *that* is something we can both understand and sympathise with.'

'Your secret is safe with us, Sally, and we have no problem with allowing the change of use. There is, however, one small proviso…'

'Okay…'

'There is?' Sukie turned to her husband, looking totally confused.

'Yes, Sally. At no time is my wife permitted anywhere near your premises.'

'Oh?'

'Pete Wallace, please explain *why* I'm not allowed to visit?'

Sally couldn't miss the hint of menace in Sukie's voice.

'Because, my darling wife, you'll take pity on all the little furballs, bring them back here and then *we'll* look like a cat rescue! In fact, we'd be cutting Sally out as the middleman and they'd all just arrive on our doorstep!'

Sukie burst out laughing as she turned to Sally.

'Actually, he does have a point there! I'm a total sap when it comes to animals but especially cats, and there's a good chance that could occur. When I come to visit – and I WILL come to visit and help out,' she looked back at her husband, 'you must promise not to let me leave with any cats in my handbag. No matter how cute they are.'

'I think I can promise to try although you do strike me as a rather determined lady…'

'Hah! She's barely known you fifteen minutes,

Sukie, and she has you sussed!'

Pete laughed as his wife swiped his arm.

'Cheeky sod! Although,' she looked at Sally, 'he's absolutely right!'

Then, to Sally's absolute astonishment, Sukie stood, walked round the table, and hunkered down in front of her while taking a hold of her hand.

'Sally, you have a very expressive face and I can see that this is a big step forward for you – moving on from the life you thought you were going to have with your husband to making a new life for yourself. I want to welcome you to the village and if there is anything at all we can do to help, you must let us know. Please don't feel alone. I hope we can be friends – heck, we love cats, how could we not be – so please do ask.'

'Well, there's one small thing – do you know of anywhere around here for rent? I can't find anything online and Fiona at the estate agents has nothing.'

'Hmmm, you're going to struggle there, I'm afraid, and unfortunately, all our holiday lets are fully booked for the summer season. Although… I may have one possible option… how would you feel about a motorhome? I have a friend who might be able to help.'

SEVENTEEN

Sally looked around the motorhome and could only exclaim at how luxurious it was. She'd been expecting something on a par with the old caravan her parents used to drag her and brother off on holiday in when they were kids. This was totally not that!

'Oh, Essie, this is gorgeous. Are you sure you want to let it out to me, a complete stranger?'

'If Sukie is vouching for you, then that's good enough for me.'

Sally looked at the soft cream leather seating and thought of Herbie's claws. She shuddered to think of the damage that could occur when they came together.

'Essie, I have a cat and while he's not destructive, I confess I am worried his claws and your leatherwork is not going to be a marriage made in heaven.'

'Oh, don't be daft. Just put some thick throws, or better still, some bed quilts over the seats and all should be fine.'

'Won't you be needing it over the summer? Isn't that when most people make use of their motorhomes?'

'Are you trying to find an excuse not to borrow Marvin because I'd rather you just came out and said so, I won't be offended. I appreciate that living in such a small space is not for everyone.'

'What? Oh, Essie, no, no, definitely not! I'm genuinely happy that you're trusting him to me, I just don't want to be an inconvenience for you or cause any damage.'

'I can assure you that all is fine. Craig, my partner, and I are off to Italy soon. My daughter is travelling and we're meeting her and her friends there before she flies to Australia. She currently has the use of Craig's little VW campervan and we'll be driving that back so by the time we get home, we certainly won't be going anywhere that requires us to sit behind a wheel for a few months.'

'In that case, I would love to rent it from you.'

'Great! Now, where, and when, do you want it?'

'Probably around a month from now, give or take. I might need it for three to four months… will that be okay?'

'That'll be fine. If we get itchy feet before then, we can use the campervan.'

'Thank you for this, Essie, I really appreciate it.'

'Hey, I'm happy to help. Now, I need to get on. Sukie's looking after our West Highland puppies while we're away and I thought I'd drop in some of their stuff while I'm here.'

'Of course. I need to get on too – I'm meeting my

builder over at the farm to confirm his services, when he can start and in what order he's going to go about things.'

'Are you using Matt O'Brien?'

'Yes, I am.'

'He's a good bloke and will do a good job for you. You won't need to worry about any cowboy work there.'

'Thank you, that's good to know.'

Sally shook Essie's hand and left her to walk up the drive to Sukie's house – could you call a manor house just a house? – as she got into Frida to drive over to see Matt.

Apologies to Frida fell once more from Sally's lips as they traversed the lumpy, bumpy lane again.

'I promise, girl, that this will be one of the first things I'll ask Matt to sort out. We can't keep doing this.'

A thought crossed her mind that even with a nice smooth lane, Frida might not be the best vehicle for countryside living. She may need to look at getting something more substantial such as a Land Rover – wasn't that what real farmers drive about in?

Matt's pickup truck was already parked when she turned in through the gate which had now been moved to allow easier access.

She pulled up alongside and was surprised to find the truck empty. Sally looked around for Matt as she got out of her car but couldn't see him anywhere. She walked over to the side of the house where she'd cleared the pathway through the brambles and walked down the steps to the yard at the back but when she got there, she found it empty.

Okay, where is he, she thought as she made her way back to the front.

'Matt? Where are you?' she called out.

A muffled reply came from the trees to the left of the house. She walked towards them and tried to peer through the thick bushes in front of her.

'Matt, are you in there?'

This time she was able to make out the words, 'Hang on, I'm coming round.'

A moment later, Matt appeared through the gate.

'Hi, Sally, nice to see you again.'

He came towards her and as he shook her hand, she grinned at the twigs which were caught in his hair.

'Matt, what have you been up to? You look like you've been dragged through a hedge backwards – quite literally!'

'Come with me, I'll show you.'

She followed him out the gate and down the lane until he stopped at the point where it turned up towards the farmhouse.

'Look here…'

He bent down and parted the overgrown grass to show her the rough tracks underneath.

'This is where the farm track used to be that went around the back to the yard. When I saw the gate between the farmhouse and the stable block, I knew there had to be an access point somewhere, it was just figuring out where.'

'Of course! That makes total sense. I hadn't given

it any thought.'

'So, do you fancy being Jane to my Tarzan as I hack my way through this jungle?'

Sally looked down at her sturdy boots, jeans, and sweatshirt – yes, she'd learnt that when it came to visiting the farm these days, thick, bramble-proof clothing was the way to go.

'Lead the way but if we come across any snakes, you're on your own.'

Matt grinned at her. 'What about any lions or tigers or bears?'

'Oh my! They're all mine! Bring 'em on!'

With a chuckle, Matt turned and began to make his way into the dark overgrowth.

Sally pulled up the hood on her sweatshirt and gamely followed behind.

EIGHTEEN

Matt held the branches back for Sally, taking great care not to let them go where they could smack her in the face. At the same time, he hacked through the grass to make sure they were following the old track and not making a new one of their own.

There were a few occasions where the brambles fought back, latching onto their clothing and he was pleased to note that Sally calmly extracted herself without any fuss. He'd been concerned that the fearless girl he'd admired from afar at school may have grown into a woman who liked to moan and groan over small issues but it seemed his concerns had been unfounded. She was showing herself to be a resilient, no-nonsense person who could face anything that came her way and he liked it. He liked it a lot.

In some ways, she reminded him of his darling Flora. His wife had been a woman who didn't shy away from hard work or difficult situations and he was picking up the same vibe from Sally. He wondered if this similarity is what had attracted him to Flora when they'd first met. Just like the first time he'd seen Sally, defending a younger child who was being bullied, Flora had been leading a protest outside Oxford University demanding better disabled access for the less able-bodied students. They'd both displayed a strong and indomitable spirit and when Flora had approached him to sign her petition, he'd done so without question. He'd also shocked himself by following it up with a request that she join him for dinner when she was finished.

She'd looked him up and down with her unusual silvery eyes, thrown her long, copper plait over her shoulder, and said she would. After that, they were inseparable. The seven-year age gap was never discussed and was never an issue. They fitted perfectly together and neither cared that she had a few years more experience of life.

'Oh, look, I can see the gate!'

Sally's words brought Matt out of his thoughts and he stopped to look back at the pathway they'd cleared.

'Hmm, it looks like the track curves away from the house before turning back in towards the gate.'

'Avoiding something, maybe? Drains perhaps? Or just preventing vibrations or noise through the house when a larger vehicle passed by?'

Sally looked at him as she voiced these thoughts and Matt found himself impressed again by her intelligent surmising.

'Yeah, both of those could be possibilities. We'll

know more once we get it all cleared.'

They climbed over the gate and made their way to the old water trough where they perched on the edge again.

Matt opened the folder he'd left there when he'd arrived, before going to explore the undergrowth for a second road track, and clicked his pen.

'Right, to business. We need to put together a timetable for what has to be done and when.'

He looked at Sally and she smiled back. Matt chose to ignore the little flip in his heart and forced himself to be businesslike.

'As I've already advised you, my solicitor has estimated a six-week turnaround but hopes to get the sale through sooner if possible. That time scale hasn't changed at this time.'

Matt wrote that onto the pad. Not because he wouldn't remember but so that he had a reason to focus his eyes elsewhere.

'Okay. I've spoken to my partner and he now thinks it'll be eight to ten weeks to complete the job he's on which will then release our team to move over here and begin your project.'

'I see.'

'However, I've spoken to a friend who does habitat management—'

'What's that?'

'They'll clear the unruly brambles, thin out your trees, remove old or dead vegetation and pretty much make all of that out there,' he waved his hand to indicate the tall trees visible over the rooftops, 'tidier and more manageable.'

'I see…'

'Is there a problem?'

'Erm, what about the wildlife that lives there? I don't want someone just coming in and ripping everything up. That's not what I'm about. I want to preserve as much of nature as possible.'

'You don't need to worry. He thinks the same as you and will take great care to ensure it's all done ethically.'

'Is it necessary to cut down the trees? Can't they just be trimmed or something?'

'Good forestry management requires tree thinning. If the trees get too tall and thick at the top, this prevents sunlight getting down to the forest floor which impacts the growth of new trees and vegetation which sustains various ecosystems. Don't worry, Freddie will do a thorough survey on the area first and he'll keep us in the loop at all times.'

'Okay.'

'You happy with that?'

'If you think he'll do a good and fair job, then I'll trust your judgement.'

'He will, I promise. Anyway, he's said he'll be able to come and have a look around next week and can put you in the diary for work to commence in six weeks. That works out good for me as it means the access to the yard here will be clear for us to bring in our equipment. It makes it easier if we can leave our stuff on site and we don't waste time loading and unloading every day. It should be pretty secure here.'

'Well, I'm going to be on site so you've no reason to worry.'

'Oh, how so?'

Sally filled him in on her meeting with Essie Walton and the arrangement with her motorhome.

'She spoke very highly of you which was nice to hear.'

'I suppose I should tell you, in open disclosure of information – or whatever they call it – that her partner, Craig, is my brother-in-law.'

'He is?'

'Yes, he's my wife's brother. And Flora's uncle.'

'Blooming heck, everyone in this village *is* related to each other? I thought those stories were urban myths.'

Matt couldn't help but laugh.

'No, we're not that bad but we are a fairly close-knit community.'

'Yeah, you're not the first to have mentioned it.'

'You'll get used to it.'

'I've been told that too!'

He grinned as he scribbled this latest development on his pad.

'Where do you want to situate the motorhome? Out the front? Or along the side? You also have those two fields at the front.'

'Hmm, no, I'd feel a bit exposed out there. I was thinking here in the yard might be better.'

'That makes sense but I'm concerned it could get a bit noisy for you. With this being an enclosed space, the banging and clattering tends to reverberate which will make it seem louder than it actually is.'

'Well, where would you suggest?'

'How about inside the barn?'

'Are you serious?'

'Come with me.'

He walked over to the five-bar gate that was located between the stables and the barn. He bent down to clear the weeds around the kissing gate at the side of it, pushed it open, walked through and then waited for Sally to join him.

As they walked round to the back of the barn, he explained.

'If you put the motorhome in the barn, but park it up by these doors,' he pointed to the large wooden doors now in front of them, 'you can open these up and get all the daylight you need, but in bad weather, they can be closed and you'll be protected from the elements. Summer thunderstorms can be rather noisy in one of those things.'

'Hmm, you've made a good point there. My folks had a caravan and you couldn't hear yourself think when it rained.'

'You've also got a small yard on this side where you could put out a table and chairs which would give you more space to work with. If you're going to be living in it for three months or so, some extra space might not be a bad thing. Furthermore, just over there, you have a water tap, there are drain facilities by the stables and I'm sure I saw plug points in the barn. If not, we can hook you up with something easily enough.'

'You make it all sound so straightforward.'

'That's because it is.'

'I just have one last concern.'

'Which is?'

'My cat, Herbert. I don't want him having too much outside access all at once.'

'Easy. These doors open into the barn – unlike the front ones which open out – so I can cobble together a frame, a sort of cat run thing, which will give him space to run about in. I'll make it large enough to fit in your table and chairs so you can both hang out together.'

'You have all the answers, don't you?'

'I try to. It's my job to find solutions to people's building dilemmas.'

Sally smiled again, the one which lit up her face and crinkled her eyes. This time, his heart clenched a bit tighter than before and his mouth went a little dry.

Matt tried to reply but found words wouldn't come to him. Thankfully, Sally came to his rescue although he didn't think she'd realised the effect she was having on him.

'Now that we have my temporary living accommodation sorted out, shall we head over to the house to discuss what you plan to do with that?'

Sally led the way this time and Matt followed behind, trying to come to terms with the feelings she was awakening in him. Feelings he hadn't felt for a very long time.

NINETEEN

Sally stood back as she guided Essie down the path and pointed her towards the open barn doors. She was so glad she wasn't driving Marvin although Essie had informed her that it was easier than she may think. She wasn't getting off too lightly, however, as she'd need to learn some manoeuvring techniques in order to take him to the drains in the yard when his tanks required emptying. Thankfully, Essie had promised to come over and help her out with this next week saying it was easier to learn "on the job".

She followed the motorhome into the barn and waited for Essie to put him into position. The barn doors at the back had been opened so Essie knew exactly where to place him and true to his word, Matt had already installed a run outside so she could allow Herbie to roam without worrying over his safety.

This wasn't the only thing Matt had sorted out for her. The ink had barely dried on the sale contracts when he'd swooped into action and his friend, Freddie, had arrived on site the very next day to begin clearing the brambles and wooded areas within the immediate vicinity of the house. As soon as they knew the sale was going ahead, she'd arranged with Fiona at the estate agents to allow Matt to have the keys for the property so he could access it for assessment purposes. What she hadn't realised, until she'd driven down today, was that he'd been popping over each night, after finishing his daytime appointments, to do some of the smaller jobs around the house. Such as repairing the upstairs window once Freddie had cut back the tree whose branches had invaded the house. He'd then removed all the damaged floorboards, cut out the wood which had rotted in the floor joists, replaced and sealed them and then put in new floorboards.

Sally was touched that he'd gone to this effort although she'd be telling him, when she saw him later, that she would be paying him for this work.

'This place is a bit out of the way, is it not? Thank goodness for satnav!'

Essie came to stand beside her and handed over Marvin's keys.

'Yes, it is rather. I'll need to look at getting a website sorted out which will provide clear directions on finding me, which means I will also need a logo designed and some sort of branding arranged. All stuff that I have got absolutely no idea on where to start.'

'I can help there.'

'You can?'

Essie laughed. 'Not directly. The nearest I come to

anything technical is sussing out how the microwave works! My niece, however, or rather, Craig's niece, Flora, is a graphic designer and I think she'll be able to help you with most of what you need.'

'Flora? As in Matt's daughter?'

'Yes, that's right. I'm surprised he didn't mention this to you.'

'Probably because I haven't discussed the business side of things with him. We've been too busy focusing on the building work.'

'Is there much to be done?'

'In the house? Not as much as I'd initially expected, which was a pleasant surprise. We've been able to work with the current layout of the house which means being able to retain most of its character. It's all the extra stuff out here that's going to take the most time.'

'May I be rude and ask what your exact plans are?'

'How about I give you a tour and explain as I go along.'

'Oh, yes please.'

They walked back to the front of the house and Sally, once she'd imparted the news of the B&B, began to talk Essie through her plans. She explained that the disabled accommodation would be on the ground floor and pointed out where the ramp up onto the veranda would be situated.

'I'm going to make this spot the designated disabled parking space so the access leads directly to the ramp.'

When they walked in through the doors, Essie exclaimed at the size of the hallway.

'Yes, it's big but rather dark and unwelcoming right now. However, once the glass panels at the sides of the front door are cleaned up, and the dark wood has been painted pale cream, it'll be considerably brighter and, hopefully, warmer.'

Essie agreed with her and gave heartening "oohs" and "ahhs" as they walked round and Sally brought her up to speed with her intentions for each room.

'These two rooms,' Sally opened the door for each, 'are going to be incorporated into my new living quarters. Matt's architect friend, Charlie Rowland, came over and suggested putting in a spiral staircase leading up to here. This room will be split in two with that side there, overlooking the courtyard, becoming an en suite bathroom and this area being a small hallway. The stairs will come up here, that door will stay there which will take me into the main part of the house and a door will be put there to allow access to the bedroom. The door currently in there, which leads out to the B&B hallway, will be removed.'

'Exciting. How long is that all likely to take?'

'Matt's making my living quarters his top priority after fixing the roof. He doesn't believe it's been leaking but several joists need to be replaced and he'd prefer to get those done when it's dry. Fingers crossed, my new apartment will be ready in about eight or ten weeks.'

'Will you move in right away?'

Sally laughed as she replied, 'It depends on how noisy the builders are! I won't be giving you notice on Marvin right away though, I can tell you.'

'Wise move!'

After showing Essie the kitchen and explaining how the layout was being configured between there and the dining room, the two women went up the stairs.

'I'm going to keep these two rooms as they are for the use of family and friends when they come to visit. They'll be freshly decorated and the bathroom at the end of the corridor will be fully renovated. This bedroom, after being stripped and painted, will have shelving put in to become my linen closet. And, last but not least, this will be my study or office. The desk will go in front of the window so I can look out over the courtyard and there'll be shelves along the walls for my books. I have a chair which will fit perfectly in that corner.'

'So, you anticipate spending a lot of time in here, do you, if you're putting in a comfy chair?'

'I'd prefer not to but when it comes to paying the bills and doing the accounting stuff, I'd like to be in a comfortable place as I pull my hair out.'

'Would you consider getting an accountant, if numbers aren't your thing?'

'It has crossed my mind but with everything else going on right now, it doesn't feel like a priority.'

'My Craig's an accountant. He used to be with one of the leading accountancy companies in Oxford but decided to take semi-retirement last year. He now looks after a handful of clients and offers a hands-on, bespoke service. If you're interested, I could ask him to come over and discuss your requirements with you. Even if you don't employ his services, he'll be able to point you in the direction of the best software to use that'll make it easier for you.'

'Essie, I would love to meet him! Please, whenever he's available, ask him to pop over.'

'I will do.'

'Now, I don't suppose you happen to know any vets, do you?'

'Not on a personal level, I don't. Why?'

'Well, in the space of a couple of hours, you've sorted out my website problem and my accounting problem... I was kinda hoping we could go for the hat-trick and get a vet in the bag too!'

Essie laughed as she replied, 'Sorry, honey. Even I have my limits!'

'No worries. In the words of the mighty, and much missed, Mr Meat Loaf, "Two out of three ain't bad!" Now, how about we lock up here and head into the village where you can introduce me to the best pub and I can buy you a drink as a thank you?'

'No need to say thank you, I'm happy to help, but I wouldn't say no to a glass of wine.'

'Then let's go.'

TWENTY

Matt was up on the roof of the farmhouse, helping to replace the broken tiles they'd discovered when the roof timbers were repaired, when a large Transit van drove into the courtyard, performed a U-turn and then backed up towards the barn opposite. He watched as Sally jumped out and ran to open the doors, stepping to the side to beckon to the driver to reverse a bit further.

He felt his heart give a little skip and he smiled as he turned back to the job in hand. Today was the day when Sally officially took up residence at Bramblebush Farm. The fact she was holed up in Essie Walton's motorhome inside the barn was a moot point. As far as she was concerned, she was now legally allowed to live on the premises and that was that. He'd grinned at the determined tilt of her chin when she'd uttered those words, remembering the day he'd first seen her in the school woods when she'd held an identical stance – hands on her hips, chin set firm and a look on her face that dared anyone to come over and bully the young boy she was protecting. Matt still hadn't told her that they shared a little bit of their past and he wasn't altogether sure how to bring it up. After all, did he really want to tell her that she'd been his schoolboy crush? How on earth would that go down? It could potentially make things rather awkward and as he was looking at the best part of four months before this job was completed, that could be a lot of embarrassing silences. No, it was better to keep it to himself – for now anyway. Maybe one day…

It was as he bent over to pick up some more nails that a movement below caught his eye. One of his workers, Darren Connors, was making his way over to the barn. Matt stopped to watch him as he was supposed to be unloading materials from the trucks parked in front of the house. He saw him approach Sally, speak to her for a few seconds and move towards the back of the van where he began carrying boxes and furniture into the barn where it was being stored until Sally could move into her new apartment area when it was ready.

Matt hesitated, unsure on what to do. He really needed Darren to finish unloading the trucks as they had to go back to pick up more loads, however, he didn't want to appear churlish by telling him to return to doing the job he was being paid for. He'd spotted Darren watching Sally when she was on site and he clearly fancied her. Matt had experienced a mixture of emotions when this realisation had hit him, jealousy being one of them, but he didn't feel it was his place to say anything.

He looked at his watch and decided he'd give Darren ten minutes and then he'd pull him back to his first task. He figured that was being fair.

'So, now it all makes sense…'

'I'm sorry? What?'

Sally looked at her brother's back as he walked past her, grinning like the Cheshire cat.

He put the box he was carrying on the floor and came to stand beside her.

'Stud Muffin out there. Good looking bloke, decent job, clearly has the hots for you… that's why you've moved down here. You've got a nice bit of country totty all lined up.'

'Christopher! Behave yourself! I have not!'

She punched her brother's arm, laughing when her fist barely made contact due to him knowing what was coming and skipping out of her way.

'It looks like it to me…'

'Shhhhh! He's coming back.'

She smiled at Darren walking towards her, another box from the van in his arms and judging by the way he was holding it, it was a heavy one full of books and not one containing her underwear. Something she was rather relieved about.

Behind Darren's back, Chris was making kissy-kissy motions and she could feel the heat rising in her cheeks. She glared at her brother before saying to

Darren, 'Oh, that looks like a book-box, probably best to put it over there.'

When he bent down to place the box on the floor, his t-shirt stretched across his back and the seat of his trousers tightened, treating her to a show of his physique that was far from unpleasant.

She was still watching him when he stood, turned around and caught her eye which made her blush even more. She quickly opened the box nearest to her and made a show of trying to locate the kettle.

Darren stepped over to her and said, 'I need to head off back to work now. The boss has reminded me that I have to finish unloading the truck.'

He was standing so close to her, the heat from his body was making the hairs on her arms rise. The smell of his sweat mingled with his aftershave or deodorant and it was a heady combination.

'Urm, err, right! Yes! Thank you for your help, I really appreciate it.'

'Anytime. You only need to ask.'

A slow, lazy smile spread across his cheeks and his blue eyes twinkled before he spun on his heel and marched out of the barn.

In the brief moment before he turned away, she was hit with a sudden twinge of recognition but before it could take hold in her mind and become something more definitive, her brother gave her a hefty nudge in the back.

'Bloody hell, sis, you don't want him making those moves on you in a hay barn.'

'Huh? Eh?'

She looked at Chris in confusion and the vague

thought slipped away.

'Well, if it got any hotter between the two of you, all combustible material would be at risk.'

'Stop it, it's not like that.'

'No? It certainly looked like it from where I was standing. Like I said, a bit of hot country totty! Mother will be pleased.'

'Oh, bugger off!'

This time her punch didn't miss.

TWENTY-ONE

Sally sat at her little table inside Herbie's cat run. Her ginger fluff monster was sprawled out on one of the climbing shelves Matt had so considerately placed for him to clamber upon. Although at this moment, Herbie was still sleeping off the sedative she'd had to give him for the journey to the farm. As such, with Matt and his workers now finished for the day, she was here on her own for the first time. Matt had asked her if she'd like to join him and Flora for dinner but she'd declined. Tonight, she needed to be alone.

The sun was setting and its warm glow settled upon her as she sat back in her seat and raised her face towards it while she revelled in the lack of man-made noise. No neighbours calling out, no children screaming, no car engines revving or doors slamming, no music being played louder than was really necessary. All she could hear were crickets chirping in the long grass of the nearby field, bees buzzing among the flowers which had taken over from whatever had once been planted there and a plethora of birdcalls echoing through the trimmed-back trees.

Matt had been true to his promise – the land management company had taken great care when they'd cut back the overgrowth and thinned out the trees. The area now looked better but hadn't lost any of its natural appearance. And going by all the sounds around her, the local wildlife didn't seem to have a problem with it either.

Sally took a sip of her wine and let the lazy, calm, country air seep through to her bones. For the first time since Steve's death, she no longer felt wound up tight enough to break. She understood that, for most of the human race, moving house was one of the most stressful things to go through but it hadn't been for her. Instead, it had given her a purpose. A good reason to get out of bed in the morning. She fully appreciated that her hurdles had been minimal compared to what other buyers had to deal with but there was still a lot on her plate to contend with.

She mentally worked through her vast to-do list, smiling at how long it was and how much she was relishing getting on with it.

Her first two tasks, while she waited for the house to be ready, was to make the acquaintance of the local vets, discuss her future plans with them and then see if she could get them on board to help her interview potential candidates. From the information she'd gleaned from Sukie, and the research she'd done online, Davies & Davies was a father and son outfit and she really hoped they wouldn't be too miffed at her muscling in – albeit just a little bit – on their territory.

Well, in two days' time, she'd find out.

A little sigh of contentment slipped from her lips as she leant forward to refill her glass. One of the first things Essie had shown her in the motorhome was the plastic, no-ice required, ice bucket and she was making full use of it now. An ice-bucket but without the slushy mess? That worked for her.

Her mind wandered back up the M40 towards home and she wondered how Chris and Evaine were settling into her old house. Her dilemma over what to do with it had been solved when her brother had announced his engagement to Evaine last month. She'd gifted the house to them, safe in the knowledge that Steve would have approved. When her parents had asked her about her financial position to be able to be so generous, she'd simply led them to believe that Steve's life insurance and compensation was enough to cover everything. As she'd never told them the values awarded to her, they didn't question her any further.

So, while Chris and his mate had helped to move her belongings today, Evaine had moved into the semi-detached with her parents' help. Tonight, everyone was sleeping under a new roof although, in her case, under two roofs!

'Come on, Herbie,' she gave the still-slumbering feline a gentle stroke before gathering him up in her arms, 'let's go and make ourselves comfortable inside Marvin. I've got a tuna salad in the fridge which I'm sure you'll be happy to share.'

TWENTY-TWO

Sally sat in the waiting room of Davies & Davies, Veterinary Surgery and tried to ignore the strange looks she was receiving from the other occupants. Well, the occupants who were of the two-legged variety and not tethered by a collar and leash or crammed into plastic baskets.

In fact, it was the absence of either of these items that was garnering her the attention. The thought crossed her mind that she could have brought Herbie in to be registered and have a check-up but she didn't know how long this would take and it wasn't fair to keep him cooped up in his basket for long, especially as she was still working on gaining his forgiveness for the long drive down from the Midlands to the farm.

She'd made a point of booking the last appointment of the day although she didn't know which Mr Davies she'd be meeting. At the point of making the booking, she'd tried to prise the information from the receptionist but was told that both were working this evening which had left her none the wiser.

On the drive here, there had been an inner debate over which Mr Davies would be better to work with. The father may not appreciate the prospect of losing business to an incomer while the son could be more amenable to new blood in the area. On the other hand, Mr D senior could be more open to the need of another surgery in the area while Mr D junior would be averse to a drop in profits.

Of course, they both might present a united front and try to run her out of town for all of the above reasons.

With a smile at the receptionist who was looking her way again for about the eighth time since she'd arrived, Sally tried to surreptitiously wipe her now clammy palms on her skirt and watched the patients around her dwindle until she was the last man standing. Or the last woman sitting to be exact.

'Mrs Edwards, you can go in now.'

The receptionist pointed her to a white painted door in the corner.

Hmm, that's a bit clinical, she thought. The vets at Herbie's old surgery in Burton had always made a point of coming out to the waiting room and escorting their clients through into the consulting area. She turned the handle and pushed the door open, glad she was trying to do it without a large, cat-filled, basket in her arms. A mental note was made to ensure that *her* surgery would be more friendly and approachable.

She turned from closing the door to see a white-coated figure standing with his back to her, bent over a desk in the corner. From the angle she was standing, she couldn't see if she was with Davies Senior or Junior.

When he straightened up and turned around, there was no disputing she was in the presence of greatness. Well, Davies Junior but... bloody hell... rock star looks had just gone off the scale!

The first thing Sally noticed was his height. He had to be the best part of six and a half feet tall. She was of average height but he towered above her.

The second thing to shake up her hormone radar was his thick blue-black hair. She'd never believed there was such a thing, considering it a trait only ever found in bodice-buster novels but she was being proved very wrong because Davies Junior had what could only be described as a mane! It was long at the back, down to the lower edge of his collar, although shorter at the sides above his ears. A fringe flopped down onto his forehead and each hair ending curled ever so slightly back on itself. It was hair which cried out for fingers to be run through it and Sally almost melted on the spot when Davies Junior did exactly that.

Eyes the colour of cornflowers peeped out from between long, thick, black lashes; the lower lashes were so long, he had the look of wearing eyeliner.

The Adonis look was completed by high, sharp cheekbones and a chiselled chin.

Chiselled?

Had she just described this man as being "chiselled"?

Well, there was a first time for everything and it was the first time she'd ever been struck this dumb by simply being in the presence of such startling good looks.

'Good evening, Mrs Edwards, I'm Nick Davies, how may I... err... help you?'

He was looking around her, clearly confused by her lack of a pet.

As she struggled to draw in a breath, Sally now understood why the receptionist had been so cagey about giving out details on which vet she'd be seeing – she'd bet most of the local female population was almost bribing the poor woman to be alone with this man for ten minutes. She dreaded to think how often poor Flopsy the rabbit or Tiddles the kitten were being dragged along here.

'Mrs Edwards?'

'Oh, I'm sorry. I was... err... just trying to think of the best way to go about opening the discussion I would like to have with you.'

'Okayyyyyyyy...' The low, deep, timbre in which the word was slowly dragged out had her all of a fluster again.

'Would you like to take a seat?'

'Oh, yes, thank you, Mr Davies.'

'Please, call me Nick. The "mister" bit is best kept for my father.'

Sally sank down onto the chair he'd pointed her towards, grateful that she didn't have to stand any longer as her treacherous knees had taken jelly wobbling to a whole new level.

'So, may I ask why you're here, Mrs Edwards?'

'Well, it's kind of like this…'

Hesitantly at first, but growing in confidence as she got into her stride, Sally filled him in on her plans for the barn and her farm.

'So, let me check I've got this right – you've bought an old farm over by Lower Ditchley which will be part B&B and part cat rescue. The cat rescue side will have its own veterinary surgery which while predominantly for the needs of the cats in rescue, will also offer a service to the local Ditchley population for small pets and you're asking me to help you recruit a vet because, in your own words, "you really wouldn't know where to start!" Is that correct?'

It was difficult not to grimace when the purpose for her visit was laid out so starkly before her.

'Yes, that is exactly correct.'

Sally didn't know where her bold attitude had sprung up from but she was grateful to it for coming to her aid.

'Unbelievable! You are openly saying that you are looking to take some of my clients away from me and you want me to help you do it!'

'Mr Davies… Nick, for reasons I can't fathom, you're the only small animal vet around for about fifteen miles which means you have a large catchment area. I had to book this appointment over two weeks ago and I have been informed that this is the norm. Trying to get your pet seen in the same week as your phone call is impossible. I think my suggestion is a win-win for all parties but most importantly, for the pets who need more immediate care.'

'We have emergency appointments available.'

'Emergencies are for animals who've been run over or ingested poison or something else equally urgent, not for little Tiddles who's off-colour due to a large hairball or a rabbit whose nails need to be trimmed. I won't be running away with your whole client list, only the smallest portion of it. I don't want a large practice but the clients we hope to have will go towards covering the bulk of the running cost of the surgery, meaning that any profits made elsewhere can go into the cat rescue.'

'Mrs Edwards, why do you want to run a cat rescue? Do you have any idea of what it entails?'

Sally looked at him for a moment, the seriousness of his question making her forget the effect he'd been having on her up till then.

'Yes,' she replied quietly, 'I am more than clued up on what it entails.'

'Really?'

'Mr Davies, I used to volunteer with a local rescue when I lived in the Midlands. I have felt the pain of seeing young cats come in, heavily pregnant, and give birth within hours of being rescued only for the kittens to die because the mother had been no more than a kitten herself and her little body was not able to provide the nourishment they needed. I've had to hand-feed day-old kittens because they were the sixth or seventh litter the mother had had and she was unable to care for them because she was exhausted. I've seen cats who've been treated in the worst possible ways by the worst possible humans – arriving at the rescue scared and scarred, traumatised and terrorised and who would shake with fear when a human came near them. I've seen care-givers sobbing tears while their hearts break when the decision is made to let a cat go on its final journey because it is too ill to be saved.

'I have also seen cats grow and develop from the loving care of the rescue workers. I've watched them become loving, purring little bundles of fur as they learn that not everyone is out to harm them. I've seen flea-ridden bags of bones turn into stunning animals worthy of any pedigree show because they've been fed decent food and received the proper level of care. And so many times, I have cried while saying goodbye as these rehabilitated givers of joy leave to go to new homes and learn what it is to be truly loved and wanted.

'So yes, I am fully aware of what this will entail. I know I'll be doing it 24/7 most of the time. I know how depressing and demoralising it can be. But I also know how incredibly rewarding it is. There is no greater feeling than when a cat who used to cower away from you comes running over and headbutts you with purring affection.

'Make no mistake, I'm in this for the long haul and I hope that I have the support of you and your father but if I don't... then fine, I'll find someone else to help me.'

Unable to believe she'd just made such a speech, Sally bent down to get a tissue from her bag to wipe away the tears which had gathered in the corners of her eyes.

When she looked up, she was startled to see a look of total kindness on Nick's face.

'I'm in! I'll give you all the help you need. Now, what do you say to getting out of here and joining me for dinner while you tell me more of your requirements?'

TWENTY-THREE

Nick pulled into the pub car park of The Drover's Arms and Sally followed behind him.

He'd told her that the pub, in the next village along the road from the surgery, had an excellent carvery if she liked the idea of that. As she hadn't eaten properly for about a week, grabbing snacks here and there while sorting out her move and then eating shop-prepared salads since she'd arrived because she hadn't yet dared to try the cooker in the mobile home, the thought of a lovely roast dinner had actually made her stomach growl.

'I'm guessing that might be a yes,' he'd laughed.

'I'm guessing you could be right. Moving house does not lend itself to eating proper meals at proper times.'

'Well, you can share all when we get there.'

She'd just picked her handbag up from the passenger footwell when the driver's door was opened and Nick was holding out his hand to help her from the car.

'Thank you.'

'You're welcome.'

He held the door open for her to walk into the pub and led her to a booth table over on the far side. She was eyeing up the vacant tables in the middle of the floor when he said, 'The darts team will be here within the hour and it gets quite noisy. The booth will help to cut out some of the furore and we'll be able discuss your plans without the need for sign language.'

'Ah! Fair point!'

'Now, what can I get you to drink? Then, when you're ready, we can go up to the carvery. Or, you can order something else if you prefer.' He pointed to the large colourful menu propped open on the table.

'No, thank you, the carvery will be perfect.'

And it would be. She'd sneaked a few peeks at the loaded plates on the tables they'd walked past and combined with the smells wafting around the room, her stomach now felt like it was eating itself. She couldn't wait to get up there and pile up the roasties.

Sally glanced around the pub while Nick went up to the bar. The olde worlde exterior was not matched on the inside which was as ultra-modern as any city centre establishment. The soft-cream floor tiles were offset against pale-grey walls and dark-grey woodwork. The fittings were shining chrome and she didn't envy the person whose job it was to polish them each day.

When Nick returned with her spritzer, she took a sip before saying, 'Well, this is a surprise! I was expecting it to be as old on the inside as it is on the outside.'

'It used to be until it was badly flood-damaged a few years back.'

'Oh, I didn't realise this was a flood area…'

Nick grinned. 'It's not. The old water tank in the roof sprung a leak and ended up coming through two ceilings.'

'No! Was anyone hurt?'

'Luckily, no. It happened over Christmas and the place was closed as the owners were having a well-earned break and spending a few days away at their daughter's. There had been a cold snap and the assumption is that the water in the tank froze, causing the old seams to split, and when the weather warmed up again, the water just poured out of the gaps. Given the extent of the damage, it was decided to gut the inside and start again. Jim, the owner, also felt that with quite a few old-style pubs in the surrounding villages, going more modern would provide a nice alternative for an evening out.'

'I am partial to old pubs myself but this is very nice. I could easily enjoy a nice night out here.'

'If we're going to be working together for a while, then I'm sure we'll end up here a few more times.'

'I'll confirm if I'm happy with that after I've eaten,' said Sally with a grin.

'Then let's not waste another minute. Time to hit up that carvery.'

'So, will you be gracing this fine establishment again in the future?'

Sally tried to discreetly rub her full-to-the-brim stomach under the table while answering, 'Absolutely! Although not before I've bought some skirts and trousers with elasticated waists!'

'I did warn you that the pudding portions were generous.'

'There is generous and there is "I'm fattening you up for the pot, my pretty!". They were massive!'

The darts teams and their entourages had arrived while they were eating and as Nick had forewarned, the noise levels in the pub had increased. They were having to lean across the table to hear each other.

'If I may ask, Sally, the setup you're planning is an unusual one – how did that come about?'

'It was a daft, throwaway reply to a question my husband once asked me but which I have since come to realise is something I really want to do.'

'And your husband is okay with it? Will he be helping you run everything?'

'I'm afraid not. He died three years ago.'

As she said this, Sally realised it was the first time she'd imparted this information without feeling like she was being stabbed through the heart. There had been a small clenching sensation but nothing compared to how it used to be. It would seem that her new venture was helping her to move on. She was finally facing forwards again rather than always trying to turn back.

'Oh, I am sorry. I didn't mean to cause...' Nick's

words drifted off as he looked down at the table, clearly discomforted by her blunt reply.

'No, please, it's okay. I'm learning to look ahead, and being able to say that without bursting into tears is a huge step for me. Please don't feel the need to tiptoe around me because that'll just make things awkward.'

'Okay, I won't! Now, tell me more about your farm, how you envisage it running and what you're looking for in a vet.'

For the next hour, Sally shared her plans with Nick and he took notes, asking pertinent questions regarding the level of experience she was looking for.

'I'd prefer someone who specialises in small animal care. I don't want anyone whose vocation in life is to stick their hand up a cow's hoo-haa as that won't be pertinent to my needs.'

Nick chuckled. 'No, I get that. My concern is that there is more demand for your kind of vet than there are vets to fill the spaces. Domestic animals continue to grow in popularity which has a knock-on effect across the veterinary industry. We have hired several small animal vets over the last five years but they don't last around here. The cost of property is so high meaning most have to commute which becomes wearisome after a few months.'

'Ah, well that's where I'm hoping to add an extra incentive – the job will come with its own accommodation.'

'Seriously?'

'Yes, I'm having one of the old outbuildings converted. I confess my reasons were more selfish in that I want quick and easy access to medical assistance in the event of an emergency but if this is the kind of sweetener that makes the role more desirable, then it works for me.'

'Sally, how big is this farm? I thought it was a smallholding but now…'

'It used to be a fully-functional farm back in the day but the farmer retired and sold off chunks of his land to survive. It now has forty-five acres left which consists of two fields to the front of the house, they're approximately six acres each, three fields behind the house with a total acreage of about twenty-two between them and a fully mature wood which is about nine acres. The final acres belong to the house which comes with a full quota of farm buildings like a huge barn, stables, and workshop / storage areas. These are being converted to accommodate the rescue.'

'I wish we'd known of this place! Dad and I have been wanting to expand for a while now because the practice has grown so large but the cost of trying to build an extension is so much along with the hassle factor when we're always so busy. I don't suppose you fancy selling, do you?'

'Err, no!'

Nick's words created a sudden ache, not dissimilar to the one she'd get when she thought about Steve and it was in that moment that Sally knew she'd found her corner in the world. There was nowhere else she wanted to be. Bramblebush Farm was home.

'Fair enough! If you do ever change your mind though…'

'Sorry, not going to happen!'

She grinned to soften her words even though she fully meant them. Nick grinned back and she knew no offence had been taken.

'Sally, as we've been talking this through, I've had a thought which I'd like you to ponder on – it's only a thought at this time but it might be feasible – how would you feel about sharing your new vet premises and your vet? You could have access to our resources – such as the receptionist taking your bookings for you – and in turn we can direct several of our small animal clientele in your direction, particularly the ones who live in the Ditchley area. This would remove the issue of you having to grow a business from scratch, you wouldn't be "poaching" our clients which may have caused some loyalty concerns and I'd be on hand on a consultancy basis if additional experience was required. I can also be on call to cover when your vet needs time off.'

'Oh! Wow! Erm…'

Dumbfounded, Sally sat back in her chair. She had not been expecting *that*!

'I don't want an answer right now and I would need to discuss it with my father as it's a fresh idea which requires more thought, so it would be better if we all gave it some consideration and then discussed it further. It may not be feasible but then… it might.'

'Okay, sure! In the first instance, I can see the advantages but it does need careful consideration.'

'It may also help in securing us a vet though because the opportunity for additional experience would be there. They'd still be your small animal vet but if they knew they could also gain farming experience, well… the role becomes considerably more appealing.'

As Nick spoke, Sally could see the point he was making and if the market was as difficult as he was suggesting, anything she could offer over her competitors could only be to her advantage.

'Well, like I said, it's not what I was expecting to come out of our meeting tonight but there is a lot of sense in the suggestion. You discuss it with your dad – he may be the voice of reason and be able to see any downfalls – and I will also give it more thought and see how I feel about it.'

'Excellent. And, in the meantime, I'll begin drafting a "Situations Vacant" advertisement, ready to be sent out once we've come to a decision. The earliest we're looking at getting someone started is three months as they'll need to give notice. Although, add on to that the time to run interviews, second interviews, come to a decision and then make an offer – to be honest, it's probably more likely to be four to five months.'

'That's fine. It'll be that long before the accommodation is ready for them. I'll ask my builder if he can do a reshuffle on the work to be done and move the conversion of living quarters up the list.'

'Good. Even if we don't end up working in tandem with each other, having that on your advert will get you plenty of applications.'

'I'll get on it tomorrow.'

Nick stuck his hand over the table.

'Here's to an enjoyable working relationship. Shall we celebrate over another drink?'

She shook it as she replied, 'Better not, seeing as how we're both driving but we can put it on ice for another time.'

'Deal!'

'Now, I had better be getting home otherwise Herbert will be pooping in my shoes as punishment for me being out so long.'

'Herbert?'

'My cat! A fluffy ginger with cat-titude oozing from every furry follicle! One way or another, you will have the pleasure of meeting him some day!'

'I look forward to it.'

'Hah! You say that now but you forget – you're a vet. Most of your meetings will be of the white coat variety and he's not too keen on those.'

'Then we'll have to look at throwing in a few non-white coat occasions so I can meet him as a friend.'

This comment had Sally looking up with surprise. Was Nick suggesting something more here? Or was he merely referring to his earlier business idea? She couldn't see anything in his expression to suggest he was expressing an interest in getting to know *her* better but she was so long out of the dating game she wouldn't know where to begin these days.

'Ah… erm… right. Yes… sure! Okay… well, I need to get going.'

As they walked out of the pub, she was aware of several pairs of eyes looking in her direction and not all of them were friendly. She could only assume the glares were coming from ladies who had their own desires to see Nick on a "non-white coat occasion" and, most likely, on their own! She just had to hope they all owned cows and horses otherwise her small animal surgery could end up being rather empty.

TWENTY-FOUR

Matt looked out into the courtyard when he heard the sound of an engine purring past. A top-of-the-range Land Rover swept over towards the barn and tooted its horn when it came to a stop by the side of the far-end doors. A moment later, Sally popped her head out and a tall, dark-haired man alighted from the vehicle. He gave Sally a kiss on the cheek before following her inside.

Matt paused for a moment, wondering who he was while also telling himself that it was none of his business. Sally had a lot going on right now and he could be anyone from a bank manager to an interior designer. Although the kiss was not what you'd expect from a bank manager but almost definitely from a designer. They were all huggy-feely that way!

He returned his attention to his current task – clearing out all the debris from the basement byre area, ready to turn it into a cosy apartment for Sally.

When Charlie came to visit and cast his architectural eye over the space, his suggestion of a spiral staircase up to the floor above and using the two rooms overhead as sleeping and bathing quarters had resulted in making the conversion considerably easier and thus quicker. The byre would be transformed into an open plan kitchen / dining / living area with a small cloakroom under the internal house stairs for convenience. The large barn doors would be replaced with fold-away glass patio doors to open the space up to the outside when the weather permitted, which was not today, and a standard door would be placed further along beside the kitchen area to permit easy access to the courtyard and the cat barn when it was complete.

The early morning drizzle was steadily growing into a full-on deluge although it had yet to reach its peak. Matt had worked and lived in the area long enough to recognise the weather patterns and he was glad they'd made the roof their priority the previous week. The building was now reasonably weatherproof although he'd be happier once the new windows were fitted – the old wooden frames were fairly rotten meaning they needed to be completely ripped out and replaced. Sally had opted to put in new double-glazed sash-windows, in keeping with the original style, but after much deliberation and discussion, had gone with the UPVC versions due to their longevity factor. He had reassured her several times over that the latest version of UPVC had advanced greatly since its early ancestors and the wood-grain effect made all the difference to its appearance.

He was on his way back from dropping a load of

rubble in the skip when he noticed Darren Connors standing off to one side, staring over at the Land Rover.

'You alright there, Darren?'

'Oh, err… yes, boss. Fine, thanks.'

'Okay. Need you to get on with removing that old, lead pipework, mate. I want this whole area cleared up by the weekend so we can get on with laying the under-floor heating next week and getting the screed down.'

'Sure thing, boss.'

Matt kept an eye on Darren and while he did get back to pulling out the old pipework, he was doing so with one eye still across the courtyard. In fact, it wasn't until the Land Rover pulled back out of the yard an hour later, that the job was attacked more vigorously. He suspected it was the second kiss on Sally's cheek from the tall dark stranger which had prompted this additional effort. There was no doubt Darren had a serious case of the hots for Sally and while Matt didn't approve of his workers liaising with the clients, he didn't feel he had the right to forbid them from doing so. If Darren chose to ask Sally out, Matt would have to stand back and say nothing. How he felt about such a situation, however, was not something he was prepared to question too deeply – he wasn't sure if he'd be happy with the answer.

Three hours later, Matt was knocking on the barn door himself while trying to avoid the rain which was now coming down like stair rods from the heavy black clouds above.

'Hey, Matt, quick, get in out of the rain. Why are you knocking? You don't need to do that.'

'I don't like to just walk in – this is kind of your home right now.'

He stepped in through the wicket door and stopped upon hearing the loud timpani of the rain on the metal roof of the barn.

'Bloody hell, I didn't realise it would be so loud in here.'

Sally followed his eyes up to the wooden flooring of the hayloft above them.

'I don't think it would be so bad if there was hay up in the loft, that would absorb the noise, but with it being empty up there, it's all just vibrating around the place.'

'Well, thankfully, the new roof along with the insulation and panelling we're putting in will resolve that. Although, it's going to be a few months down the line now that we've brought forward the renovation of the workshops.'

'It's fine and once I'm in Marvin with his door closed, I can barely hear it. Mind you, I don't think Herbie's so keen. He's been under the covers of the bed since the rain began coming down like this.'

'Poor little thing.'

It had been quite a revelation for Matt when he'd found himself drawn to Sally's large, opinionated cat. Even though Flora had asked many times over the years if they could have a cat or a dog, he'd always refused because he knew he'd be the one who'd end up looking after it and there had been times when he'd just about managed to look after himself and Flora. Adding another body to the mix hadn't been an option. As such, he'd never considered himself an animal person. Whenever he worked in homes with resident four-legged creatures, they were usually kept out of his way so he had little interaction with them. Therefore, the first time he'd come to give Sally a progress report and Herbie had jumped up on his lap and settled down to sleep, he could barely move from the shock. And, of course, from the ginger lump snoring on top of him. When Sally had told him how honoured he was, as Herbie didn't do strangers very well, a little thrill of pleasure had run through him. Since then, whenever he dropped by, Herbie made a point of coming over and rubbing himself around his legs or jumping onto his lap, his loud purring vibrating through Matt's hands as he petted him.

'Would you like a coffee? The kettle has just boiled.'

'If it's not too much trouble, that would be great, thank you.'

He took a seat in front of the motorhome's large windscreen, swivelled it round to look through to the bedroom area and watched as the lump in the middle of the bed slithered over to the edge. Two fluffy ginger paws stretched out from under the quilt before hitting the floor. They were soon followed by a snout, whiskers, a fluffy face, and a body with a vast brush of a tail bringing up the rear. Quite literally! Another stretch ensued before Herbie padded down the step and clambered onto Matt.

'Hey, little dude, is all this noise too much for your

little sensitive ears? It's not nice, is it?'

The cat pushed his head up against the palm of his hand, butting it several times.

'Here you go.'

Sally set the mug of coffee in front of him and then sat down on the opposite side of the table.

'I know I say this every time, but it never ceases to amaze me when I see how Herbie responds to you. The only other person he did that with was Steve. When Nick was here earlier, Herbie did a disappearing act so you truly have something going on that no one else has.'

Matt saw his chance to satisfy his curiosity over the stranger from earlier and he quickly grabbed it.

'Nick?'

'Yes, Nick Davies. He's the vet who's kindly helping me with recruiting a vet of my own. Have you never met him?'

He shook his head.

'No, I can't say that I have. But as I don't have a pet, that's not really a surprise. Never had the need of his services.'

'Oh, I kind of thought that everyone around here knew everyone else. That's certainly the impression I've been getting.'

Matt laughed. 'I know it can feel like that, especially within the village itself, but it's not always the case. Like I said, if I'd ever had the need of a vet, then I'm sure our paths would have crossed but as I haven't…'

'I suppose.'

'So, was he here with good news?'

Matt didn't know why he felt compelled to know more about this "Nick" bloke's visit but the question was out there before he had a chance to consider if he should.

'Well, there's been an unexpected development…'

'He's not trying to cause trouble because you'll be taking over some of his area, is he?'

'No. Quite the opposite as it happens. He and his father would like to offer a kind of partnership. They know the area they cover is too big for them and they've tried employing small animal vets in the past but for different reasons, they don't stick around for long. Nick thinks that what I'm offering – accommodation, their own surgery which they can build to their own requirements – could be a game-changer and bring in someone who'll stay the course. They would like to farm out their small animal clients to my surgery and I would pay them a small yearly administration fee to cover the costs of the additional services provided. The use of their receptionist for example. She'd make the appointments and keep the records updated which means I'd save on the cost of having to employ someone to do that here.'

'Well, that sounds good so far but I can't believe they're going to hand over a chunk of their clients just like that without any kind of recompense. What's the catch?'

'I can't see one. The Davies acknowledge that they're likely to lose a portion of their clients anyway but if we do it like this, they can use my vet as extra cover for their surgery and vice-versa. One concern I've had since Nick first mentioned it, was what to do if my vet was on a day off and an emergency case came in – I'd be stuck. Now we'll have a rota system going on so that everyone gets time off but there is still cover. They are fully aware my rescue animals will always be the priority and any emergency cases will supersede booked appointments.'

'And the loss of profit? They're not okay with that, surely?'

'Again, it goes back to accepting they'd lose a number of clients anyway but Nick reckons that the time being freed up by having my vet here for the small animals, will enable them to dedicate more of their time to the new racing stables which have opened up on the other side of the county and which Mr Davies Senior is very keen to get the business for.'

'It sounds like it's all working out well.'

'So far, it's good. Nick has been so helpful. That's why he was here earlier – looking around the hayloft to see the space we'll be working from and to provide a fresh set of eyes for the planned setup of the rescue down here. He's already suggested we look at putting in interlocking doors at the entrance to the rescue hall, as I'm now going to call it, to make sure we don't have any escapees.'

Matt bit back an exclamation. He'd also had this idea but had been saving it for when they got round to renovating the barn as he hadn't wanted to overload Sally with too much detail all at once. Now this "Nick" one was getting the credit *and* Sally's starry eyes. Bugger!

'I agree, that's an excellent idea. It makes a lot of sense. I'll look into them for you and get you some information.'

'Thank you. Now, Essie mentioned that your Flora is a graphic designer – is that correct? And if so, do you think she'd be interested in doing some work for me?'

'Yes, she is a graphic designer and I'm sure she'd be thrilled to work for you. I'll leave her number with you before I go and you can give her a call.'

'Brilliant! Thank you.'

'No problem. Now, let me update you with where we're at with the house…'

When Sally leant forward to look at the notes he'd placed on the table, her light floral perfume filled his head and he felt a slight dizzy sensation. It only lasted a few seconds but it was enough for Matt to know that he was going to have to sit down with himself and work out exactly what it was he was feeling for this woman, although he suspected he already knew the answer.

TWENTY-FIVE

Flora drove slowly up the road towards the farm. Her dad had warned her that despite the interim fixes made to it, it was still quite rough. Given how much she was bouncing about, she dreaded to think what it had been like previously.

She came to the fork and took the left-hand option, following it down to the five-bar gate. When her dad had been discussing the job with her the previous night, he'd told her this would be Sally's private entrance once all the work was done and the track would be extended past the back of the old stable block where a small car park area was being put in for the vet surgery.

She parked up, grabbed her laptop bag from behind her seat and slipped through the quaint little kissing gate, coming to a standstill as she rounded the corner into the courtyard.

'Oh, my!' she muttered.

When her father had been talking about this job over the last month or so, she hadn't really appreciated the scale of it. Until now! Seeing it for herself brought home how big a task this was. She looked to her right, at the main house, and saw her dad through the open barn doors, half hidden behind what looked like kitchen units. She walked over and stuck her head inside.

'Hey, Dad.'

'Hi, sweetie, are you here for your appointment with Sally already?' He looked at his watch as he stood and walked over towards her.

'Yes, I am. Guessing you've had a busy morning, then…'

'I have! I totally didn't realise that was the time. So, are you all set?'

'As much as I can be. It all depends if Sally has something in mind or if she's a blank canvas, wanting me to do all the creating.'

'Well, she hasn't said much to me on the branding side of things so I'm afraid I can't help, although she is pretty on the ball with everything else so I'd be surprised if she doesn't have a couple of ideas to throw in the pot for you.'

'Blimey! Now I'm nervous… she sounds hyper-organised!'

'She's lovely and I'm sure you'll both work together very well.'

'Then I had better get on with it. I don't want to ruin my chances by being late for our first appointment. Where do I go?'

'Across to the old barn, through the wicket gate

there on the far right. There's no need to knock, just go in and head over towards the motorhome.'

Her dad pointed the way and gave her a smile of reassurance as she walked off.

Flora felt her heartbeat quicken as she approached the barn. This had the potential to be a lucrative consignment with there being three businesses on the same site. She was here to pitch for the B&B initially but if it went well…

She pushed the wicket gate open and stepped inside. Having expected the barn to be dark and gloomy, she was surprised to find it quite bright and sunny due to the large doors on the opposite side being wide open.

She made her way towards the motorhome but slowed her step when she heard voices floating over the top of it towards her.

'Look, Darren, I appreciate you asking, I really do, but I don't want to go out to dinner with you. I'm just not in the right place for that at the moment.'

The woman's voice held a note of exasperation.

'It's only dinner I'm asking you for, not your hand in marriage. What's the big deal?'

Hmmm, she didn't like the aggressive tone that was said in. She drew closer to the large vehicle and came to a halt just out of sight around the side.

'The big deal is that it wouldn't feel right. You're a nice man, Darren, but it would be wrong for me to accept. I've already said this to you twice before. Please, stop asking me, it's not fair to keep doing so.'

'Then just say "yes" and we're all good. It's not that difficult.'

Flora decided that this was as good a moment as any to make her presence known. She stepped out and marched quickly towards Sally, practically barging Darren out of the way, stuck her hand out and said, 'Hi, Sally, I'm Flora. I'm here for our meeting. Oh,' she donned an innocent expression as she looked at Darren, 'I hope I'm not interrupting... I was worried about being late. Didn't want to create a bad impression, you know.'

'No, no, you're not interrupting anything. Thank you for coming over. Darren, I think Matt is probably looking for you.'

Flora watched both Sally and Darren carefully as he turned and strode towards the door back to the yard. There was no mistaking Sally's relief at seeing him leave but Darren's body language screamed that he was annoyed by the interruption.

'Can I get you a drink, Flora? Tea, coffee, something cold?'

When the wicket gate closed behind Darren, Flora held up her hand to say "wait", placed her laptop bag on one of the garden chairs by the van, and stealthily made her way back to the main barn door. As she'd suspected, the small door hadn't been closed fully and when she yanked it open, Darren was hunched up with his ear pressed against the small gap.

'Seriously, Darren... I think you'd better report back in at the farmhouse PDQ before there's trouble!'

'Pah!' he spat out before moving away. She watched until he'd disappeared up the side of the main house before closing the door behind her. As a precaution, she dropped the latch to ensure they wouldn't be disturbed.

'He's definitely gone now although he was trying to earwig at the door.'

'You are kidding me… seriously?'

Several emotions passed over Sally's face – annoyance, exasperation, and fear. It was the latter which prompted Flora to ask, 'Are you having a problem with him? I wasn't eavesdropping,' well, she had a little bit, 'but I couldn't help but overhear some of the conversation as I was walking over from the door. It would appear the word "no" doesn't sit within his vocabulary.'

'You would be right, Flora,' Sally sighed. 'That's now the third time he's asked me out and just won't accept my refusal. I've tried to be polite about it and let him down gently but his persistence is wearing me out. The thing is, I can't risk being rude or blunt to him because I'm a bit isolated in here and well… some blokes… you know…'

'I do. You should tell my dad – he'll get it sorted for you.'

'I don't want to get anyone into trouble. I just want him to do his job and leave me alone. Anyway, do you mind if we drop the subject and move on? Let me start again – it's lovely to meet you, Flora, and can I offer you a drink?'

'It's very nice to meet you, Sally, and something cold would be lovely. It's a warm one today.'

'How about a St Clements – deliciously refreshing when feeling a bit parched.'

'That sounds good to me.'

'Please, take a seat and I'll be right back.' Sally

gestured towards the garden table and chairs she had set up outside the motorhome.

By the time she returned with a tray of ice-filled glasses and a jug full of orange juice, bitter lemon, ice and slices of fruit, Flora had her laptop set up and some folders open which show-pieced her abilities to maybe provide Sally with a few ideas if she didn't have any of her own.

'I like this little setup you have here, Sally. What a good idea to put your garden table and chairs outside the motorhome like this, to give you more space.'

'Thank you. I've also got a set out in the run so I can enjoy the sun when it's not too hot, sit in here in the shade when it is or, if it's cold, I stay in the van. It's great to have options.'

The smile she gave Flora was so bright and sunny, it was easy to see why Darren Connors was infatuated with her. A little part of her wondered if her father was too but she pushed that thought away – this was not the time or place to be thinking such things – pulled her laptop towards her and began finding out what Sally was looking for.

Two hours later, after the jug had been refilled twice and the filled rolls Sally made for lunch had been devoured, they sat back, satisfied they'd come up with something that did what Sally needed it to do.

'And you're sure the website will be easy to navigate? I've been on some which were horrific and had you jumping through all sorts of hoops before you got to the end of your booking.'

'I promise you, Sally, this one will be straightforward. With only three bedrooms, there shouldn't be too many issues. And you're quite sure you're happy with the name?'

'Yes. I think "Bramblebush B&B" is perfect. Putting "farm" in there made it a bit of a mouthful. Plus, it's not a farm anymore and could be misleading. I don't want people turning up expecting to see cows and sheep in the fields. Equally, I don't want people looking elsewhere because they think it'll smell of cows and sheep!'

'Indeed! I quite agree. So, I will get on with that and once the interior is finished, we'll get photographs taken and loaded up so your future guests can see what you have to offer.'

'I'm hoping it won't be too long now. Your dad said that when the new windows have all been installed, they'd be able to crack on with the inside.'

'You're having your own small apartment built, aren't you? Dad mentioned something…'

'Yes. What used to be the byre under the house is being transformed.'

'How's it looking?'

'I don't know! Your dad has told me I'm not allowed to see it until it's completed. I am allowed to visit before it's decorated though so I can decide what colours I want and where.'

'Blimey! That's kind of him, the bossy old sod!'

Sally laughed along with her before going into the van and coming back with another tray of juice and a few bowls of nibbles.

'Oh, Sally, you don't need to keep feeding me. I'll be getting on now and let you get back to sorting things out here – you must be so busy.'

'Oh, do you have to go? Sorry, that must sound strange but... well... it's rather nice to have some female company. As nice as your dad is, he's the only person I've spoken to for ages. Darren doesn't count and I don't know anyone else around here yet. While I've "met" Jenny and Sukie, I've not been in a position to sit with them for a natter. Essie is the only person I'd say I sort of know but she's been away in Italy for the last few weeks and only got back two days ago.'

Flora placed her laptop bag by the side of her chair, picked up some crisps and gave Sally a big smile.

'Well, as I have nowhere else to be right now and this is a lovely spot to sit and chill,' she waved her hand towards the field outside the barn door, 'I'd be delighted to chew the fat with you for a while.'

Sally refilled their glasses and as she handed one to Flora, asked, 'What made you choose to be a graphic designer?'

Flora gave a small shrug. 'I kind of fell into it. I love art and all things that are arty but I'm not an artist. Not in the traditional sense. I'm no Picasso or Danny Delaney but I seem to have an eye for design and colour. I think "putting things together" is a good way of describing what I do and enjoy most. I also dabble with interior design – my uncle went travelling last year and I redecorated his house while he was away. At his request, I should add. I didn't break in and just do it!'

Sally giggled at that.

'So, you do interior design too... that's interesting to know.'

'It is?'

'Yes. You see, I have several ideas for the B&B but I don't know which way to go – do I keep it traditional to give the full-on, English country cottage experience or is that a bit twee and overdone, in which case should I go all out modern instead? Or, do I try to find a way of fusing the two together?'

'Have you checked out what the opposition are doing?'

'I've been on the websites for the nearest establishments and it seems to be a fifty-fifty split. The Inn on the Green in the village is totally traditional while the Dog & Duck at the other end is full-on modern.'

'And looking further afield?'

'The same – half traditional and half modern.'

'Then you go for the fusion option. This will enhance your USP.'

'My what?'

'Unique selling point. So, for example, if your bathrooms can accommodate it, have a walk-in shower area but also a traditional free-standing bath which could be a spa bath and thus providing your modern twist.'

'Oh! I like the sound of that…'

'Yeah, me too! Unfortunately, Dad won't put one in at home. Boring or what?'

'I'm sure he has his reasons.'

'Yeah! He's boring!'

'Maybe when you get your own place…'

'Hah! That won't be happening anytime soon. Properties around here come up once in a blue moon and even if something did come along, I'd never be able to afford it. No, I'm stuck at home for the foreseeable.'

'I'm sure your dad likes having you there.'

'Oh, we get along fine. It's just been the two of us for the last couple of decades – we've got it pretty much sussed by now.'

'It must have been difficult at times though, for you both.'

'We've had our moments and I do know it's been hard for him to be both mum and dad to me. I've been hoping since forever that he'll meet someone but he's never shown the slightest bit of interest in getting back in the saddle. I thought he might get his act together when I went off to art college but nope, I came home three years later and nothing had changed.'

'He's clearly happy as he is or was so in love with your mum that he feels it would be wrong to be with anyone else.'

'Maybe. I just think it would be nice for him to have someone special again. He's an amazing bloke and it's a shame to think of him going to waste.'

'I've got a meeting with your Uncle Craig at the end of the week, is he an uncle on your mum or dad's side.'

'Oh, he's on my mum's side and currently "Persona-non-Grata" with my dad these days.'

'Oh?'

'Yeah. Basically, my dad blames my maternal grandmother for my mum's death. Uncle Craig didn't have much to do with my grandmother for many years – she lives in Scotland, you see – which was fine with my dad. Last year, however, Uncle Craig reconnected with her and they've grown closer over the months since. My dad sees this as a betrayal by Uncle Craig and now won't talk to him either. However, I am very fond of my uncle and Essie so visit them often. My dad doesn't like it but he accepts it as I'm old enough to make my own decisions. It's probably best that you know this because if they cross paths when Uncle Craig is here, it could be interesting.'

'It would seem so.'

'Anyway, enough about my crazy family, if I'm going to be helping out with your interior designing, is there any chance I could get a sneak peek at what we'll be working with so I can begin to do some research and put ideas together. After all, if you're going down the lines of posh spa baths, you'll need to ensure Dad knows ASAP so that the plumbing is all in the right places.'

'Good point.' Sally looked at her watch. 'Tell you what, they should have finished working in the house for today – would you like to go over for a look round?'

'I thought you weren't allowed?'

'Oh, that's only for my new apartment – nothing was said about the rest of the house.'

Flora stood up and grabbed her laptop.

'Lead the way! This I really want to see.'

TWENTY-SIX

Matt switched off the oven when he heard Flora come through the front door. The potatoes were baked and could be kept warm in there for a few more minutes.

'Hi, Dad.' She walked into the kitchen and placed a kiss on his cheek. 'How long till dinner is ready?'

'The spuds are cooked and the salad is tossed. It'll only take a few minutes to finish off the chops and we're good to go.'

'Great. I'll quickly change if that's okay?'

'Of course. Off you go.'

When Flora came back into the room, his heart missed a beat – in her long, floaty summer dress, she looked just like her mother. Well, current hairstyle aside. But, in every other way, it was like seeing his own Flora for the first time all over again.

'Well, how did it go with Sally?' he asked, making a point of moving his head-space on – he'd only become maudlin if he let it rest on his wife and he was beginning to grow weary of it now, although it had only taken twenty years for him to get to this point.

"Hmm, are you sure it's not the presence of a certain woman called Sally, that's brought you to this…" asked a sneaky little voice in the back of his head.

Matt ignored it and looked at Flora as she laid the table.

'Really well. She's lovely and so friendly.'

'See, I told you there was nothing to worry about.'

'You did. And you were right. Although, it's a good thing I arrived when I did.'

'What do you mean?' He flipped the chops over on the grill, spooned a little of the juice from the drip tray over them to keep them moist and dropped the lid back down. Another couple of minutes and they'd be done.

'Well, one of your workers – Darren? – was in there with her when I walked in. Apparently, he's asked her out three times now and even though she turned him down, he's not taking no for an answer. I got the feeling that, if I hadn't arrived when I did, things may have turned a little nasty. Certainly, Sally was relieved to see me. And even after he left, he was hanging around the barn door trying to listen through it.'

The oven door slammed closed as Matt kicked it shut.

'Dad?'

'Oh, sorry, Flora. The tray was burning my hand through the towel and I hit the door with more force than I intended.'

'Right. And not because you're angry with the information I've just passed on?'

'Okay, yes, I'm annoyed at what you've told me. I've already had words with Darren about pestering Sally and hanging around her all the time.'

Matt hoped he was doing a good job of hiding his true feelings from Flora because, inside, he was absolutely seething. How dare Darren Connors intimidate Sally in this manner. He was furious on two levels. One – she was the client and should not be subjected to this behaviour which could cost them the job if she was of a mind to cancel the contract due to harassment and two, which was far more important – because it was unacceptable for a man to try and coerce a woman into going on a date. Or anything else for that matter! Bloody hell! Hadn't anything from the last few years, where the rights of women were taking centre stage across the media, touched Darren at all? Was he *that* unaware of how inappropriate he was being?

'So, what do you intend to do about him, Dad? You can't keep him on site after this – that's not fair on Sally.'

'Oh, don't you worry about that, Flora. I'll have a word with Robbie tonight. Darren Connors can swap places with Lucy Flemming.'

'He won't like that.'

'Tough!'

As Flora spooned some salad onto her plate, Matt took a bigger gulp from his bottle of beer than he would normally but he needed it to try and calm the fury which was rocketing around inside. Darren

Connors had gone too far and he was lucky to be getting away with just a transfer.

The following morning, Matt was still fired up over what Flora had told him. He had to bide his time before speaking to Darren though, as he needed to ensure he finished the plumbing in Sally's basement. It was no secret that Darren had a temper on him – which is why he knew Flora hadn't exaggerated her concerns for Sally the day before – and so Matt had to carefully choose his moment to inform Darren he was off this job. With the crush he'd developed on Sally, he was most definitely not going to take the news well.

The opportunity finally arose that afternoon when Darren came to tell him that he'd finished the last of the pipework, the sink was now draining properly and the kitchen appliances were also up and running.

'Great stuff, Darren. Let me just do the checks on them so I can sign them off.'

Twenty minutes later, he was satisfied that Darren had done a good job. He sighed inwardly. Darren was a great plumber and he was sorry to lose him from this job but there was no way he could stay. He'd gone too far.

'Darren, come outside please, I need to talk with you.'

Matt walked out to the courtyard and waited for Darren to catch up with him.

'Alright, boss? Any problems with the sign-off?'

'No, Darren, none at all. A fabulous job as always,

well done!'

'Thanks, boss.'

'You're welcome. I just need to let you know that from tomorrow, you'll be working with Robbie over at Burford.'

'Why?'

'He needs your particular skills for the job there.'

'But I like working here.'

'I'm sure you do but you're needed over there. So, please be on site for eight-thirty tomorrow morning.'

'Okay, boss.'

The surliness of the reply did not go unnoticed and he was about to address it when one of the other lads called over to him.

'Hey, boss, there's a delivery of plaster here which needs your signature.'

'Cheers. Be right there…'

He looked back at Darren.

'Are we good here, Darren?'

'Yes, boss.'

'Very well.'

He nodded to him and then turned towards the house, pleased the situation was resolved and hadn't been as traumatic as it might have been.

A quarter of an hour later, having checked and signed for the latest batch of building supplies, Matt decided he'd let Sally know that she'd have no further problems with Darren and advise her of his reassignment. He would also stress to her that she must tell him if there were any further problems of this nature. He was grateful Flora had brought it to his attention this time but it shouldn't have been up to her and he had to ensure Sally took this on board.

He was about to knock on the wicket gate when he remembered again that Sally had insisted it wasn't necessary. He wasn't yet used to just walking in.

As he opened the door, the sound of shouting flew towards him.

'YOU BITCH! HOW DARE YOU COMPLAIN ABOUT ME. WHAT THE FUCK DID YOU DO THAT FOR?'

'I didn't do or say anything. Now get away from me or I *will* be making a complaint!'

'DON'T FUCKING LIE TO ME! THERE'S NO OTHER REASON WHY I'D BE GETTING TRANSFERRED. IT'S ALL YOUR FAULT AND NOW YOU'RE GOING TO PAY FOR THAT…'

Matt ran across the barn and came around the motorhome in time to see Darren push Sally up against the wall by her throat.

'Oi! Get your hands off her, now!'

He grabbed Darren's collar, pulled him from her and all but threw him across the barn floor.

'She deserves a punch for what she's done!'

Hearing this pathetic apology for a man saying a woman deserved to be hit, never mind that it was Sally he was referring to, was too much for Matt. With no thought of the consequences, he pulled his arm back and gave Darren the punch *he* deserved – square on the nose! Blood spurted over his hand as the man landed on the ground.

With the red mist now fully descended, he found a strength in his arms that enabled him to drag Darren over to the door by the scruff of his collar and throw him out onto the cobbles.

'GET OUT OF HERE, NOW! YOU ARE FIRED! DON'T YOU EVER SHOW YOUR FACE AROUND MY BUSINESS AGAIN.'

'YOU CAN'T FIRE ME! I'LL SUE YOU FOR PHYSICAL ABUSE.'

'Go right ahead! And I'll be sure to let the police know that you were halfway to strangling a woman. Whose side do you think they'll be on when they hear that? Now fuck off and get out of my sight before I land another punch on you.'

Their raised voices had brought the rest of his employees running out of the house and they were all standing watching the spectacle in front of them.

'Jimmy, Harry – please get this scumbag out of here and make sure he leaves. He was about to hit Sally.'

He added the last bit on purpose as he knew this would anger them and they'd make sure he was gone. When they stepped across and roughly man-handled Darren to his feet, Matt knew it had been the right thing to do. Darren would get no sympathy from either them or from any of the other lads, which was exactly as it should be.

He watched Darren being dragged off and once he was out of sight, he turned and walked back into the barn, shaking his bruised and aching fist. He was glad he'd arrived in time to come to Sally's assistance but, damn, why did it have to be so bloody painful?

TWENTY-SEVEN

Sally braced her back against the wall and used it to push herself up from the floor which she'd slumped down upon when Darren had been pulled away.

With great tenderness, she touched the back of her head and was relieved when her fingers came away dry. It had hit the rough brick wall with such force, she wouldn't have been surprised to find it bleeding. But thankfully, it wasn't – just incredibly sore.

Her hand came round to her neck and she didn't need a mirror to know it would already be sporting some glorious bruising – the pain in her throat was enough to bring her to that conclusion. She leant over, one hand on her knee for balance, the other still rubbing her neck as she coughed and gasped. Darren had only pinned her against the wall for a few seconds but he'd done so with some force and it had been long enough to inflict damage.

Her eyes were still watering and she was wiping

the tears from her face when she heard footsteps. Looking up, she saw Matt coming towards her.

'Than—,' her voice came out in a dry croak. She stopped, coughed, and tried again.

'Thank you,' she managed this time.

'Sally, I am so sorry. I never for a moment thought he'd come at you like that.'

She slowly made her way over to the iPad, lying where it had skittered across the floor by the barn door when Darren had overturned the table to reach her.

A small prayer of gratitude went up when she saw it was undamaged and she walked back to the table, righted it and put the tablet down on it. She scooped up the plastic outdoor jug and glass which, as luck would have it, had been empty and took them into the motorhome. A moment later she returned with two glasses of water. She placed one on the table, pushing it towards Matt, and took small sips from the other, trying not to grimace with pain when she swallowed.

'Why?' She looked at Matt as she whispered, the pain in her throat feeling like shards of glass were lodged there. 'Why did he think I'd put in a complaint against him? I don't understand.'

'I reassigned him to our other project and told him this afternoon.'

'Why did you do that?'

'Because Flora told me he was harassing you and that is not permissible.'

'She shouldn't have done that.'

'No, she shouldn't have done, YOU should have!'

Sally blinked in surprise at the harsh tone of Matt's voice.

'I'm sorry, what?'

'YOU should have told me, Sally. YOU should have been the one to let me know there was a problem, not Flora. It was her concern for you that brought it to my attention but I don't appreciate my daughter being in that situation.'

'Matt, with respect, do you think anything about this situation would have played out any differently if I'd been the one to tell you?'

For a few seconds they glared at each other and then Matt's shoulders dropped, his eyes fell to the floor and his hands slowly unclenched.

'No, you're right, it wouldn't have made any difference. Darren Connors has a short fuse and the outcome would most likely have been exactly as it was.'

The movement of his hands caught her attention. 'Your hand? What happened?'

'I may have felt it was necessary to punch Darren in order to subdue him.'

'Oh! Ouch!'

'Yeah, just a bit.'

'Sit!' She pointed to the wooden garden seat she'd just straightened. 'I'll be back in a moment.'

When she returned, she had a Tupperware box in her hand which she upended onto the table and shuffled the contents about until she found what she was after.

'Here we go – arnica cream. This'll do the job.'

'Seriously? You believe all that nature stuff?'

'Absolutely! Natural healing was here long before all your chemical, pharmaceutical drugs and humanity survived so there must be something in it.'

'But new drugs are much better than this nonsense.'

'Are they? You don't think they can work alongside each other, that we're better when we embrace the old along with the new? Here, give me your hand.'

She gave another small cough as she took Matt's hand in hers. The pain in her throat was easing off although her neck still throbbed. She gently rubbed the cream across the bruised knuckles and down the fingers. She put another dab on the back of his hand and soothed it over his skin.

'There, that should help. If you have gloves, I'd recommend wearing them for a bit to protect you till the bruising eases.'

'What about you? You have bruising…'

Matt pointed at his neck and moved it from side to side.

'Ah yes, my turn now.'

With the same care she'd given to her patient, Sally applied the cream to her own wounds. When she was finished, she looked at the water glasses on the table. 'You know, I think I could really do with a strong cup of tea. Care to join me?'

'Err… yes, I will, thank you. I'll just go and tell the lads to finish up for the day. It's nearly time anyway – half-an-hour early won't hurt anyone.'

Sally had the teapot and mugs on the table when he returned. She'd also wrapped a light, chiffon scarf around her neck to hide the bruises which were more severe than she'd expected. The sight of them, when she'd checked herself in the mirror, had not been pretty at all.

'Everything okay?' she asked.

'Yes. Darren has gone and the boys have asked me to pass on their wishes to you. They're all angry at his behaviour and they've said if there's anything you need, you only have to ask.'

'I'm not some defenceless little lady, you know…'

'No one is suggesting you are. We're all just showing you the same level of kindness and respect that we would for anyone. Besides, with your dad's judo skills, the last thing I'd expect you to be is defenceless!'

She chuckled. 'Yeah, well, there is that I suppo— Hang on! How do you know about my dad's judo skills?'

'Ah! Oops!'

Matt's face turned a fine shade of red under her stare.

'I knew you from school. You used to go to Queen Vic's in Lichfield.'

'I did, though… I don't remember you. Sorry.'

'Don't be! We never spoke and as I was two years above you, our paths rarely crossed. You came to my attention one day when I was walking home through the woods. You were defending one of the first-years against a bunch of bullies. I watched for a moment to see what was going on and was all set to step in to help when they began dispersing. I heard one mutter, as they walked away, that your dad taught martial arts and it wasn't worth messing with you.'

'Gosh! Yeah… I remember that day now. The kid

was my brother's mate and next-door neighbour. He was a right geeky little thing – perfect bully bait!'

'After that, I kind of noticed you around more often and—'

He stopped.

'Yes?'

Matt sighed before carrying on speaking. 'And I was going to ask you come with me to the end-of-year school dance. But you went and left and I didn't get the chance.'

'Oh! Right! My… err… dad got a new job over towards Derby and decided it was a good time to move. Unfortunately, I didn't get a say in the matter. I was pretty pissed off about it, let me tell you. I'd been so looking forward to going to that dance. I'd chosen my outfit and everything!'

'I know. I heard you raging about it to one of your friends.'

'Why didn't you mention this sooner?'

Sally was surprised by Matt's revelation and wasn't sure if it felt a little creepy too. Or was she just being over-sensitive after what had just happened?

'At first, I wasn't sure if it was you. You looked familiar when we first met but it was a while later when the penny dropped and I realised who you were. The thing is… there never seemed to be an appropriate time to say "Hey, I remember you from school, how you doing?" – it felt a little weird to me, if I'm being honest.'

'I suppose. Well, that just shows what a small world we live in! Who would have thought it?' She nodded at his mug. 'Would you like a top-up?'

He looked at his watch. 'I'd better not, time's getting on and I should be getting home. I'm going to have to explain this,' he lifted his bruised hand, 'to Flora and then listen dutifully as she reads me the riot act.'

'Is she a bit bossy, then?'

'Er, yeah! Sometimes I find myself asking exactly who the parent is!'

Sally found herself smiling. She'd liked the no-nonsense Flora and despite her young age, she had a sensible head on her shoulders. She could easily see her ruling the roost despite her dad's senior position.

'You know, Sally, you could actually help me out here…'

'I could? How so?'

'It's pub quiz night at The Inn on the Green and Flora likes to go along. However, our little team of two doesn't do so well against the teams of four. If you would join Flora and I for dinner there and stay to do the quiz afterwards, I might just about earn enough brownie points to get past this.' He raised his hand again.

'Oh, urm… I don't know…'

'Look, if you're alone tonight, you're most likely going to dwell on what happened and you'll be not up to dick tomorrow.'

'Excuse me? Not up what?'

'Not up to dick! It's an old expression my Grandfather John used and it's carried on down through the family. It means not well. If you hang around here on your own, you'll give too much headspace to this afternoon. The distraction, if you come out with us, would be far better. And it'll be a good opportunity to meet some more people from the village. It won't do you any harm to get out there and mingle a bit – after all, aren't you hoping the local residents will become new customers for your surgery? You stand a better chance of that happening if they get to know you.'

Sally had been all set to decline Matt's offer until he'd thrown his last statement into the mix. He was right – she *had* been holing herself up here at the farm and had barely ventured into the village at all since she'd moved in. She'd found the fact that everyone seemed to know everyone else a bit daunting and she hadn't wanted people prying into her past under the guise of "getting to know her". One of the reasons behind her move had been to start again and she'd rather do it without the spectre of her dead husband, and the pitying looks which came with that discovery, hanging over her. There was no longer a "Sally & Steve" situation – it was now just a "Sally" situation and she needed to get on with dealing with that.

'Okay, I accept the invitation to join you and Flora for dinner. It's very kind of you to ask.'

'Cool! And it's not really kindness, I genuinely am looking after my own skin here! Flora is less likely to verbally flay me if you're around.'

He stood up.

'I'm going to pop home to grab a shower and change into something that doesn't smell of blood and sawdust.'

Sally burst out laughing.

'Blood and sawdust! That sounds like something

you'd hear in the Wild Wild West!'

'The way I was brawling today, Flora would probably say that's where I belong!'

They walked over to the barn door which led out to the courtyard.

'I'll call you when I'm on my way back to pick you up.'

'There's no need for that, Matt, I can drive myself.'

'You could but not when you've sustained a bang to the head. Don't deny it – I've been watching you rubbing it over the last hour. It would be irresponsible for you to drive and even more irresponsible for me to let you.'

'But you're happy to let me join you in a pub quiz?'

'It's the fact you agreed to join us that tells me you're definitely in no fit state to drive!'

They both laughed at this and Sally could still hear Matt chuckling as she closed the wicket gate behind him, making sure the lock was secured before she walked back to the van.

TWENTY-EIGHT

The ebb and flow of conversation surrounded Sally as she looked around the quaint little pub. Despite admiring it from the outside each time she'd passed by, this was the first time she'd been inside and it couldn't have been more different to The Drover's Arms where she'd had dinner with Nick Davies. As modern as that had been inside, The Inn on the Green prided itself on maintaining the traditional old English-style interior. Age-darkened oak beams were highlighted against white painted walls and the bar itself looked like it had been in situ since the dawn of time.

Matt and Flora had picked her up from the farm and filled her in on the eccentric landlady, Percy, and the history of the pub. It had stood on this spot for several centuries and had once been just a mere watering hole until a fire had caused the main inn in the village to close back in the 1800s. While travellers to the village were on the decrease due to the advancement of the rail services, they were still sufficient enough for the then owners of The Inn on the Green to move out of the rooms they'd occupied above the pub and upgraded the inn's hospitality facilities by doing so. And it had continued to be thus to this day.

Sally, who was partial to a bit of history, had loved hearing this and vowed to bring her best friend, Karen, here for lunch the next time she came up.

'Here you go, Sally, one lager shandy, light on the lager and heavy on the lemonade as requested. Our food will be over shortly and I've put us on the list for the quiz later. The good thing about arriving early is that we'll have a table.'

'Does it get very busy, then?'

'Oh yes!' Flora leaned across the table, clearly thrilled at the prospect of them joining in later. 'Most of the village comes out for it. Even Sukie and Pete Wallace show up most weeks.'

'What? Pete Wallace joins in with the local pub quiz? Seriously?'

'He sure does, when he's not away on tour.' Matt took another drink from his pint before placing the glass on the table and licking away the frothy moustache from his top lip. The action gave Sally a surprising little jolt in her stomach.

'The villagers all love Pete and Sukie. They don't have any airs or graces and try to be a part of the day-to-day living as much as possible, which means everyone is especially protective of them and any strangers who come asking too many questions get short-shrift and sent on their way.'

'I met them when I had to discuss the change of use for the farm. They were very kind and welcoming.'

'I'll also wager that Sukie was totally on board with your plans for the cat rescue. Her love of cats is well known.'

'Yes, she was. Whenever she visits the rescue in the future, Pete has ordered me not to let her leave the premises without a full body search first as he doesn't trust her not to try and sneak some of the residents home with her.'

This comment caused Matt and Flora to laugh and Sally found herself joining in.

While they waited for their meals, Sally realised that this was the first proper night out she'd had since Steve's death. There had, of course, been the occasional family dinner celebrating her parents' anniversaries or birthdays but they didn't really count. This was a night out with non-family members and pretty much under her own steam. Okay, Matt had been required to bring in a little persuasion but she'd agreed to join him and Flora with no further coercion and she'd found herself looking forward to it when she'd been getting showered and changed.

'Dad tells me he got these bruises coming to your assistance this afternoon, Sally.'

'Er, yes, he did.' She glanced at Matt, not sure how much he'd told Flora and what she could safely say.

'It's okay, she knows the full story. I told her everything.'

'And the verbal flaying?'

'Not as painful as I was expecting.'

'Excuse me, you two, I am here! It's not my fault I'm rather protective of my dad – I've already lost one parent, not quite ready to get rid of the other. Although,' Flora sneaked a side-peek at her father, 'there are some days when I could happily see the back of him.'

'Is that so, young lady?'

'Yes, it is, old man.'

Ribs were elbowed on both sides and Sally couldn't help but smile at their antics and banter which only ceased when their meals were placed on the table.

'Hi, Sally, how lovely to see you here. Are you joining in the quiz tonight?'

'Sukie, hello. Yes, I am. Matt kindly invited me to join him and Flora.'

'That's wonderful. I've been wanting to pop over and see how you're getting on but I didn't want to come across as being all "lady of the manor-ish", if you get my meaning? It's so easy for these things to be misconstrued.'

'Sukie, I would never think that and you will always be a welcome visitor. Please drop over anytime. Although, it's still a bit of a building site at the moment, so bring a hard hat.'

Just then, three other women came over to join Sukie.

'Sally, these are the rest of my team-mates. Jenny, whom you already know, Sam, who runs the tearooms and Molly, whose partner, Charlie, does most of the architectural work for the area.'

'A ladies-only team?'

'Yes,' Jenny replied, 'our respective "others" head up their own team. They're called the "Rock 'n' Rowlands" and we're "Sukie's Sassy Cats". What's your team's name?'

'Oh! I don't know.'

She turned to Flora and Matt.

'We're the "Three Bees",' said Flora, smiling.

'Three Bees?' Sally racked her brain trying to figure where that had come from.

'Yeah!' Flora laughed. 'Bramblebush B&B. The Three Bees!'

A warm happiness flowed through Sally upon hearing Flora's words. This small gesture of inclusion touched her more than she could have expected.

'Well, Sally, you are now officially a member of our team. That's the best result we've had for ages.'

Flora smiled at her over the table.

'Oh, I didn't do that much.'

'Sure you did,' Matt said, 'don't sell yourself short. Have you had a nice evening?'

'Matt, thank you so much for inviting me along. I've had a great time. I can't recall the last time I laughed this much. Even though everyone is super-competitive, listening to all the patter and chatter this evening has been so much fun.'

'Hey, you didn't just listen. Telling Pete Wallace that just because he had the sharpest cheek-bones in the room didn't make him the sharpest knife in the drawer was brilliant!'

'Oh gosh! I can't believe I came out with that. I must go and apologise…'

'Hey, don't you dare, lady!'

Sally looked up to find Sukie grinning down at her.

'That has to be one of the best lines I've heard delivered to my husband and don't you dare take it back.'

'But I was rude.'

'No, you weren't. You just joined in with the flow of the evening. Everyone takes little pot-shots at each other but it's never nasty or malicious and we don't ever take the words exchanged to heart.'

Sukie bent down and whispered in her ear.

'Don't worry so much. You're doing great. You've got this.'

She straightened up, gave a small wink and then, with much noise, went off to locate her husband.

The kind words of support were more than Sally had expected and she felt tears well up in her eyes. She looked down at the table, blinking hard to prevent them from falling.

'Hey, Sal, you okay?'

She glanced over to Matt who was looking at her with concern.

'Yes, yes, I'm fine, thank you. It's been quite a day and Sukie being so lovely has just tipped my occasionally wayward emotions slightly over the edge. I'll be alright.'

He watched her for a moment before giving a small nod.

'Fair enough. It has been rather action-packed so maybe it's time we all headed home.'

When they got back to the farm, Matt opened the car boot and pulled out a large duffle bag.

'Dad, what are you doing?'

'I'm making the barn a little more secure for Sally.'

'Excuse me?' Sally looked at Matt with surprise.

'Sally, all you have on these two wicket gates are silly little Yale locks which couldn't keep out a cold, never mind anyone with intent to harm.'

'Thanks, Matt, for that lovely thought. It's really going to help me sleep tonight!'

'By the time I'm finished, Sally, it'll be like the Tower of London in there and you'll be completely safe.'

'Sally, just let him get on with it. We won't get to leave here until he's done whatever he has planned. He's stubborn like that.'

'There's nothing wrong with being cautious.'

'Fine! Fine! Just do what you need to do!'

She threw her hands up and walked over to the barn, Flora, and Matt behind her. Using her phone torch, she unlocked the little gate and stepped inside, flicking the light switch as she entered.

'Would you like a drink of something while you're doing whatever you're doing, Matt?'

'No thanks, I'm good. This'll only take me fifteen minutes.'

'Flora?'

'No, thank you, Sally. I'm good too.'

She turned to see what Matt was up to and did a double-take when he pulled a cordless drill out of the duffle bag at his feet.

'Matt, what ARE you doing?'

'Just putting some bolts on these doors, Sally, to make them sturdier against any unauthorised access.'

'While I appreciate your concern for my well being, and I really do, your actions are not exactly helping me. I'll be lying awake all night now, shaking under my duvet, while waiting for some form of evil to come and get me.'

'Then you can take comfort from knowing that nothing and no one will be getting through these gates unless they're invited. There, that's the first one done already. See, no time at all.'

And sure enough, while they'd been talking, Matt had put two good sturdy bolts onto the first of the wicket gates in the barn doors. He walked across to the one in the back doors and repeated his actions.

'There you go. Now you can sleep sweetly and have happy dreams. And I will too because I'll know you're safe.'

Sally walked over to the back doors where Matt was standing.

'Would you mind putting this bolt down for me, please. It's rather stiff and I usually leave it undone because it's such a bother.'

'No problem.'

He did as she asked and when he'd forced the bolt into the notch in the concrete floor, he simply said, 'I'll bring some oil over for that tomorrow.'

She watched as he checked the other set of thick wooden doors on that side of the building and made sure the bolts were fully engaged. This small action calmed her skittish insides as she became aware she was now completely safe.

When Matt and Flora stepped out into the courtyard to leave, Matt turned back to her.

'Just so you know, I'll be installing a couple of security lights out here tomorrow. I should've done it sooner. Sorry about that.'

'Matt, please don't apologise for anything. My security really isn't your concern though I am deeply grateful that you have made it so.'

'Nothing wrong with looking out for folks, Sally, and I'm looking out for you. Sleep well and I'll see you in the morning.'

'Sure, see you in the morning. Good night, Flora, and thank you again for a great evening. I really did enjoy it.'

'Good, because I'll be expecting you to do it all again next week.'

Sally closed the little door, snibbed the lock and threw the two shiny new bolts into place. Even though Matt had just checked the other barn doors, she went round them again and, satisfied that all was good, stepped inside Marvin, locked his door, and got ready for bed.

She'd only been under the quilt a couple of minutes when Herbie came up and curled into her stomach. With his little warm body pushing against her, and knowing the barn was quite secure, she soon drifted off into a deep and dreamless sleep and didn't stir until her alarm went off the next morning.

TWENTY-NINE

Sally looked down at the CV in front of her and tried not to yawn. This was now the third interview she'd sat in on with Nick and it was as tedious as hell. So far, they'd had three young men who'd spent most of the time talking themselves up and not really taking on board what the position was truly about. To make matters worse, she'd had a hand in choosing these potential candidates.

She'd been in the middle of reading through the CV's Nick had sent over for her feedback when Darren had decided to cause trouble and she was blaming the after-effects of the trauma for her poor choices.

When Nick finally wrapped the interview up, it took all of her willpower not to do a happy dance although given how tiny the office they were sitting in was, even a happy shuffle would be a challenge.

'Now I remember why I usually let my dad do

these things!'

Nick walked back in from showing the candidate out, arms high above his head and a large yawn stretching his mouth.

'I have to say, I hadn't expected the task to be this onerous!'

'Well, three down and three to go – any thoughts on those we've seen so far?'

'Yeah! If I never see them again, it'll be too soon. Talk about loving the sound of your own voice.'

'That can be a problem with junior vets who've trained up in the city – they think we're all a bunch of country bumpkins!'

'Who's next on the list?'

Nick looked down at the next CV on the pile.

'Juliet Turner. She's due in twenty minutes.'

'Ah, yes, the only woman in the pile you sent me. Any reason for that?'

'She was the only one experienced enough for the position. We had others but they weren't yet ready for the level we need.'

'I see.'

'To be honest, Sally, of all the vets we're seeing today, she's the weakest candidate.'

'So why are we seeing her?'

'Because you chose her and this is as much your gig as it is mine. I didn't want you to think your opinion wasn't valid.'

'Okay, thank you for that. Let's see how it goes.'

It took Sally less than ten minutes to know that she liked Juliet. The woman had a kind vibe, a gentle tone of voice and both were entirely in keeping with her no-nonsense appearance. Her mid-brown hair was pulled back in a simple ponytail at the base of her neck, and her brown eyes, which were the colour of milk-chocolate, seemed to draw you in and you instantly felt you could trust her. Her makeup was minimal and in keeping with the tailored dark-grey trouser suit and white blouse that she wore. The ensemble was finished off with a pair of ankle boots whose heel was solid and low. Furthermore, she didn't make any attempt to blow her own trumpet and so far, her answers had been concise and to the point.

'Juliet, may I ask you a question?' Sally leant forward. This was her own personal test question which she hadn't bothered to ask the previous three candidates because she'd written them off pretty much from the start of their interviews. 'If you had a poorly animal in front of you, which required a high level of care that would be very expensive, how would you approach it? Would your first thought be to try and save it at all costs or would you weigh up the expense and decide if the costs involved would be worth the effort?'

Juliet looked her straight in the eye and answered, without even a breath of hesitation, 'I would do absolutely everything in my power to save the animal. While I appreciate that cost must be considered in some aspects, it would never be my first thought. I do this job to help animals first and foremost.'

'Thank you.'

Sally worked really hard on keeping her face poker straight but inside she was skipping like a three-year-old! This was exactly the kind of vet she wanted to work with. Someone who understood that their first priority was to do everything possible to save the animal and to hang with the cost.

She sat back and let Nick lead the rest of the interview but she'd already decided it was Juliet whom the remaining two candidates would have to match up to.

'Hmm, I'm not sure about her,' Nick said after he'd shown Juliet out.

'Why not?'

Sally wanted to hear his thoughts before she voiced her own.

'Well, there's the eighteen-month gap in her work history for a start.'

'She explained that. She was doing voluntary work overseas with various small animal sanctuaries, helping them to understand more up-to-date procedures. I thought that was rather commendable, actually!'

'Hmm… also, she's too soft. I don't think she's got what it takes to be a country vet.'

'But she's not going to be a country vet – her primary role is for small animals. That's what we agreed.'

'But she may need to cover in an emergency.'

'Then you will have to either give her additional training or be on the end of the phone to talk her through anything that might come up. But, for what *I* am looking for, she's perfect. And I would like you to keep in mind that this is *my* vet, not yours. I know we agreed to share resources but if that means compromising on the kind of vet I want to deal with on a daily basis, then we need to rethink the situation.'

This was the moment when it came home to Sally just how much she'd grown to love her prospective new ventures. She was looking forward to getting the B&B up and running but her passion lay with the rescue and that was where she knew she'd get the most satisfaction even if it meant having to put her foot down with Nick.

'Okay, it's your call. We've still got two left to see and we can discuss it further after that.'

It was with no small amount of irony that Sally acknowledged to herself that she'd fallen in-dislike with their next candidate, Simon Groves, in the same amount of time she'd taken to fall in-like with Juliet.

Simon was loud and bombastic. So much so, it actually felt as though he was interviewing them! While she appreciated interviews were a two-way street, the arrogance of this man was beyond belief.

She decided to test him and so put forth the same question she'd asked Juliet.

'Well, naturally, I'd assess the cost first before administering treatment to ensure the owners could afford to pay.'

The answer was directed at Nick even though she'd asked the question and such was her annoyance with this, her hands had to be shoved under her thighs because her self-control was clinging on by a fingernail.

'And if they couldn't afford to pay? Or could only pay a partial amount?'

'Then I'd recommend they have the animal put down. After all, we're here to make money.'

'Actually, Mr Groves, we're here to save animals!'

The ice in her reply could have sunk the Titanic but the pompous oaf in front of her ignored her and centred his whole attention on Nick. Thankfully, her business-partner-to-be wrapped the interview up rather quickly after that which gave her enough time to grab a coffee and calm down.

'Well, he wasn't too bad.'

'Excuse me? Come again…'

Nick looked up from the notes he was writing on Simon's CV.

'He was a decent candidate. He has the experience we're after and he can be available in two months.'

'I don't care if he's available in two hours – that man does NOT get to set foot on my property.'

'Why not? I thought he came over well.'

'Nick, were we just in the same interview? He's an arrogant, loud-mouthed ass, and I know for a fact that he'd be a patronising asshole when dealing with me and the owners of our clients.'

'You can't say that—'

'Yes, I can! I've met enough vets in my time who seem to think they know more about my cat after five minutes than I do after living with him for five years! I will not have anyone like that in my surgery. I want to see kindness and sympathy over costs and expenditure.'

'That's not how you run a business, Sally.'

'Then it's a good thing I'll be running a rescue centre, isn't it!'

She glared at him over her mug, both hands gripping it tightly to prevent it suddenly flying across the room.

Nick held her gaze for a moment before sitting down with a sigh.

'You're right. I'm sorry. I've made this whole process about what we're looking for, not what you are looking for. And I agree, Simon would not be a good fit for your needs.'

At his admission, her anger flowed away.

'Look, Nick, I don't want to seem ungrateful and I do appreciate the time and help you've given me for this, I really do, but I have to make sure the person I'm going to be working so closely with is a good fit for me and what I want to achieve.'

'You're right. Look, let's see this last one and then, after that, would you like to discuss everything over dinner? It's steak night at the Drover's and they're pretty darn tasty.'

'Sure, okay. That would be nice. Thank you.'

'Right then, let's see what Keith Melon – is that for real? – has to offer us and then we're done for the day.'

'Bring him in. The sooner we start, the sooner we get fed!'

THIRTY

Sally placed her knife and fork together on the plate and pushed it away.

'That's it! I'm done!'

'But you haven't eaten all your chips.'

'Nick, when you told me the steaks were tasty, you omitted to mention that they're big enough to give Desperate Dan a run for his money! The chips were collateral damage tonight!'

'Mind if I take a few?'

'Knock yourself out! I'm stuffed!'

She watched Nick scoop half of the remaining fries onto his plate and wolf them down.

'How can you possibly be that trim while hoovering up not only your own dining-table sized steak, but most of my chips too?'

'The fun side of being a country vet is the amount of time you spend traipsing over fields, climbing over walls, gates, and fences, and running from angry cattle. All that soon works off any extra calories.'

'But I bet you enjoy every moment of it and wouldn't change it for anything.'

'You're right there. I love it.'

'You know how doctors can garner a lot of "attention" from some of their lady patients, is it the same for vets?'

'We do get our fair share of that, it has to be said. I mean, Daisy over at Waterford Farm, fair shakes her udders when she sees me crossing the field!'

'Oh you!' Sally laughed at his silly comment. 'You know what I mean.'

'I do but you made that too easy for me,' he grinned.

When he smiled like that, Sally could see again why his receptionist had to fend off the female clients and she liked how he'd batted away that he did in fact receive a lot of "attention"!

'The problem with being a vet or a doctor or a policeman etc, is that people see what they perceive as the glamorous side. They don't take into account the long hours, the emergency call-outs at three in the morning, being late for dates because an operation was more complicated than expected and took longer than anticipated and they sure as hell don't understand how it affects you when one of your patients doesn't make it. It doesn't matter if it's a cow, a dog, or a human being – a life being snuffed out hurts on every level.'

He looked over the table at her.

'Sorry, I probably sound quite bitter but it was all of the above that caused my marriage to break down.'

'Oh, no, I'm sorry. I didn't realise.'

'No reason why you should. I was working in London, met my wife there and she simply wasn't prepared when I moved back to work with my father. A vet's life in Clapham is a lifetime away from life in the country.'

'Yes, I get that. I haven't seen many cows grazing on Clapham Common any time I've gone by…'

Nick smiled at her comment.

'I wouldn't fancy their chances, to be honest! They'd be steak before the day was out!'

'So, not missing London much, then?'

'No. I enjoyed it while I was there but I love the life I live now, even if it's a single one.'

'I'm sure there are plenty of young ladies in the Ditchley area who'd be happy to un-single you.'

'Maybe, but I'm not ready to go there yet. I still need time.'

'I understand that. So, to completely change the subject in the least subtle manner possible, we have six candidates to talk about and decide if we want to offer second interviews to any of them. And since you're the expert around here, why don't you go first. From a professional viewpoint, who would be your two choices out of the six?'

'Simon Groves gets my first vote and Juliet Turner at a push.'

'Well, I think you already know what I'm going to say… Juliet Turner, hands down, and Simon Groves only if he was the very last vet left on the planet!'

'Even if he is the most qualified?'

'He can have all the qualifications in the world but

if people don't like him, then they won't come to us.'

'I think they will, given the size of our catchment area.'

'Not a good enough reason, so let me put it another way. Tiddles is under the weather so his owner, trusting what we represent, brings him in to be seen. It turns out that Tiddles has pancreatitis but it's been caught early and is treatable. All because he was diagnosed at the first sign of a problem. Now… you put a bloke in charge who looks at the profit margin and thinks women are second-class citizens… Tiddles won't be brought in early because his lady owner doesn't feel comfortable doing so. She's worried she'll be made to feel she's a time waster because of how the vet speaks to her. So Tiddles suffers through and eventually looks to be doing okay. The owner believes she made the right decision. Except a few months later, Tiddles collapses, he's rushed to the surgery where it transpires he has pancreatic cancer and due to the speed at which this variant of cancer can spread, it's game over for him. It's too late.

'I won't work with someone who intimidates and patronises the clients. I've already told you before that I've dealt with vets of that ilk in the past and believe me when I say, they weren't my vet for long. Do not underestimate the need for trust and faith in this.'

She stopped to take a sip from her wine glass and to give Nick a chance to speak after her little speech.

'I see your point. Because I work with farmers who, while they care for their animals, have a different way of looking at things and I can be remiss in remembering that small animals are generally considered to be members of the family these days. Yes, you're right, we would benefit from someone with a more empathetic nature.'

'Exactly. So, while Simon Groves may be perfect for sticking his hand up a cow's arse – as long as he's taken his head out of his own first – I wouldn't let him within a mile of my Herbert.'

'Then I think that leaves us with Juliet Turner.'

'I believe it does.'

Nick smiled at her before taking another drink of his beer. As he placed the glass back down, he said, 'You took to her almost immediately. Why?'

'She's a straight talker, which I always like, she answered my question honestly and without hesitation and she said what I wanted to hear. For her, the animals come first, not the profit. I want to be sure that if an elderly person comes to the surgery, who cannot afford expensive treatments, they will still be given the same high level of care than if they'd arrived dripping diamonds from every finger.'

'But you're not a charity, Sally—'

'Once again, Nick, that's exactly what I'll be! You need to remember that my rescue is the foundation to all of this. Without the rescue, I have no need for a vet or a vet's surgery. I'm doing this for purely selfish reasons but if other people can benefit from it too…'

'Very well. So, I guess we're asking Juliet back. If we decide she's not for us, what then?'

'We go back to the drawing board and re-advertise the position. And we keep doing that until the right person comes along. I'm not prepared to compromise on this, Nick, it's too important to me.'

'If you insist…'

'Nick, I must be comfortable with my vet because I could be dragging them out of their beds at silly o'clock in the morning due to a young cat having difficulties with a pregnancy, or a stray that's been badly treated and needs immediate attention. I must know they will step up to the plate without huffing and puffing at me or making me feel inferior. I'm sorry to keep harping back to this but it has to be someone I have trust and faith in.'

'No, I get it. I really do. I can see this means a lot to you and as they will technically be your vet, you get to make the call. Quite literally! You get to call Juliet to invite her back.'

'Cool! I will do that first thing in the morning.'

'I just want to check one last thing…'

Nick took his tablet from his briefcase and spent a couple of moments scrolling through it. Sally took another sip of her wine and waited, enjoying the feeling of relief that she'd managed to bring him round to her way of thinking. Urgh! The thought of having Simon Groves anywhere near her precious rescue made her stomach churn. No way! Not ever!

'Hmm, it is as I thought…'

'What is?'

Nick slid his tablet over the table.

'Juliet is on a six-month maternity cover contract and still has four months to work.'

'I'm happy to wait, it's only an extra month to what we expected.'

'Oh, I have no problem with that but didn't you want to allow whoever came on board carte blanche with organising the surgery and setting it up to their own spec?'

'Yes, that's supposed to be one of the sweeteners for the role. That it really would be "their" surgery.'

'Well, by the time Juliet – assuming we're all good and she takes the job – gets here, decides what she wants, puts in her orders for the equipment etc, then add on delivery time and installation… it could easily be another seven to eight months before the surgery is completed. Which means you won't be able to take in any animals until February – at the earliest.'

'What? But that's going to be almost a year in total from when I first found the farm. I thought I'd be good to go within about six or seven months. I really wanted it to be open by Christmas.'

Sally felt her heart fill with dismay as she thought of the rescue centres she knew who were crying out for spaces because they were already full beyond capacity. She'd hoped to give them a degree of respite by taking some of their feline occupants off them.

'There is another option. If Juliet takes the job, ask her to spend a day with us both where we can go to the site and discuss it with her. Once we know what her preferences are, we – or you – can get on with arranging the building work and I can get the equipment ordered. That will save us time.'

'Now that sounds like a good plan and I get the feeling Juliet would be okay with doing that. I also wouldn't want to keep Matt hanging around unnecessarily.'

'Matt?'

'My builder.'

'Of course. Those guys are always in high demand – if he gets caught up on another job, it could take even longer.'

'Oh hell! I didn't even think of that. Right, what's Juliet's phone number, I'm calling her now!'

THIRTY-ONE

Sally shook Craig's hand and, once in his car, watched him perform a rather nifty three-point-turn before driving out of the courtyard. It had been a productive morning with the accountant and they'd both agreed they would like to work together. He would look after the books for all three of the businesses, taking each one on as it started up. He was also going to look at registering the charity on an official level because while he knew there were hoops to jump through to get an official charity number, the long-term benefits made it worthwhile.

She knew she'd have to share her secret with him somewhere along the line but it would be a little while yet. She had to be absolutely sure she could trust him and she wouldn't know that until she'd spent more time with him.

'Hey, Sal, you okay there? Looks like you have all the worries of the world on your shoulders.'

'Oh, hi, Matt.' She gave him a bright smile. 'I'm fine. In fact, I'm more than fine. I've just ticked another box on the never-ending list.'

'Accountant?'

'Yes. I'm guessing you saw Craig, then…'

'I did.'

'But you didn't come out to say hello?'

'No, I was busy.'

'Or, maybe avoiding him…' She raised an eyebrow along with the corners of her mouth.

Matt sighed. 'Flora's been talking, hasn't she?'

'She may have mentioned that you don't see eye-to-eye with your brother-in-law.'

'Hmm…'

'Fair enough. None of my business.'

She went to turn away when a thought struck her. Looking back at Matt, she asked, 'Can I ask one question?'

'Sure.'

'Would you say Craig is trustworthy? If he has confidential information, would it remain confidential?'

'Yes! To both of your questions. He is more than trustworthy. While I may have family issues with him, they are just that – family issues. His work is beyond reproach and he's excellent at what he does. If it puts your mind at ease, he looks after the books for our business. Robbie asked him last year and he's been a godsend.'

'Yet, you didn't recommend him…'

'I didn't feel it was my place. Also, with him being family, it can sometimes make things awkward.'

'No problem. Thank you.'

She was halfway over the old cobbles when Matt called over, 'Sally, why did you ask me that question?'

She turned back.

'Because I knew you'd tell me the truth. The fact that you could still speak honourably about Craig, despite your personal issues, is very reassuring.'

'You trusted me.'

'I did. I do. Thank you.'

They exchanged smiles and moved off in opposite directions – Matt back towards the house, Sally towards the barn where she had approximately – she looked at her watch – twenty minutes to tidy up and grab a bite to eat before Nick and Juliet Turner were due to arrive.

She rushed over to the motorhome and threw together a slapdash apology for a cheese sandwich which she carried back out with her into the barn as she went over to the garden table and pulled together the folders she'd been showing to Craig. He'd been impressed by how meticulously she'd filed all the receipts for the work being done around the farm. Little did he know that her filing was once a thing of legend between her and Steve – for NOT being done! The bills, receipts and insurance documents had always been tossed onto a pile which would only be tackled when it was at risk of toppling over. It was having to work her way through the pile after Steve's death, trying to locate the various pieces of paperwork she needed, that had her vowing never again! From that day, absolutely everything went into files and folders and she could lay her hands on whatever she needed within seconds.

She carried the files over to the garden storage box she was using until the office area was ready in the main house and placed them inside. After locking it, she returned to the table, took a bite of her sandwich, and then cursed the crumbs she'd dropped.

The loud knock echoed around the barn just as she swallowed her last crust. She quickly glugged back a mouthful of water and then ran across to open the door.

'Hi, Juliet, please come in.'

Sally stood back to allow Juliet to step through the wicket gate and when she looked out again, Nick's car was just pulling up by the side of the house. She gave him a wave and left the door open.

'Thank you for coming out to see us, Juliet. Nick is just parking and will be here in a moment. Can I get you a drink? Tea? Coffee? Something cold?'

'Something cold would be perfect, thank you. And thank you for asking me back. I know it's probably not professional to say so but I was thrilled to receive your call.'

'Well, I hope you're still as thrilled once you've seen the currently uninspiring site where the surgery will be located.'

By the time Sally came back out of the motorhome with a tray of cool drinks, Nick and Juliet were seated at the table, chatting. Juliet appeared relaxed and it made Sally feel better. She was so hoping this woman would accept the job because everything about her felt right.

'Here we are, folks. Something to keep our whistles wet as we talk.'

'Nick was just explaining about the need to press ahead with getting the surgery sorted out.'

'Yes, when we looked at the timing of everything, it wasn't going to be practical to wait until you, or whoever takes the job, to join us. Would this be an issue for you?'

'No, not at all. It makes perfect sense to get on with it, especially where ordering in equipment is concerned. Sometimes, that stuff can take ages to arrive!'

'Well, if you'd like to come with me, I'll show you the space and you can give us your thoughts.'

Sally led the way and soon they were standing directly over where they'd been sitting previously.

'So, all of this area is being given over to the surgery?'

'Yes, Juliet, it is. What do you think?'

'I think it's a great space and will be more than accommodating.'

Nick stepped forward. 'I was thinking we could put in two consulting rooms, two operating theatres and a specialist recovery room which would be separate from the holding area.'

'That would be perfect. It can be bothersome waiting for the operating room to be cleaned before you can get onto dealing with your next patient. Two rooms will minimise that waiting time and we can do more.'

'That was my thinking too.'

Sally stood back and let Nick point out to Juliet

where he thought each room or area would be and was happy to hear Juliet give her own opinions in a confident manner. As much as Sally liked Nick, he could occasionally be a bit domineering and she liked that Juliet was showing no signs of being intimidated by him.

'There is one thing I would really like to see included in the plans and it needs to be in a specific location.'

Sally stepped forward to hear more.

'Sure, what is it?' she asked.

'I'd really like us to have a Peace Room.'

'A what?'

She looked at Nick but he looked just as puzzled.

'A Peace Room, well, that's what I call it.' Juliet looked at them both in turn before continuing. 'When owners have to say their final goodbyes to their beloved pets, it's often in the clinical environment of a consulting room. They have to make their peace surrounded by surgical steel and antiseptic smells. It would be nice to have a room which has a more sensitive and soothing atmosphere for them. Somewhere less clinical to help take some of the trauma from them. It should also have a separate exit so the distraught owners don't have to walk the gauntlet that is the waiting room where everyone else can see their distress. That's something which should remain private as much as possible.'

Sally listened to Juliet's words and each one resonated with her. She had been in the very position currently being described and even now, had moments of sadness as she thought back to the cats who'd come before Herbie and how it felt to say goodbye to them. The fact that this woman had pinpointed the issue and wanted to do something about it, spoke volumes about her character.

She looked at Nick and gave him a small nod before turning to Juliet and saying, 'Juliet, the job is yours if you want it. And I hope you do because, even though it may not be professional to say it, I really want you here.'

THIRTY-TWO

Sally stood by the gate and waved as the two cars turned around and drove away.

'She seems decent,' Matt said, standing waving beside her.

Sally turned to him with a smile.

'I think so. There's something about her which feels real and genuine. I can't wait for her to move in.'

'I liked her suggestion for the additional room being added to her cottage. Are you okay with it?'

'Absolutely. If she hadn't already won me over by that point, she most certainly would have done so with that request.'

Sally thought back to the conversation half an hour earlier when she'd been showing Juliet where her live-in accommodation would be. She'd asked Matt to join them so he could answer any questions Juliet may have or address any requests she wanted to make in how she'd like the space to be set out. When Matt had shown her the plans, she'd been more than happy with them but had had one request – would it be possible to add another room next to her bedroom where she could keep any animals which required through-the-night care such as hand-rearing kittens or intensive care patients.

'So, you don't mind losing that storage space you planned to keep at the end of the block?'

'Not in the slightest. It would only have ended up full of junk anyway – far better it be put to good use and a small ICU space is as good a use as any. Besides, it makes perfect sense. The last thing I want is my vet to leave because she's having to traipse across the yard every four hours to check on patients. No, I wholeheartedly approve. Are you okay with the request to fence in the area between the corner of her cottage – which, I have to say, is by far a nicer name for her accommodation – and the barn so she can let her dog run about safely?'

'Yes, that's no problem at all. In fact, the second fire escape for the surgery will be going in at that end of the barn and will be in her garden so she can use it to access the surgery and, if she wants to let her dog have the freedom to run around, she'll be in a position to keep an eye on it. I'll ensure the fire exit gate and fencing is good and sturdy in case she has a dog who likes to jump up.'

'She's come up with some good suggestions today and I feel more than justified in fighting Nick to have her.'

'He didn't approve?'

'He's concerned her CV isn't quite as thorough as

another candidate we saw but I didn't like him and as I'll be paying the wages, the final call was mine.'

'Well, if it helps in any way, I think it was a great call. I liked her too.'

Sally smiled again.

'It shouldn't make a difference but it does. I'm glad you like her and can see what I see.'

'Talking about "seeing" things – I have a surprise for you.'

'Oh, what?'

'The last of the plastering was finished today. You can now see your flat AND the house!'

'Noooooo! Seriously? I thought there would be another three weeks… that's the timescale you gave me.'

'I did but that was allowing for unexpected surprises that many houses like this can throw up, but this old girl played nicely and didn't cause any unexpected hiccups. She needed some rewiring in areas where the mice had had a nibble and there were several areas where timbers had to be replaced and treated but, in the grand scheme of things, she's been a bit of a dream to work with.'

'Even the plumbing, which had you shaking your head when we first walked around?'

'Apart from the new bathrooms we put in and your kitchen, her plumbing was in all the right places. It simply turned out to be a case of replacing the old pipes with new ones.'

'Then, kind sir, if you don't mind, I'd love to see the finished result.'

'Let's start at the front door. Also, bear in mind that

much of the plaster is either still wet or in the process of drying so it does look quite dark. Once it's all painted, however, it'll be much brighter.'

'How long is that likely to take?'

'I want to give it a week to ten days – to be sure it's completely dried out. This lovely warm weather is set to carry through into next week so our timing couldn't have been better.'

'Does that mean I'll be on my own here next week?'

'Hah! No chance! We'll be getting to work on clearing out those old workshops so we can begin getting Juliet's pad sorted for her. Then, once you're out of the barn and properly ensconced in your new home, we can get to work on that. I'm afraid we're here for some time to come – you don't get rid of me that easily!'

'It also means I'm stuck with Bob's awful singing too!'

They both burst out laughing. Matt's second-in-command liked to do more than "whistle while he worked" even though he had a singing voice that should never see the light of day.

'It keeps him happy.'

'I wish we could say the same for the rest of us!' she replied although, inside, she was thrilled the workmen were still going to be around for a while. She'd grown accustomed to their presence and rather liked having them about. They were always cheery and smiling and seemed to fill the space with joy. As they made their way to the front of the house, she wondered if the old girl hadn't put up much resistance to her makeover because she was happy that Sally was there. Or was that just fanciful thinking? Sally was inclined to think not because she couldn't deny she'd felt connected to this glorious building from the first moment she'd set eyes on it.

'Right, are you ready?'

Matt had his hand on the freshly sanded and varnished front door.

'I sure am!'

Sally held her breath as Matt slowly pushed the door open. She couldn't wait to see—

'Oh!'

'What's wrong?'

'Err, the flooring?'

'Ah! That's only a protective covering. It's all through the house at this time until the painting and decorating has been done. The last thing you want is big dollops of paint on your lovely, freshly restored floors. The decorators will also have special coverings on their shoes for added protection.'

'I thought they would be done after the painting was finished.'

'But then you'd be washing all the dust off your nice, new, clean walls.'

'Hmmm, true. I guess I kind of always thought of working from the top to the bottom…'

'It depends on what's lying in wait at the bottom. If it's something dusty and dirty, then you reschedule it.'

'So, I see!'

Sally looked about her. Truth was, apart from the floor, the only alterations in the hallway had been blocking up the doorway further along where that room had been turned into the en suite bathroom and putting in doors to close off the corridor on either side of the grand staircase as these wouldn't be required for public use.

She walked into the disabled room first and was delighted at how different it now looked with the new windows in place. She walked over for a closer look at the frames.

'You know, even though these aren't wooden, you'd be hard pushed to tell. They look great.'

Matt came to stand beside her.

'They were definitely the best option, in my opinion. They won't require painting, and should last a good fifteen to twenty years. Less work is always a result.'

'Puts you out of a job though!' She gave him a soft nudge in the side and his grin produced a warm sensation in her tummy.

'By the time we're finishing up here, I don't think I'll want to see the place again for fifteen to twenty years!'

'Hah! Cheeky. Don't be surprised if the house gets you back for that one.'

'You know,' he turned to look at her, 'I love how you refer to the house as though it's a living being. I often feel that way when I work on buildings which come with a past and it's nice to meet someone who shares that.'

'I wouldn't normally be so inclined but… I don't know… there's been something about this place which touched me from the first moment I saw it…

saw her! I believe it's a "her". A glamorous old lady who's been woken from her slumber and is being all dressed up so she may dance once again.'

Matt stared at her but said nothing. The heat began to build in her cheeks and she pulled her gaze away from his.

'I couldn't have put it better myself,' he finally replied. 'Now come, you have much more to see.'

He took her hand and began walking her through all that had been done and what was still to be done once the decorators were finished. Much of what he said, however, went over her head as her eyes kept looking down at the hand holding hers. She knew the action had been an involuntary one, in his excitement to show her around, but that didn't stop the warmth of his fingers wrapped around hers seeping up her arm, across her chest and down through her stomach. His touch felt nice… more than nice, in fact, so that when they reached her new kitchen – the one where she'd be cooking for her guests – and he released her hand to give her entry into it an arms-wide-open "ta-da", she suddenly felt as though she'd been cast adrift. It took a couple of seconds for her brain to catch up with what he was showing her although, when it did, she couldn't help but gasp loudly.

'Oh…WOW! Just…WOW!'

She spun around, taking in how different the kitchen looked from that first day. When she'd brought Flora round for a look, it hadn't yet been touched but now, with all her lovely, white, shiny units, marble tops, new tiles, and the much longed-for island unit, it looked stunning and she knew she was going to enjoy working in here.

Over in the fireplace area, the new, ten-ringed, double-oven, chrome gas range sparkled in the sunlight coming through the window. Sadly, the old range hadn't been properly maintained and trying to bring it back to life hadn't been a practical option. While Sally had been sad to let it go, deep down there was a spot of relief as she didn't know how well she'd have gotten on with it.

'You like it?'

'I do, I do! It's just so bright! And the tiles,' she looked down at the terracotta tiles under her feet which had once been grimy and dirty but now looked brand new, 'are fantastic. How on earth did you get them so clean?'

'Ah, we have many tools at our disposal. It wasn't so difficult.'

'Well, I love it. You've done a great job. Thank you.'

'No problem. Now, do you want to go down to your new apartment? It was the first area to be plastered which means it's almost dry and that'll be the starting point for the decorators so you can get moved in once they're done.'

'Lead the way, I can't wait!'

Sally followed Matt out of the kitchen, along the corridor and through the two, new, glass and wood panelled fire doors on either side of the staircase. In this corridor, there were only two other doors – one leading outside at the far end and the other on her right-hand side. Matt opened this and they walked through into a small hallway. Directly in front of her was a wrought-iron spiral staircase with a matching banister. The two doors at the opposite end led into her bedroom and bathroom. She hadn't seen either of these so was pleasantly surprised to find a set of French windows leading out onto the porch directly from the bedroom.

'I don't recall seeing these on Charlie's plans.'

'We put them in afterwards once we'd cleared all the greenery and saw how far back the porch extended. I'm going to put a trellis gate up just on the other side of the outside door to give you your own private sitting area and your own entrance to the house.'

'Oh, thank you. That would be lovely.'

'And now for downstairs.'

The lounge and kitchen area were less of a surprise although she hadn't fully appreciated how bright and airy it would be when the old wooden barn doors had been replaced with floor-to-ceiling, wide, glass ones. The tall expanse of glass ran the length of the lounge area but came to a stop where the kitchen began. Here, the original stonework had been retained and a standard kitchen door fitted which would allow her direct access to the courtyard without having to navigate her way through the catio when it was put in.

'Oh my! This is glorious!'

'Hang on a minute, wait until you see this.'

Matt walked over and flicked a couple of switches.

Suddenly, all the glass turned from opaque to clear and she could see across the yard to the barn.

'What on earth?'

'Special glass so you can have privacy when the

217

yard is in use during the day. When I put Herbert's catio in place, that'll reduce your exposure but there may still be a nosy client or two who'll think nothing of wandering over the cobbles to try and peek in your windows!'

She laughed as she walked over to the kitchen area.

'You think they'd do that?'

'I've lived here for the best part of twenty-five years – I *know* they will!'

Sally came to a stop on the edge of her kitchen and her soul sang with joy as it couldn't be more different from the one upstairs. The units in her B&B kitchen were all flat and shiny for practical reasons but down here she'd allowed her heart to lead the way. The dark, air-force blue, wooden units were beautifully set off against the pale lemon tiles on the wall behind them and the cream porcelain floor tiles which ran the length of the room.

'You like?'

'I do, very much.'

'Have you decided on your lounge colours yet?'

'Now that I've seen the room, I think I'll stick with the pale lemon – after all, there's only two walls – and look at dark blue furnishings. It'll pull it all together nicely. I'll need to grab Flora so we can go shopping. We thought we'd have more time.'

'Well, if you like, I'm happy to join you both. I'll bring the van along so you can take home whatever is immediately available.'

'That would be a massive help! Are you sure you don't mind?'

'Not right now but I can't promise to be in the same

frame of mind when you're both finished!'

Sally laughed. 'I'll try to make it as painless as possible. Let me call Flora and find out when she's available.'

As she stepped outside to make her call, she stopped for a moment to ponder if the rapid beat of her heart was down to the excitement of seeing the house looking so good or the thought of spending even more time with Matt away from his workplace. While she waited for Flora to answer, Sally couldn't help but suspect it was the latter.

THIRTY-THREE

Flora hopped from foot to foot in barely concealed excitement. And to keep herself warm as it was absolutely freezing. Mind you, it was the 21st of December – the shortest day of the year and one not known for being hot and balmy.

'Hurry up, Dad, they'll be here soon and you can't keep everyone waiting in the cold while you tie a pretty bow!'

'I'm nearly done, stop moaning at me.'

'Where's Sally? Maybe she'll be able to produce something better.'

'She's in the house, getting everything ready for later, when this is over. Now, how does that look?'

Her dad stepped out of the way and Flora got her first glimpse of the dark purple satin ribbon which stretched across the doors into the rescue hall. They'd chosen purple to match the logo and colours the rescue had adopted, using the hue of ripened brambleberries as their inspiration. Today was the day the rescue facility was being officially opened although no four-footed residents would come in until January.

'Yes, that looks great. Let me get some photographs for the website and social media pages.'

She clicked away with her camera, laughing at her dad as he made a hasty exit out of the way to ensure she didn't click him too. He'd never been one for having his picture taken.

'When is everything due to kick off?'

'In approximately,' she twisted her wrist to look at her watch, 'twenty minutes. Which means they're going to begin arriving any time now.'

'Okay. So, are you happy with how it all looks?'

Her dad walked over to stand beside her and they took in the new appearance of the barn. The old, heavy wooden doors had been removed and replaced with light-weight, automatic, cream coloured, composite doors with glazed windows on the upper half. The other doors and windows on the building had been replaced to match and the barn now looked fresh and inviting. When you walked through the doors, into the little vestibule, a left turn led you to the lift for the surgery upstairs. They'd agreed this would be beneficial not only for disabled access but also for elderly dogs or clients who might struggle with the stairs and any heavy deliveries which needed to go up.

Directly in front, as you walked through the outer doors, was a vast window which reached right up to the ceiling above. This gave potential new feline slaves the opportunity to view the cats within without disturbing them unnecessarily.

To the right of the window, were the interlocking doors. A security feature which ensured none of the inhabitants could make a break for freedom.

Across the top of the refreshed entryway, the new signage had been hung. It was dark purple with cream writing which declared this was the "Bramblebush Cat Rescue" and a picture of Herbert's handsome ginger face adorned the bottom right corner. Four brass, swan-neck lights were placed above it to light it up on the darker nights.

The rescue looked smart and professional which Sally was hoping would inspire confidence in the public and bring them forth to make adoptions.

'I think it looks grand, Flora, I really do.'

'Me too, Dad.'

Just then, they heard the rattle of the cattle grid in the distance.

'I think our guests are beginning to arrive.'

Flora grinned at her dad.

'I would say they are. We'd better go and let Sally know. I'm sure she won't want to be greeting Pete Wallace with her pinny on!'

'It gives me the greatest of pleasure to declare the Bramblebush Cat Rescue officially open.'

Flora moved this way and that, clicking furiously on her camera to ensure she had plenty of photographs of this momentous occasion. She knew that the more she took, the better the chance of getting a couple of good ones.

She stood back to one side as the small crowd gathered in the courtyard applauded Pete before following him and Sally inside where a small buffet and refreshments had been set up. She continued to take photographs of the smiling guests and, once inside, she would hand out small flyers with the website address on so they could go online later and view them. With a bit of luck, some sharing may also be done which would help to spread word of the rescue.

After grabbing a cup of tea to warm herself up, Flora continued taking photographs as she strolled among the guests. After about half an hour, she couldn't believe her luck when she saw Pete standing alone and quickly moved across before someone else could step in and claim his attention.

'Er, excuse me, Mr Wallace…'

'Oh, hi Flora, how are you? Are you involved with this venture?'

'You… you know who I am?'

Flora gulped in surprise as she felt her cheeks warming up.

'Of course I know who you are. In my position as Lord of the Manor, it's my duty to know all the residents in the village.'

'Oh, right… I see…'

Pete burst out laughing.

'Flora, I'm messing with you. I know who you are because your team keeps giving the "Rock 'n' Rowlands" a run for their money on the Tuesday night pub quiz. They say you should know your opponents but that doesn't seem to be helping us win against you that often.'

'Sorry about that, Mr Wallace. I'll see if we can dumb ourselves down a bit.'

Flora felt herself relax as she bantered back.

'Thank you, we would appreciate that, we need all the help we can get. And please, call me Pete. Only my solicitor calls me "Mr Wallace" and that's usually when he has bad news for me.'

'You're too kind. Anyway, I was hoping to ask you a small favour if I may and if it's not too rude…'

'Ask away, how can I help?'

'I've volunteered to manage the website and social media side of things for the rescue as Sally's already tied up with the B&B and will be even busier once the cats begin to arrive. One thing that could give us a real boost is if you would agree to be our patron. I appreciate it's a big ask and understand if you would like some time to consider it—'

'No, you're fine. I'll do it.'

'You will?'

Flora had to stop herself from shaking her head to check she'd heard correctly.

'Absolutely. In fact, I'm honoured to be asked.'

'You are?'

'I am. When I met my wife, she came as a package deal with two rescue cats, Tony and Adam. Until then, I'd been very much a dog person but they have taught me just how special cats are and I am thrilled to be able to help this great cause in any way. I should also add that Sukie would throttle me if I were to decline.'

'So, you don't mind if I tag you across social media when I load the photographs up onto the website?'

'Not at all. And, if you pass me one of those flyers, I'll get my IT dude to add you to my website. Hopefully, that'll get you more attention.'

'Oh, wow! Thank you. I wasn't expecting that.'

'Like I said,' he gave her a small wink, 'my wife would kill me if I didn't!'

Flora couldn't help but laugh at Pete's cheeky expression and understood then why half of the world was in love with him.

'Now, talking of my darling Sukie, I must go and find her before she signs our home up for fostering duties. I dread to think what I could be going back to.'

He gave her a soft pat on the arm and wandered off, peering over the heads of the guests as he looked for his lady.

'You okay there, Flora? You're looking a bit shell-shocked.'

'Err… yeah… yes. I'm… errr… fine. Sorry!' She turned to Sally who was looking at her with a bemused look on her face. 'Pete Wallace has just agreed to be our patron. I can't believe I *actually* asked him and, more to the point, I can't believe he *actually* said yes!'

'Oh, Flora, that's fantastic news. Thank you so much. What a coup that is. The publicity his name will generate will be immeasurable. Well done! He's even nicer than I originally thought.'

'He was. He was nice and kind. I'm glad he's agreed to help.'

Just then, Essie came over to join them and they were sharing the good news with her when a commotion over by the large jungle-gym style climbing frame Matt and Bob had built for the cats caught their attention. They looked across to see three women standing together, trying to look innocent, although they suspected one had just attempted to clamber up onto the small chute. The first lady was elegantly put together in her pressed slacks and twin-set, the second looked like she'd just parked up her Harley Davidson in her jeans, Motorhead t-shirt and leather jacket and the third was a tiny bird-like creature wearing an incongruous combination of a long flowery-print dress with a pair of Doc Marten boots.

'Flora,' Sally whispered, 'who are those women?'

Before Flora could reply, Jenny Rowland appeared by their side and said with a sigh in her voice, 'I'm afraid those three are with me.'

Flora, along with Sally and Essie, spun round to look at her.

'The one who looks like she's stepped off the front page of "Vogue for OAPs" is my mother, Bernice. The woman who looks like Boudica with a bad case of PMT, is my old neighbour and now my mum's best friend and partner-in-crime, Sadie, and do not be fooled by Rose's frail, delicate appearance – that woman has a stubborn streak wider than the English Channel and she's tougher than those boots she's wearing!'

Jenny moved her gaze away from the octogenarians behaving badly and turned it towards Sally.

'You will also be thrilled to know that all three have signed up as volunteers for the rescue when it opens.'

The four women turned their heads as one to watch the antics of Rose trying to fit on the cat slide and Flora, never one to miss an opportunity, lifted her camera and took a shot. This one was definitely going on the website. After all, who didn't want to see photographs of happiness, be it cats or, in this case, old ladies?

THIRTY-FOUR

Matt sat on the top step of the porch and looked out across the small car park to the trees which stood between the house and the field beyond. He raised his beer bottle and took a deep swallow, watching the fairy lights twinkling in the dark beyond the tall, leafy sentries.

He smiled as he remembered when Sally had done her "recce" of the fields on either side of the road leading up to the farm. It was the day he took her and Flora out shopping and he was driving his Transit van. They were bumping their way down the farm track to the main road when she'd suddenly asked him to stop. Much to his amazement, she'd then asked him if he would mind greatly if she stood on the top of his van. Naturally, he'd asked why and she'd explained that she couldn't get a clear, elevated view of these two fields from the house and although she had an idea of what she wanted to do with them, she needed to see them from above to decide if her hopes were feasible.

Deciding that her slight frame was unlikely to cause any damage to his van he agreed although the shenanigans of getting her up there without a ladder had almost caused him a hernia! Common sense told him that they could have come back later with one in the van but she was already half on the roof by that time.

After she'd taken a number of photographs on her phone and they'd helped her back down again, he'd asked what her plans were for those two fields and was pleasantly surprised when she said she wanted to leave them as they were – more wild meadow than fields – and build raised decked walkways around them with a couple of gazebos in each field where guests could go and have some quiet time with nature. Her intention had been to keep any disturbance of the wildlife which had taken over the fields in the years they'd lain dormant, to a minimum and she'd succeeded. She'd also had various sized tunnels put in before the new road surface went down, to allow the wildlife to traverse safely to either side. This small act of trying to ensure the safety of the animals around her had hit a soft spot inside him and he now found himself having to face up to the fact that his schoolboy crush had grown into something considerably deeper. He couldn't quite bring himself to say he was in love with her but he would struggle to find any other description if someone were to question him hard enough.

He heard the door click open behind him and looked over his shoulder to see Sally walking out with a blanket in her hands.

'Here, put this over you. It's blooming cold out here and I don't want you catching anything three days before Christmas! Flora would do her nut!'

She draped the blanket over his shoulders before sitting down on the step next to him.

'How did you know I was here?'

'I saw you slip out and had a quick look out of the window to see what you were up to.'

'I needed a bit of breathing space. I'm not the best in a crowd.'

'I understand that. I have to be honest and say that it's strange having so many people here. I'm not sure how I feel about it.'

'So why on earth did you decide to have a Christmas party?'

'It's not a party, as such. More of a social gathering and I wanted to say thank you to everyone who's been kind, welcoming and helpful. Ten months ago, I'd never heard of this village and now I've become a part of it. In two weeks, my new business opens to the world, the vet surgery will be taking in its first clients and I'll have any number of stray or unwanted cats to look after and find homes for. Everyone in there,' she pointed over her shoulder with her thumb, 'has shown me kindness in every way possible. I mean, for example, Essie has told me that my plan to give away all the berries picked in the summer is daft and that I should stick to the old tradition of keeping some, which I have to pass on to her and she will make Bramblebush Jam and Bramblebush Chutney that I can serve up to my guests and, hopefully, sell to them too. Now, I wouldn't have thought of that!'

'Essie is rather clued up. I've heard she runs the local WI with a hand of steel.'

'She's been very supportive in all of this and has become a good friend too.'

Matt tipped his bottle towards the trees and the field in front of them.

'I was just remembering the day you climbed on the van to survey those fields.'

'Oh yes,' she laughed, 'it was like something from a Carry On movie.'

'Worth it though – they're a lovely little haven of tranquillity now.'

'Yes, I think so too. What's more, Sukie came up with a great suggestion of placing a fold-up table and chair in the gazebos and advertising the B&B on writers Facebook groups as a writing retreat. Apparently, that had been her plan for her windmill until Charlie fell in love with it and moved in before the paint had barely dried on the walls!'

This time it was Matt who laughed.

'Yes, that one took us all by surprise. It was the second time I'd worked with him and had him pegged as being a true city boy – London through and through I thought – but it just goes to show you never can judge another man. He adores living here and I think Sukie will be hard pushed to get rid of him.'

'The way she spoke, I don't think she's in any hurry to.'

'She's very good friends with Molly, Charlie's partner, so is probably more than happy with them being close by.'

'I'm hoping she'll be a good friend of mine too – I like her a lot.'

'Sukie's very much a "Marmite" gal – you either love her or you don't. Her straight-talking, no BS manner can rub some folks up the wrong way while other people love those traits the most. You always know where you stand with her and she's no gossip either.'

'I like her for being to the point. People like that are the best kind.'

'For sure. Now, to completely change the subject, are you still joining Flora and I for Christmas dinner?'

'I absolutely am and looking forward to it.'

'Well, you might regret that as I'm doing the cooking but—'

'Hey, you two! What're you doing out here? I've been looking everywhere for you, Sal – do you have any more of the fruity pickle? There's a bloke called Bob looking for some and he's threatening to sing if I don't find any.'

'Oh, good grief, Karen, don't let him do that – he'll empty the place within minutes. I'm on my way.'

'Fab. Oh, and by the way, you do realise you're both sitting underneath a large bunch of mistletoe, don't you? Don't be bringing bad luck on yourselves by breaking the tradition, now!'

Karen grinned wickedly at them before disappearing back inside.

'Has she forgiven you yet for keeping all this a secret from her?'

Sally looked over her shoulder at the now closed door before turning back to face him.

'I think so but I'll find out for sure later when everyone has gone home and we're here alone.'

'Can I ask why you didn't tell her? She is your best friend after all.'

'I… I want to say it was my secret but that makes it sound like I deliberately withheld from her, which wasn't the case. It's more that I just didn't want to tell *anyone*. Apart from my brother, who was sworn to absolute secrecy or I'd take my old house back off him, the rest of my family don't even know yet – I led them to believe I needed a change of scenery to help me move on from Steve's death. I suppose… I guess I was doing something for me and wasn't in the right place for sharing that with those close to me.'

'Would they have tried to talk you out of it?'

'My parents may have done – I don't know. Karen? Nah! She'd have been right behind me from the off. Which is why my conversation with her later could be awkward.'

'Well, we'd better get inside before Bob starts to warm up those pipes of his which could piss her off even more!'

He took the blanket off his shoulders, stood on the step, and held his hand out to help Sally up. When she stepped onto the porch, it brought her face directly in line with his and he inadvertently glanced up at the mistletoe above their heads.

'Erm…' he gave a small cough. 'Err, do you think we should… you know…'

He looked up again and Sally followed his gaze.

'Is it bad luck, not to kiss?'

'I don't know. I wouldn't put it past Karen just to

say that in order to make sure we did.'

'I suppose we had better then, why take the risk?'

'Good point, I suppose we should.'

Matt leant in, closing the distance between them. His intention had been to place a gentlemanly peck on her cheek – he would never be so bold as to go straight for the lips – but Sally moved at the same time and before he knew what was happening, their lips were touching and darts of electricity were coursing through him. Startled, his eyes widened and he saw Sally's do the same. Had she felt it too? Every nerve ending in his body was tingling but he couldn't bring himself to pull away. They both simply stood, lips barely touching and neither of them moved.

Eventually, after what felt like an age but was, in reality, merely seconds, he felt himself leaning in closer, putting more pressure on the soft mouth under his. His pleasure, when the pressure was returned, knew no bounds and of their own volition, his hands found their way to Sally's waist and he pulled her closer until their bodies touched. Her hands came to rest on his upper arms and their warmth seeped through his shirt sleeves, sending pulsing shots of heat across his chest. A small moan vibrated against his mouth—

'Sally, we're getting desperate for that pick— Oops, sorry! Bad timing…'

Karen's voice was the verbal equivalent of a cold shower and they pulled apart just as the wooden door clicked closed.

'Oh… err… I…'

Matt didn't know what to say or where to look.

'I'd better… urm… get inside… Bob… singing…'

'Ah, yes. You need… you need to nip that one in the… err… the bud…'

Sally bent down, scooped the blanket up off the porch and with a wan smile, scurried off inside, leaving him standing alone once more.

He picked up his beer bottle and looked out once again towards the twinkling lights behind the trees, willing his racing heart to slow down. He didn't quite know what to make of what had just happened but it looked like the time had come for him to face up to the feelings he'd been making such an effort to ignore.

He let out a sigh, drained the dregs of his beer and turned to walk back inside, the jelly sensation in his legs seeping away with every step.

THIRTY-FIVE

'Right, lady, I think it's about time you spilled some beans! What on EARTH have you been getting up to since I last saw you?'

Sally looked at Karen, whose arms were buried in the soapy water which filled the sink, and tried to gauge if she was annoyed or not. The sound of water swishing around in the dishwasher prevented the room from being completely silent.

'Where would you like me to start?'

'I suppose from the beginning. Chronological order works best for me.'

'Would that be your inner barrister perhaps?'

'I *am* a barrister, Sal, and we never have a day off. Stop prevaricating and get on with it before I end up clunking you with one of these pots! And, being a very nice solid copper, they'd clunk you rather well.'

As Karen washed the pots and roasting pans which had cooked the finger food for the buffet, Sally brought her up to speed on all that had occurred since they'd last met.

'Why didn't you tell me? All those phone calls and you never even hinted at any of this. I thought you were just being evasive after I gave you the third degree on your birthday and figured you didn't want to see me in case I did it again.'

Sally placed the tea towel on the rail to dry and wiped down the island worktop before taking two wine glasses from the cupboard and splitting the remains of a bottle between them as she tried to find the words to explain.

'No, I can assure you, it wasn't that, not at all. It's just… I don't know, honestly, I don't. I was trying to explain this to Matt earlier – I wasn't intentionally keeping it a secret; I simply didn't want to tell anyone. Does that make any sense?'

'I suppose it does, in a way. It would have been nice to share it with you, though.'

'I understand but that's the thing – I didn't want to share it. For a while, it belonged to me and only me. No one else. And I liked how that felt.'

Karen stared at her but said nothing.

'What? Why are you staring at me?'

'What about Matt? Where is he fitting into all this? You talk about him as a friend, you've told me how helpful he's been but that kiss I interrupted was not the sort of kiss friends give each other. Heck, you and I have known each other since school and *we've* never kissed like that!'

'I didn't think you'd want us to kiss like that but if you insist…'

She puckered up and leant over the island towards her friend who swatted her away amidst a spurt of laughter.

'Get away with you, ya daft moo! You know what I mean and stop trying to evade the question. What gives with you and Matt?'

'Tell me, Karen, are you a good barrister?'

'Damn right I am, what gave it away?'

'The fact you're currently like a dog with a bone over Matt.'

'I just wanna know what's happening to my bestie's heart. Is the little icicle beginning to thaw? Is it starting to feel love again? After all, it has been a while. And yes, I do appreciate the circumstances made it difficult but after nearly four years, you are long overdue having someone special in your life once more.'

'Then, to answer your question, nothing "gives" with Matt and I! Apparently, he had a crush on me at school—'

'Whoa! Back it up… he knew you at school? I don't remember him.'

'He was a couple of years above us. I don't remember him either but he remembers me. He was going to ask me to the end-of-term dance but we moved away before he had the chance.'

'Damn! He could have asked me, then I wouldn't have been stuck with snotty-nosed Tommy Haxton.'

'That was your own fault! You kept knocking back all the lads who asked you because you were waiting for Philip Vickers to request the pleasure of your company. Except he'd already asked Katya

Middleton which left you high and dry. No one to blame but yourself there, girlfriend.'

'Humph! Your sympathy is underwhelming! Anyway, stop changing the damn subject – we're talking about you and Matt here.'

'There is no "me and Matt" to talk about. We're good friends and he's been an amazing help with getting this place all sorted out but I've paid him for that. It's amazing how friendly folks are when you're paying their wages.'

'Look, I know what I saw tonight and there were no "wages" involved there.'

Karen took a swig of her wine and as she set the glass back on the worktop, she pinned Sally down with a firm expression on her face.

'Okay, I'm going to drop this for now, Sal, because I don't want to make you uncomfortable but do me a favour – have a good think on how you feel about Matt and where you would like this to go. Be totally honest with yourself because he seems like a good bloke.'

'He is.'

'Then don't risk losing him, love. The good guys are few and far between.'

'I'll drink to that!'

They clinked their glasses before emptying them.

'And on that note, my little chickadee, I'm off to catch some winks in that glorious bedroom you've put me in. I'll see you in the morning.'

'Goodnight, Karen, and thank you for understanding.'

'No worries. Goodnight.'

Karen walked over to the door but then stopped and turned back.

'Sal, I just want to say one last thing – when I arrived earlier, the first thing I noticed was how fantastic you look. You are positively glowing! I don't think I have ever seen you look so vibrant and happy. You've smiled and laughed all night long. I know you were happy with Steve and I don't want to undermine what you had with him but this…' she pointed her finger at Sally and moved it up and down, 'this is way beyond that. I think you've finally grown into your own skin and it's looking mighty fine!'

She gave her a smile and walked into the hallway.

Sally listened to the footsteps going up the stairs and pondered on what Karen had said as she placed the glasses on the worktop by the sink, switched off the light and made her way along to her own bedroom. Herbert was already curled up in the middle of the bed and as she twisted her body to fit around him, Karen's words kept repeating themselves in her head.

Two hours later, after much tossing and turning which was so bad, Herbie had growled at one point, Sally got up and padded down her spiral staircase to the kitchen. Maybe a glass of milk might help her to sleep but she knew she was clutching at straws. The truth was, Karen's words had struck deeper than she'd expected and she was now questioning herself in ways she hadn't done before.

Was she really now finding herself? She'd always thought of herself as being a fairly complete person and when she'd married Steve, her belief was that they'd enhanced each other. She'd never been a woman who felt a man was required to make her "whole" – Steve had merely been the icing on the cake of her happy existence.

She stopped dead, the carton of milk half-tilted in her hand, and took heed of her thought process. "Happy existence!" Those very words summed it up and she had been completely unaware. She had been "existing" – not in a bad way although the years after Steve's death were in a different league entirely. But Karen was right – nothing about her life had made her feel fulfilled. She'd left school with okay grades, got a job as a secretary, and worked up to being a PA and then met and married Steve. Nothing about any of that was exceptional.

The microwave pinged and she took the cup of warm milk over to the sofa where she sat in the dark and looked out into the courtyard.

Maybe if they'd had children, she'd feel differently about her life. She knew from friends that children changed everything about your perspective and your place within the universe but she'd never had the urge to be a mother and Steve hadn't fancied being a father, citing his own poor example of one as being enough to put anyone off the idea.

Suddenly, one of the courtyard security lights came on and Sally found herself looking into the eyes of a beautiful, red-furred fox. It stood still, clearly startled by the light and was looking right in Sally's direction although she knew it wouldn't be able to see her sitting inside in the dark.

She watched as the fox sniffed the air and the ground before slowly moving across the cobbles and through the gate on the other side.

A sense of fulfilment flowed through Sally then – seeing such a glorious creature in its natural environment brought home to her how much of a privilege it was to be living in this place.

A few minutes went by as she finished her drink and thought some more about where she now was in her life. Matt also crossed her mind but she pushed him to one side – there was only so much soul-searching she was prepared to do at silly o'clock in the morning.

Finally, after placing the mug in the dishwasher, she wandered back up to bed and as she slipped between the sheets again, she concluded that while her good monetary fortune had led her to this house and new episode in her life, she now also had an overwhelming sense of peace and that was something which money could never buy.

THIRTY-SIX

'Oh, I hope she hasn't got lost…'

Flora bounced over to look out the window again.

'I'm sure she hasn't, love. Just relax.'

'But, it's nearly twelve…'

'And your invite was for any time between twelve and half-past. If Sally was able to find that farm of hers, in the middle of nowhere, she'll be able to find us.'

'Dad, you know as well as I do, she found that by accident. Did I remember to tell her to take the first left AFTER the sharp bend in the road? That's where people always go wrong.'

'Flora, just calm down. You did tell her, several times. Anyway, what's the panic? We're not eating until after the King's speech – there's plenty of time.'

'I simply want her here so we can all just chill and relax.'

'Fine! You continue to keep an eye while I go and

baste the turkey.'

Flora looked back out towards the road. She couldn't share with her dad that much of her excitement was down to having a new person to share Christmas dinner with and that person was a woman to boot! She wasn't blind and had been watching from the sidelines as her father and Sally appeared to be growing closer. Furthermore, the longer she'd been working with Sally and spending time in her company, she'd become really fond of her and wouldn't be in the least bit upset if her dad and Sal became an item. Although they were going at it so slowly, they'd be using Zimmer frames when the time came. And, if they wanted to do the old "hoochie-coochie" they'd most likely need a bed-lift to make it happen!

Therefore, Flora had invited Sally to join them for dinner today in the hope of moving things along but she couldn't help the little twinge of fear that she'd cancel at the last minute, having sussed out what Flora was up to.

A few minutes later, she saw the red roof of a car over the top of the hedge and let out a loud sigh of relief when it turned into their driveway.

'She's here!' she yelled out to her dad before running to the front door and throwing it open.

'Sally! You found us. Welcome, welcome!'

She grabbed Sally up in a big hug.

'Hey, Flora, your directions were perfect and I found you with no problem at all although, I have to say, it is gorgeous around here. This side of the village is still uncharted territory for me.'

'Our little lane is rather well hidden and the few residents on it like it that way.'

'I adore your house – it's stunning.'

Flora turned and looked at her home through Sally's eyes. The old, detached building dated back to the seventeenth century and sported the timbred look so prominent from that time. Her dad had recently repainted the outside and had gone for pale blue plasterwork alongside the black wooden timbers. The window frames had been painted white and were vivid amongst the blue. The front door had been repainted in deep cornflower blue, with all the black cast-iron trimmings refreshed, making it a feature in its own right.

'Dad will be pleased to hear you say that. He recently redid the exterior – it was traditional black and white before – and hasn't been able to decide if he did the right thing.'

'Oh, he did. I love it. And it looks so good alongside the other house I passed just back a bit.'

'You mean the yellow one?'

'Yes.'

'That's what inspired dad to be brave.'

'Well, I think they look stunning and they make your little well-hidden nook an extra-special find.'

'Sally, hello, glad you found us okay.'

'Hi, Matt, I was just telling Flora that her directions were perfect. I was also admiring your stunning house. I adore the shades of blue.'

It amused Flora to watch her dad swell with pride at Sally's words. No matter how often *she'd* told him that his bold move was a success, it had only taken one sentence of praise from Sally to make him accept it.

'Come, let me help you inside with your stuff.'

'*My* stuff? I travel light – I have one overnight bag! His Royal Highness, Prince Herbert, on the other hand… he's the one who needs everything bar the kitchen sink!'

Flora walked over to the car to help her dad.

'Hey there, Herbie, how are you, you gorgeous boy?' she cooed, as she bent down to grab his bag of litter and tray. Her dad picked up Sally's holdall and a carrier bag of tins which she assumed was Herbie's food. She hoped he'd be allowed some turkey later – surely cats were permitted to have a Christmas dinner too.

They filed into the house and she led Sally to the lounge where she placed Herbert, in his carrier, in the middle of the room.

'Are you sure you're both okay to let him just wander around? I'm happy to confine him to my room – it's only for one night.'

'Don't be daft – of course it's okay,' Flora replied quickly before her dad had a chance to say anything different and bent down to let the cat out of his basket. She wanted Sally to be as relaxed as possible while she was here and she knew that was more likely if Herbert was around them and she didn't need to pop up the stairs to check on him every ten minutes or so.

'We need to keep an eye on any open windows, in case he's tempted to go exploring, although, truth be told, he'll most likely find a corner somewhere and hide away. Like most cats, he doesn't travel well and isn't too good in new spaces.'

'We've got the skylights in the kitchen open but I think he'll have a job getting up to those!'

'Skylights? Right.'

'Dad, why don't you take Sally through to the kitchen and get her a glass of wine while I take her bag up to her room. Sally,' Flora gave a little wink, 'I'm sure if you ask him nicely enough, Dad will give you a tour of the house. It's worth seeing and is the reason he became a builder.'

'Oh, is that so? Please tell me more and I'd love to look around if it's not too much of an imposition.'

Flora smiled to herself as she walked up the stairs and overheard her dad begin to explain the history of their home. She heard a soft padding behind her and looked over her shoulder to see Herbie following her.

'Hey, little man, so far, so good, eh?' she whispered as she bent down to give him a scratch under his chin. 'Things have started off quite nicely.'

Herbert didn't answer her back but she was sure there was an element of understanding in his bright green eyes while he waited for her to lead the way.

THIRTY-SEVEN

'Blimey! I am stuffed beyond belief! That was exquisite. Thank you both so much for inviting me here today.'

Sally sat back in her chair while wondering if she felt relaxed enough with Matt and Flora to undo the top button on her trousers. The meal had been perfectly cooked which had resulted in her eating considerably more than was usually the case. Her mum, much as she loved her, wasn't graced with the ability to cook and what came out of her kitchen most of the time required a government health warning attached.

'You don't need to keep thanking us, Sally, it's been a pleasure to have you here. I think Flora's enjoying having another lady around. It makes a change.'

'Oh, I see. Is it usually just the two of you, then?'

'It varies.' Flora glanced at her father before

continuing. 'Sometimes, it's just us and sometimes my Grandfather Archie joins us. We alternate Christmas with him and my Uncle Craig.'

'Oh, wouldn't you just have dinner altogether?'

'We used to… until Uncle Craig became chummy with his mummy again and my lovely father here had a problem with that.'

Sally looked at Matt but said nothing.

'That's a chat for another time. Besides, I think Archie likes the new setup where he goes to Craig and Essie one day and comes to us the next. The wily old codger gets two Christmas dinners out of it and he's not complaining about that.'

'Then I only hope he doesn't eat as much as I have today because I can't see me eating again for a week!' Sally gave her bloated stomach another rub.

'Hah! You say that now but give it two hours when Flora breaks out the Christmas cake and mince pies – you'll soon change your mind.'

Matt grinned as she groaned at the thought of more food.

'Nooooo, don't! I can't even bear the thought.'

'Can we go into the lounge and do pressies now? Please?'

'Oh, go on then.' He turned to her as he said, 'Flora might be twenty-four but she's still like a four-year-old when it comes to presents.'

'Then let me just pop out to Frida and bring mine in.'

'You didn't need to bring gifts, Sally.'

Sally felt her eyes do an imaginary roll! Only a bloke would come out with such a statement.

'Of course I did, Matt. I wasn't arriving empty handed. That would have been rude. Now, excuse me for a moment.'

Thirty minutes later, they were sitting on the floor in the lounge surrounded by balls of discarded wrapping paper. Sally was pleased that her gifts had gone down so well. She'd bought Flora a bottle of perfume which she'd mentioned she liked and a new external hard drive for her computer. The girl had been thrilled with both and said how impressed she was that Sally had been listening while she'd chattered away.

When it came to Matt opening his gift, she'd held her breath in the hope that he would like what she'd bought him. Men were always so difficult to buy for. She needn't have worried, however, for the antique toolset had gone down a treat.

'Oh, my, Sally! These are fantastic! I love them.'

'I'll be honest, I'm not exactly sure what they all are – obviously, I know the chisels and planers – but some look more like implements of torture than a tool.'

'Well, this one is—'

'Dad! No! I don't want to hear it today.' Flora looked over at Sally. 'Don't start him on his tools – you won't be able to shut him up.'

'Oh, do you have a lot? I'd hoped these would be a bit more unusual…'

'Sally, these really are wonderful. I have plenty of tools but not antique items which can occasionally be a nuisance because given that I specialise in restoring old buildings, I sometimes would benefit from an old tool to do the job. This fabulous collection will be well used, I can assure you of that. Thank you so much.'

He leant over to kiss her cheek and she could feel the heat turning them pink as her thoughts went back to the last time his lips were near her face.

'Now, I need to go and get your gift, Sally. Give me a moment…'

There was a bang and a thud as doors were opened and closed before Matt called through the door, 'Right, Sally, close your eyes.'

She did as she was asked and soon felt his presence in front of her.

'Okay, you can open them now.'

Slowly, she opened her eyes and let out a gasp of delight.

'Matt! Oh, my goodness, it is BEAUTIFUL!'

Leaning up against Matt's legs, was the most stunning wrought iron sign. It was rectangular with the shape of a bush cut out and a cat sitting beneath it. Bramble fruit had been coloured in red and dark blue and the word "Bramblebush" had been engraved along the bottom and picked out in gold. Above and below the rectangle was the most exquisite scroll work she had ever seen.

'I hope I haven't overstepped the mark with this. My friend who made the staircase for your apartment also does this type of work and I knew he'd do a good job for you.'

'No, you absolutely haven't. I adore it and never even gave any thought to a sign. I'm guessing this is for the end of the lane by the main road?'

'That's correct. I also have the post out back from

which it will hang but thought it might be too much to bring everything in. That and the fact that it's really blooming heavy. You won't be able to take this home with you, I'm afraid. I'll have to bring it all over in the van.'

'Matt, I honestly can't tell you how much I adore it. And I have no objection whatsoever to you doing the heavy lifting!'

Sally couldn't take her eyes off the sign and put her hand out to trace around the words and the raised brambles. It was so tactile and it was a shame that once in situ, she'd only be able to look at it. Unless she went clambering up a ladder, of course, but that would be most impractical.

'How about I place it over here against the wall and you can admire it for a while longer,' Matt grinned at her as he bent down to pick up the iron work. From her position on the floor, she was perfectly placed to notice his shirt straining across his chest and the tops of his sleeves as he raised the sign off his legs and moved it to the side of the room. Something twinged in the pit of her stomach and it was nothing to do with overeating. This was the first time she could recall seeing him wearing anything other than jeans and a polo shirt. She most certainly hadn't seen him in a dress shirt before.

She looked up to find him watching her and feeling her cheeks growing hot again, she quickly diverted her eyes back to the sign which now looked even lovelier against the pale cream of the wall.

'Flora, do you want to sort out the coffee and cake while I clear up this mess?'

'Sure, Dad. Sally, would you like tea or coffee?'

'Oh, coffee for me and, please, let me help.'

'No, Sal,' Matt said, 'you're our guest so grab a seat or a sofa and make yourself comfortable.'

'Actually, Dad, I was wondering if you and Sally fancied playing a board game.' Flora turned to look at Sally. 'Because it's usually only ever the two of us, board games aren't that much fun but now we are three…'

Her voice tailed off and she gave her such a look of hope that Sally knew she couldn't possibly say no.

'I think that would be great fun. Why don't I clear the dining table and we can play there? What game did you have in mind?'

'Monopoly?'

'Flora, no, that goes on for ever. We'll still be playing it tomorrow!'

'Aw, Daaaaaaaad…'

'D'you know, I haven't played that for years. It was my favourite when I was a kid but no one would ever play it with me.'

Matt looked at her as he replied in a tone which was resigned to a marathon gaming session, 'Probably because the damn thing is never-ending! Fine! We'll play Monopoly. I can see I'm clearly outnumbered here.'

'Yay! I'll pop the kettle on to boil while I go upstairs and grab it.'

Sally found herself smiling as she cleared the remaining tableware from the dining table and straightened the tablecloth. She replaced the coasters for their drinks and put a few mats back down for the cake plates to sit on.

As she moved about, she watched Matt clearing up on the other side of the room and, for the first time, really took in how he looked. His light-brown hair was shorter than she recalled which meant he'd probably had it cut for Christmas. This thought made her grin as her father and brother had always had a "Christmas cut". The shorter style emphasised the strength in his jaw and the straight line of his nose. The shirt he was wearing was the perfect shade of blue for highlighting his blue eyes which always seemed to twinkle. The same shirt which kept showing off the muscles across his back and chest as he picked up the rubbish was causing her to have little electric shocks each time.

She turned her back and straightened the tablecloth again even though it was lying perfectly flat already. She just had to do something to try and take her mind off Matt even though she could hear his every move behind her.

Sally decided she was laying the blame for this new awareness of Matt firmly on Karen's doorstep! She'd tried to push her friend's observations of their mistletoe kiss to the back of her mind but the conversation kept popping up and it was here again now, wishing her a Merry Christmas and telling her to get her act together, which would be all very well and good if Matt was giving off the "come hither" vibes but as he wasn't, she was most certainly not about to launch herself at him like an in-heat, jet-propelled missile.

'Here we go, one Monopoly game. Sally, do you

mind setting it up while I bring through the stuff from the kitchen.'

'Of course, no problem.'

She all but snatched the box from Flora's hand, glad to have something else to do.

As she laid out the board and sorted the money into piles on the lid, Sally wondered what kind of player Matt would be and made a small deal with herself – if he was the patient sort who took any losses with a pinch of salt, she'd give further consideration to Karen's urging of moving the friendship forward. If he was a sore loser, then it stopped here.

A wee voice hiding in the corner of her brain muttered something about how she already knew he was a good sport in these things from being part of their pub quiz team each week but she told it to be quiet – board games were another matter altogether and were not even in the same league as a pub quiz.

THIRTY-EIGHT

'That's it! I'm bankrupt! I no longer have a single fake pound to my name. I'm out.'

Matt sat back and grinned at Flora who was now sitting with all of his money on her pile.

'I think you're wasted doing graphic design, Flora, you should be a property mogul. Judging by the fact you now have all your dad's money and most of mine, you're certainly cut out for it.'

'Nah! I think property on Park Lane and Mayfair is considerably more expensive in real life. Plus, there's too many wheelers and dealers in that game – not for me at all. I'll stick to the board game version and just be content to wipe the floor with my opponents.'

'Matt, I think we've uncovered a ruthless streak in your daughter. You may need to do something about that.'

'I reckon it's too late, Sally, the beast has been

unleashed and I doubt it'll go back in its cage.'

'Oh, you two! Behave! Are we done here?'

Matt looked at his watch and was surprised to see it was after eight o'clock.

'Yes, I'd say we're done. We've been playing for almost three hours.'

'My, Dad, doesn't time fly when you're being forced to play a board game you didn't want to play.'

Flora grinned cheekily across the table at him and he couldn't help but grin back as he replied, 'Anymore of your cheek, young lady, and I'll be putting that box in the bin.'

'Sure! Of course you will!'

Flora rolled her eyes while she packed the game up and Matt slid a glance at Sally, pleased to see her smiling at the daft chatter going on.

He pushed back his chair and stood, stretching his arms out as he did so. He wasn't used to sitting in one place for so long and he felt cramped up.

'Anyone for a brandy? Seeing as it's Christmas and all…'

'Not for me, thanks, Dad. I'm off upstairs to FaceTime some of my mates. I'll see you both in the morning.'

'Okay, sweetheart. Sleep well when you get there.' He leant over to give her a kiss on her cheek.

'Goodnight, Flora. Thank you for a truly lovely day. It was kind of you to invite me and I've had a great time.'

'Sally, you are most welcome. It's been a pleasure having you here.'

Matt watched the two women embrace and felt a

warming glow to see Flora looking so happy. His conscience pricked him a little by making him question if he'd been right to stay single all these years. Maybe he should have considered remarrying, if only to give his daughter some female company and guidance.

'Sally, can I tempt you with a brandy?'

When she smiled and accepted, he walked over to the drinks cupboard and told his conscience that marrying someone just to make his daughter happy was wrong and would not have been fair on the lady in question – whoever she may have been.

'Shall we take these over to the sofa and put a film on?'

'Sure, that sounds good.'

'I also have a tin of chocolates hidden away so Flora didn't find them. We can nibble on those.'

When they were settled on the sofa, Matt at one end and Sally at the other with the big tin of sweets in the middle, Sally turned to him and said, 'This is just how Christmas would be at home, although without the board game.'

'No board games? Why not?'

'My dad and brother are too competitive and always take the fun out of them so Mum banned them when I was a teenager. She said Christmas was stressful enough without listening to them going at it.'

'May I ask why you didn't go home for Christmas this year?'

'My brother and his fiancée recently moved into my old house and wanted to host Christmas dinner this year. However, the dining room is tiny and getting six people in there is an accomplishment. Seven would have been a step too far and that's where I would have ended up eating – on the hall stairs!'

'Your mum didn't want you all together under her roof, then?'

'I'm sure she'd have been delighted to have us all home but her cooking is never going to win any prizes unless they're for who can desecrate a meal the best. Evaine, my sister-in-law to be, however, was desperate to celebrate Christmas in her new home and with her parents adding to the numbers, someone had to take a side step. I was happy to be the one.'

'Fewer questions about what you're doing down here?'

Sally smiled at him. 'You're very astute, Mr O'Brien, that's exactly it.'

'You'll need to let them know what you're doing at some point, surely. After all, your brother helped you move down here. Didn't he ask any questions?'

'Chris takes discreteness to a whole new level. While we may have had our fair share of sibling quarrels over the years, the one thing he has never done is tell tales to our mother. He knows about the farm, obviously, but I can trust him not to say anything to the parents. There's also the small threat of booting him out of my old house if he did, which I mentioned to you previously. Of course, I'd never do that and he knows it.'

'Wasn't he even a bit curious?'

'He probably was but he'll wait for me to divulge everything when I'm ready. He's not one for probing into other folks' business.'

'He sounds like a decent brother.'

'He is. I've been lucky. What about you – do you have siblings?'

'No, I'm an only child. Apparently, I was such a painful birth – Mum was in labour for over thirty hours – that she vowed never again.'

'Blooming heck! I can't say I blame the woman!'

'I agree although there's been many times when I wished I'd had them, if only so Flora could have had some cousins to play with while growing up. I think she found it rather lonely at times although I did my best by allowing lots of sleepovers with her friends.'

'Not quite the same though, is it, as having family.'

'No, sadly not.'

'And her Uncle Craig – no nieces or nephews there?'

Matt felt his chest tighten at the mention of his wife's brother.

'No, he married late and it was a short-lived affair. No time for kids and, even if he'd had any, they'd have been too young for Flora.'

'You really don't like Craig, do you?'

'What makes you ask that?'

'Your face changes, almost like disgust, when his name comes up. When we spoke before, I didn't fully notice it – my mind was full of B&B stuff – but there, just now, it was really obvious.'

Matt felt himself squirm under her gaze. Sally had twisted round so her shoulder was against the back of the sofa and she was facing him. The film on the television had been completely forgotten so he picked up the remote to turn down the volume before mirroring Sally's actions to look back at her.

'It's… it's difficult.'

'Look, you don't need to explain anything to me. I was just observing.'

'I know. But you're going to be working with Craig and you'll inevitably wonder what the problem is.'

'Probably but that still doesn't make it any of my business.'

Matt felt something topple inside him, a sensation like bricks tumbling down. He'd always been aware that he'd built a wall to hold in his pain and anger but now it was ready to be set free and he instinctively knew Sally was the right person to share it with. She'd had to deal with her own pain and loss – she would understand.

'Flora, my wife, was close to her family and by default, so were we. Gerald, as Craig was known back then, and his father Archie were central to our lives. Archie developed bad arthritis quite young and it fell mostly on Craig – I'll just call him that to avoid confusion – to care for him. Their mother left when they were both young so the three of them had become a close-knit unit. As far as I know, the communication between the family and their mother – also called Flora due to the tradition thing I previously mentioned – was sparse but they did maintain contact.

'Anyway, not long after our baby Flora was born, my wife received an invitation to visit her mother in Scotland, where she now lives.'

'Have you met her, your mother-in-law?'

'Only twice. The first time was at our wedding. It

was a bit weird, to be honest.'

'Why?'

'Because she was the spitting image of my wife! I mean, you expect there to be similarities but they looked like twins. And my daughter is the same. She is the absolute spit of her mother and grandmother.'

'Are you sure that's not just how you see her because of your memories?'

Matt stood and walked over to the corner dresser and returned with the photograph which adorned the top shelf. He handed it to Sally.

'You tell me…'

'Bloody hell! I take it back. I have never seen such a familial likeness before.'

While Sally looked at the photograph in her hand, he guessed at what she would be thinking – how the woman being held tightly in his embrace could easily have been his daughter. Her gold wedding dress set off her beautiful vibrant auburn hair which although longer than young Flora's current style, was still the same dazzling colour and the pale blue, almost silver, eyes gazed back, shining with joy and happiness.

'As you can see, it's our wedding day so my wife was a few years older than Flora is now but the resemblance is off the scale.'

'That must be difficult for you.'

'It is and it isn't, if you know what I mean.'

'Yeah, I do.'

'Anyway, my wife got this invite to go to Scotland but she declined, saying she wasn't ready to travel that far with a baby and she wasn't leaving her behind.'

'Were you not included in the invite?'

'I was but Flora didn't want to go so she used my work as an excuse. Time passed, the invites kept coming and became more frequent until, eventually, Flora gave in and said she'd go. By this time, little Flora was three years old and could have gone with her mum but for some reason, I really don't know why or what, my wife decided she would go on her own. Little Flora and I waved her off one sunny, spring morning and never saw her alive again.'

'Oh, Matt…' He looked down to see Sally's hand resting on top of his and became aware that they were now sitting next to each other. He must have closed the gap when he sat back down from bringing over the photograph.

'She arrived safely at her mum's place in the middle of nowhere and called to tell me that things were okay. She was planning to stay for a week but suddenly, on the third night, I got a call from Flora saying she was on her way home. She was crying and sobbing but I couldn't get out of her what had caused this upset. She just kept saying she'd tell me when she got home. I tried to talk her out of travelling at night but she was adamant that she had to leave immediately.'

Matt drew in a deep breath to help him face the next few sentences, one of which he'd never shared with another human being.

'That was the last time we spoke. What she didn't tell me was that a storm had broken over the area and the rain was coming down in sheets. Her car was found crashed into trees by the side of the road. She was still alive at the time but due to the remoteness of the location, the ambulance arrived too late. The police believe the car aquaplaned because the road was more like a river and she was found just past a sharp bend.'

The pressure on his hand increased as Sally gave it a gentle squeeze and Matt found the gesture comforting.

'What no one knows, and what I have never shared with anyone until now, is that Flora was pregnant. Eleven weeks. She hadn't shared the news with me yet. That was the last straw for me. I could have accepted the loss of one life but the loss of two... well, I'm sure you can imagine.'

'Oh, Matt, I don't think I can. That is just... there are no words.'

'Her mother came down for the funeral – that was the second time I met her – and I asked her why Flora had been so distraught, what had occurred that would have made her want to leave immediately and not wait till the morning or until the storm had passed. To this day, I still don't know. Her mother clammed up and said she was unable to say and her father did likewise. I just know there's more to it all but no one will give me any answers. I've asked Craig but he's saying nothing either.'

'Do you think he knows?'

'I'm honestly not sure. Anyway, after the funeral, I broke all contact with that side of the family. It was only when little Flora became a teenager, and wasn't so little anymore, that some contact was re-established but it was purely for her benefit. She was asking questions and wanted to know more about her mother. As you know, she's developed a good relationship with her grandfather and uncle but I always tended to keep my distance as much as was possible. Once a year at Christmas was about as much as I could stomach. There was a sort of truce for a few years when I found out that Archie and Craig didn't have much to do with Flora Senior but then Craig re-established communication and that was it. Back to how it used to be.'

'What about your mother-in-law? Is there any contact there?'

'No, there isn't. This was the agreement I made with Flora – I was okay for her to be involved with her grandfather and uncle but her grandmother was a no-go area. Until the woman tells me what happened that night, I want nothing to do with her and the same for Flora.'

'Flora was okay with that?'

'She accepted the compromise. She knows why I feel the way I do and respects that. She's never made any mention since of wanting to know more, or meet her grandmother so I have to take it as read that she's still okay with things as they are.'

Matt leant forward, picked his brandy balloon off the coffee table, and drained what was left in it.

'I think I need another one of these. You?'

'Yes, I think so too.'

'Sorry for off-loading all that on you.'

Sally held onto his hand and pulled him closer to her.

'Matt, don't apologise. There's no need. I'm pleased you felt you could share this with me.' She gently placed her other hand on his cheek. 'You've carried this pain for so long, it's time to get it out there. I hope speaking about it eases some of the burden for you.'

He looked into her eyes which were looking at him with such caring concern and unable to stop himself, moved forward just enough to let his lips make contact with hers. Once again, he felt the electrical frisson when their mouths met and wondered if Sally felt it too. He waited for her to pull away but she didn't, she merely moved closer and the hand which had been on his cheek slipped around the back of his neck and pressed him against her. In that moment, he felt the greatest surge of freedom. By telling Sally of his pain, he'd set it free and its release meant he now had space in his heart to fall in love again.

And he knew exactly who he wanted to fill it.

THIRTY-NINE

Sally lay in Matt's spare bedroom, staring up at the ceiling while trying to make sense of the last few hours. She placed a finger gently on her lips and felt the soft, swollen skin tingling against it. It had been a very long time since she'd sat on a sofa, in semi-darkness, and kissed like a teenager. It had felt both good and strange in equal measure.

Part of her felt guilty, however, and it was this that was preventing her falling asleep. She knew there was no need to feel this way, Steve was dead and would never have expected her to become a nun in his absence but that didn't alleviate the sensation that she was cheating on him. The other part of her, however, was thrilled she and Matt had stepped onto the bridge which would lead them from being friends and take them, hopefully, towards something more meaningful.

In between kisses, and sips of brandy, they'd talked

about where they were headed and both had agreed they'd like to find out but at a gentle pace. Neither of them wanted to rush forward into a full-blown relationship. Sally was sure that Matt was most likely battling with the same emotions as herself, through the wall in his own bedroom. They were both coming into this with baggage and needed to be sure it wouldn't impede them over time.

They'd also talked at length about his wife and the rift in the family. Sally felt his judgement had been clouded by the grief he'd been dealing with.

'I'm not saying you were wrong,' she'd said to him, 'but perhaps, with the passing of time, now would be good to begin mending things. For Flora's sake, if nothing else. It can't be easy for her.'

He'd acknowledged this but the main turning point had been when she'd gently pressed home a point about his wife.

'Matt, I can't help but feel, given what you've said, that you blame your mother-in-law for not stopping Flora from leaving that night. That, even though something had occurred which made her want to leave, you think more effort should have been made in keeping her there until the morning.'

'I do! I blame her for upsetting my Flora in the first place and for not keeping her safe.'

'Look, this is only a thought and forgive me if I'm talking out of turn here but as an outsider, there are two things which have come to mind. The first is that, with being pregnant, is it possible your Flora was maybe just a bit more emotional than would normally be the case? While I've never been pregnant myself, I know plenty of women who have and this seems to be something they've all had in common due to the hormonal changes going on.'

Matt had looked at her in surprise and after a moment, agreed it was possible and a fact he'd never thought to consider.

'The second thing that jumped out at me straight away, however, is when you mentioned how strong willed your Flora could be. Short of tying her up, do you honestly think there is any way your mother-in-law could have stopped her from leaving that night once the idea was in her head? Be truly honest here – do you?'

Matt had been holding her hands at the time and his grip had tightened considerably as he thought this over. When they finally relaxed, she knew he'd come to terms with what she'd said.

'You're right. Wild horses wouldn't have stopped her from getting in that car once she'd made the decision.' He'd let out a long quiet sigh. 'It looks like I've been blaming all the wrong people.'

'From experience, I know that putting the blame on others makes it easier to cope with the grief. Blaming the person who's died feels all wrong so we shift it somewhere else. The thing is, in many cases, there is no blame. These things just happen. That's how life works.'

'But, your husband... he was killed by a stupid boy-racer who lost control of the car he was driving too fast. Surely you must blame him?'

'I did, at the time, but now I see he was just a stupid, immature little boy who will have to live with what he did for the rest of his life. He's now in prison and due to stay there for a few more years but his punishment will never remove the horror from his mind.'

'How do you know that? How do you know he cares about what he did?'

'Because he sends a letter of apology to me every year on the date of the accident. That boy is never going to forget.'

'And that doesn't upset you?'

'Not anymore. It did the first time but after that, it kind of helped. Thinking about it now, it's helped me to move on. Once you forgive, you break the chains that are holding you down. I think I can say my chains are well and truly broken.'

Sally thought about the answer she'd given to his question and was comforted in knowing she truly had moved on and as she turned over, pulling the quilt tighter around her shoulders, she felt the bed dip lightly in the bottom corner as Herbert jumped up to join her. He'd been asleep on Flora's bed for most of the day, moving only for some turkey, and was still there when they'd come up the stairs but clearly felt he needed to remind her that he was still the number one man in her life.

He padded up the bed towards her pillow and she raised the quilt for him to slip underneath. Once he had taken up his position in the crook of her bent knees, she gave a little sigh of happiness and drifted off to sleep while thinking how Karen was going to pee her pants in joy when she filled her in on this latest development.

The following morning, Sally was delighted to find no awkwardness between her and Matt. Their conversation was light-hearted although there were odd moments where his gaze lingered on her a little longer than normal or she caught him looking at her mouth with a hint of desire in his eyes. She really hoped Flora had suddenly been struck blind through the night because there was no way she was going to miss these signs – that girl was sharper than a Gordon Ramsay Henckels knife!

'So, Sally, I keep meaning to ask, what are you planning to do with the rest of the land around the house? How many acres are behind it – thirty? Thirty-five?'

'I understand it's about thirty, Matt, but I'm not very good with large land measurements. I prefer to go with "a lot" – I can work with that!'

Matt chuckled. 'It's still quite a bit though.'

'Yeah, it is. I'm thinking of allowing it to stay wild, the same as I've done at the front. I've had a few walks out on it and I'm sure some foxes and badgers have moved in and set up home. It would be a shame to move them out.'

Flora sat down at the table and poured out some tea from the pot in the middle.

'The badgers could be protected so you may not have an option there,' she said.

'I think you'll find they're both protected – by Sukie and Pete.'

Sally looked at Matt over her slice of toast.

'Oh, how so?'

'They hadn't long moved into the manor when they received a visit from some toff over in the neighbouring county advising them that he was the leader of some hunt group or whatever they call themselves, and that their ride outs often took them across the bottom of Pete and Sukie's land. As such, he was there to advise them of this and ensure they didn't have a problem with it.'

'I thought fox-hunting was banned now?'

'It is and instead they're *supposed* to do a form of drag racing where they lay out a scent for the hounds to follow but their excuse is that, if a fox crosses the path and the hounds go after it, there's nothing they can do.'

'What a load of bollocks!'

'Yes, Flora, I agree. Just repeating what they say.' Matt turned back to Sally. 'Anyway, from what I've heard, Sukie went ballistic at the bloke and told him in no uncertain terms that his hunt would never be permitted to cross their land and any foxes on it were now her protected property. The same goes for the badgers. Pete refused permission for any culling on his land and has gone as far as to advise he is willing to take on any setts which require relocating.'

'D'ya know, Sukie goes up and up in my estimation every day.'

Matt smiled at her. 'When it comes to animals, and their welfare, I'd say you are both cut from the same cloth.'

'Which takes me back to your question, Matt. I have no need of the land from a farming perspective so I'm happy to leave it as it is. Besides, given the shape and lie of the fields, I think they'd be difficult to work with today's modern machinery which is quite large and bulky. It's probably why they weren't sold off with the rest of the land. However, Essie mentioned something about a bloke in the village who's into beekeeping so I may offer him the use of a field for his hives if he's interested. No rental costs but he can provide me with honey which I can sell alongside my bramble products. What do you think?'

'Personally, I think it's great. You know how I feel about over-development but you could make some good revenue by allowing neighbouring farmers to farm it.'

'Nah! I'd rather give it back to Mother Nature. Her need is greater than mine, these days. Although, there's one thing I want to pick your brains over – I found a couple of old huts on my travels and after what Sukie said about writer retreats, I wondered if I could do anything with them. Would you mind having a look and giving me your expert opinion? If it's possible, they could be another revenue stream.'

'Of course, I'd be happy to check them out for you and advise.'

Her tummy gave off a little "squeeeeeeeee" sensation at the thought of spending more time with him in a totally private environment because the middle of a field, which she owned, was pretty darn private.

'Sally,' Flora cut into her thoughts. 'Further to your writer's retreat thing, you could also include photographers, birdwatchers, and wildlife enthusiasts.

I'm sure you'd gain a good deal of interest from them too.'

'Of course! That's a great idea. Thank you, Flora.'

'Any time, happy to help.' She gave Sally a grin and a wink as she stood and left the table.

Sally smiled back at her but couldn't help wondering what the wink was all about. Had the girl already clocked the shift in the relationship with her father. If she had, then her discretion was much appreciated as Sally didn't think Matt was quite ready to share this change with his daughter just yet.

'Okay, you two. It's time for me to make a move and get out of your hair so you can prepare for your next visitor's arrival. Are you looking forward to seeing your grandfather, Flora?'

'Yes, I am. He's always fun and I know he'll enjoy the day out.'

'I'm sure you'll all have a lovely time together.' She looked at Matt as she said this, a subtle reminder of their conversation from the night before and was reassured when he gave her a small nod.

'We'll make sure a good time is had by all. Flora, why don't you give Craig and Essie a call and see if they fancy joining us. I'm sure there's enough food to feed a couple of extra mouths.'

Flora was throwing herself into her father's arms while squealing with joy as Sally left the room. When she looked back, Matt caught her eye and mouthed, 'Thank you' over Flora's shoulder. Sally gave him a big smile, happy that the fractures in this family were now slowly healing.

FORTY

'There you go, sweetheart, make yourself comfy in there. Auntie Juliet will be down to check you out soon and after that, we can give you some nice tasty food. Good girl, there, there…'

Sally gently stroked the trembling, long-haired tabby she'd just put into a quarantine pen. She'd received a call from another rescue asking if she could help because the location of this poor girl was closer to her than them. She'd been in her new van and out the gate within five minutes of ending the call. A woman had found the cat in her garden that morning but had drawn a blank when she'd asked her local neighbours if it belonged to them. Sally had a suspicion the cat may have been dumped because she could see the poor thing was in her senior years and the area where she'd been found was quite rural. Juliet would scan her for a chip when she checked her over.

She grabbed the Polaroid camera and took a

photograph that would shortly be attached to the form she took from the tray on the desk and began to fill in with the details of where the cat had been found along with the date and time. Juliet would add further notes on the state of health and general condition along with any meds and treatments she had to administer.

'Now, what shall we call you?'

She looked at the cat for a moment before scribbling "Tabitha" on the top line of the form.

Satisfied she'd filled in everything she had to at that time, she signed her name, put the form in a plastic folder and dropped it in the slot on the front of the cage.

Sally's eyes settled on the cat again, who had now made her way into the little igloo in the pen, and felt once again the combination of pain and rage that always came with rescue cats. The pain for the distress they were in and the rage for the people who'd let them down.

She spun on her heel and walked over to switch on the softer, low light in the pen and turn off the bright overheads. Matt hadn't been kidding when he said her cats wouldn't ever want to leave because they were getting every possible luxury here.

As she walked through to the sluice room, where the carrier cage Tabitha had been transported in would be washed down and disinfected, Sally knew he had a point. She had gone to town on trying to make everything as perfect as possible but these poor creatures deserved the best she could give them after the horrors most of them would have experienced.

There was, of course, the small matter of her not-so-small bank balance which, despite her massive spending over the last year, had barely even had a small ding put in it, never mind any kind of a dent!

Thinking of her bank balance had her suddenly checking her watch – Craig the accountant was coming over this afternoon and she was going to have to tell him everything. January was when tax assessments had to be done and she didn't know where she stood with that.

She picked a clean carrier cage off the shelf and took it out to her specially fitted van. The words "Bramblebush Cat Rescue" were emblazoned along the sides in cream and they stood out beautifully against the dark purple of the van. Inside, it had been modified to allow up to six carrier cages to be securely transported along with a small first-aid area in the event of immediate assistance being required.

After she'd disinfected it and moved it into position under the car-port area Matt had erected, she walked over to the new surgery to see how Juliet was getting on. When she walked into the reception area, she found Essie sitting manning the phone and appointments.

'Hiya, Sal, everything okay? Juliet said you were off to pick up a stray, how is the poor little mite?'

'Scared at the moment, although her overall condition doesn't look too bad, but the prognosis could change after Juliet has seen her. If she's old, and I suspect she is, she could have a condition and that's why she's been dumped because people can't always afford the treatment.'

'Oh, that's cruel.'

'Yeah, well… that's people for you.'

'I hope she's okay. Anyway, I've made up a rota of who'll be manning the reception for the next month. My ladies from the WI were all very keen to do their bit in volunteering to assist you once I explained to them that all profits from the surgery were going towards the rescue.'

'Hmm, are you sure about that? I reckon most of them will be hoping to see more of Nick Davies…'

Essie chuckled. 'I think you're absolutely right about that, especially as I did happen to let it slip that he's involved with the surgery but as it's all for a good cause…'

'You're incorrigible, Essie!'

'It has been said, I confess, and mostly by my Craig!'

'Who I'm due to sit down with soon so I'd better get on. I just wanted to check that everything was going okay, this being the first day of business and all…'

'No problems so far. Jools's on her last patient now for this morning and everyone she's attended to so far has come out singing her praises. I think she's going to be an exceptional asset.'

'Oh, that is good to hear. Can you let her know, please, that she needs to go over to the QU when she's finished here?'

'Queue?'

'Quarantine unit. Too many syllables in there!'

'Of course. I'll be sure to do that.'

'Thank you. Right, onto the next task. It's never ending.'

'You do have a lot going on, Sally, but the good news is that I've found two candidates who'd be happy to do a few hours of cleaning each morning in the B&B. A husband-and-wife team who are now retired but would like to have a small part-time job. They'd like to rotate if that's ok with you.'

'Sure, I don't mind. As long as the beds are changed and the rooms are cleaned, the seven dwarves can come along too!'

'Oh, you also want dwarves… leave that one with me!'

This time it was Sally who burst out laughing.

'Essie, with your skills, nothing would surprise me!'

She turned away with a small wave and made her way down the outside steps, thinking again on what a blessing Essie had turned out to be. As the opening day for the surgery had drawn closer, Sally had realised that she wasn't happy with the idea of the appointments being managed by Nick's surgery because it meant there was no one to greet the clients when they arrived, however, employing a receptionist would eat into the profits which would take money out of the rescue. It was Essie who'd suggested getting in volunteers and said she knew exactly who would be reliable candidates to ask and she hadn't let her down. It was another thing she no longer had to worry about although there was plenty she did, such as having everything ready for Craig's arrival and dealing with the daunting task which lay in front of her.

'Oh, Sally, I know I've said it before but I'm saying it again – your filing skills are quite exceptional. If only all my clients were this conscientious with their receipts, it would make my job so much easier.'

'I never used to be, I can assure you. I learnt the hard way.'

She looked at the box files all lined up in their respective months and she knew the receipts inside were arranged in date order with notes attached if more details were required. She actually felt quite pleased with herself.

'So, the first thing I need to look at is the current bank balance for the business and then I can work my way back from there, matching the receipts against the outgoings.'

'Ah, right…'

'Is there a problem?'

'No, Craig, absolutely not. I just think… well… oh, I'm just going to show you…'

She pulled the keyboard towards her and logged onto her bank account. She noted the balance before turning the screen towards Craig and saw that it had increased again. It didn't seem to matter what she spent, the interest – even at the current ridiculously low rates – soon pushed the total back up again.

She waited quietly for Craig to take in what he was seeing. When he looked back at her, his surprise was clear to see.

'For real?'

'Yup,' she nodded, 'for real.'

'Wow! That was unexpected. I mean, don't get me

wrong, I've worked with values considerably greater than that when I was doing accountancy full-time but they were attached to business accounts, never one individual.'

'It was a lottery win that we chose not to make public.'

'I can't say I blame you. Wow!'

She watched him take off his glasses, give them a wipe and put them back on again.

'Doing that won't change the numbers, Craig,' she grinned.

He chuckled. 'So it would appear.'

Sally quickly explained that the account had been opened purely for the winnings and pointed out to him the sparse values which had been taken out prior to Steve's death – a sum to pay off their mortgage and the cost of the fatal Aston Martin along with a few grand to cover a holiday they were planning to take but had never happened. After that, it had lain untouched until she'd bought the farm and every outgoing since had a receipt to match it.

'I'll be honest, this does make things easier from a start-off point of view. I'll look at some different options on how best to do this and then discuss them with you once I have the relevant information collated.'

'Good. Easy is good. Now, I'm going to go and refresh these coffee mugs while you get your head around it all. Once you're done here, I'll introduce you to Juliet, or Jools which she says she prefers, as she'll oversee the invoicing for the surgery and meds used for the rescue.'

'Just one thing, Sally, while I remember, I believe you told Essie that the profits from the B&B will be going towards the running of the rescue?'

She halted at the side of the desk. 'That's correct.'

'Do you think the B&B will generate enough business to make that feasible? I mean, I'm guessing that's your cover story to hide this…' Craig pointed at the balance on the computer screen.

'I'll be honest, it was a concern I had too but no more. The website went live on the second of January and from next week, I'm fully booked, Monday through to Friday, for the next three months!'

'Seriously? My goodness… well done!'

'Yeah, it turns out I fall into the catchment area for the large conference centre a few miles up the road and while they do provide in-house accommodation, it would appear not everyone wants to stay on site. Lucky me!'

'That's a great result. And it'll stop the locals from being too nosy.'

'And that can only be a good thing, yes?'

'Oh yes!'

FORTY-ONE

'So, how was your first day, Jools?'

'Not too bad, not too bad at all although a number of the owners looked disappointed to see me – what's that all about?'

'Ah, they were probably hoping for Nick. He's considered to be the "Catch of the Area" in these here parts.'

'Right! I see. That would explain it.'

'I wouldn't worry about it though – Essie tells me they were all singing your praises when they came out. Your first impressions went down well.'

'Let's hope they stay that way.'

'Did you have a look at Tabitha? Anything to report?'

'On the outside, she looks good. Healthy coat and clear eyes but I've taken a blood test to check out her innards. Unsurprisingly, no microchip. Once I have the results, we can take it from there.'

'Had she stopped trembling by the time you arrived?'

'No, but she quickly perked up when I put some food down for her. She'd also used the litter tray and that's a good sign.'

'Fab. I'll pop over later to put more food down and settle her for the night.'

'Thanks. I can get on with sorting out my unpacking. Peggy was most put out that we couldn't find her favourite dolly last night.'

'Oh, the poor love. I hope she soon feels at home.'

'I think the nice, secure garden Matt has provided for her to run around in will help with that.'

'Look, I've got a stew going in the slow cooker and there's plenty of it – why don't you come over for dinner. I'm sure cooking is the last thing you want to do after your first day on the job and surrounded by cardboard boxes. Bring Peggy with you.'

'Won't your cat object to a dog being in his home?'

'He can go upstairs if it's a problem but I'd really like the two of them to grow used to each other given the close proximity we're living in here.'

'Then we both accept your kind offer, thank you. Is half-an-hour okay? I'd like to take a quick shower first – get rid of the smell of the surgery.'

'That'll be perfect.'

By the time her guests arrived, Sally had set up the small table Matt had cleverly concealed within the breakfast bar, sliced the fresh crusty loaf into doorsteps and opened a bottle of Merlot to breathe.

The good thing about Juliet being just over the courtyard was that she didn't have to drive home.

'Ah, great minds…' Jools placed the bottle of wine she'd brought over on the table alongside the Merlot.

'Oh, there was no need to do that but thank you.'

'I couldn't possibly arrive empty-handed, that would have been very poor form. Although, I'm now worried you'll think I'm a complete lush because most of my stuff is still packed up yet I managed to lay my hands on the alcohol!'

Sally burst out laughing. 'Jools, I'd have been more concerned if you'd managed to move house without resorting to alcohol!'

She poured them both a glass and handed one to Jools.

'A toast. Here's to you, your good health and to helping a great many cats find happier, healthier lives. For the cats!'

'For the cats!'

Once they'd sat down to eat, with bowls loaded with rich hot stew, and Peggy lying in front of the wood burner with a hopeful look in her eyes, Sally asked, 'Do you find it hard being a vet at times?'

'In what way?' Jools replied while dunking some butter-lathered bread in the thick, beefy gravy.

'Well, seeing animals that are poorly or suffering? Or worse, being asked to put healthy animals to sleep? I just couldn't face that.'

'I agree that having to deal with sick animals is difficult but knowing I can ease their suffering in some way does help. I can't express how it feels when you've had an animal come to you in a bad way but you save it and bring it back to health. You can feel the animal's gratitude and there's no better feeling in the world.'

'But, what about the flip side of the coin? That must be tough?'

'Like you wouldn't believe, Sally, but that's the Yin and Yang of life – for every up there must be a down. When an animal is in pain, and there's nothing I can do to make it well again, then the kindest thing is to let it go to its eternal sleep. It hurts like hell and I've cried more tears than I'll ever be able to count for them but I find solace in the knowledge they are in a nicer place.'

'You believe that?'

'I have to.'

'If it's not too rude, may I ask what made you choose to be a vet?'

'I love animals. I always have done, ever since I was born. We had a family cat, Tilly, when I was a baby and I've been told that I wouldn't go to sleep until she was lying beside me. My mum panicked in the beginning, scared the cat would harm me, but then she saw Tilly's presence soothed me and after that, the cat and I slept together for the next ten years. When she began to grow old and frail, I saw how the vet did his best to help her and when it was her time to go, he talked my mum into letting me be there with her at the end. He understood that I *needed* to be with her, that it was important for me to be allowed to say my goodbyes. That was the day I decided I would be a vet. I wanted to give to other animals and owners what he had given to us. Although I suspect the calling was always there, that was simply the day it became set in stone.'

'Oh, how so?'

'Other little girls had dollies, I had animals. Stuffed kittens, puppies, horses… you name it, if it was an animal in toy form, I wanted it. I still played nurses like other girls would do but it would be my animals lined up with bandages on or getting injections to keep them well. Clearly the latter came from Tilly receiving her yearly boosters. One story, which I was never allowed to forget when growing up,' Jools gave a small laugh, 'happened when I was about six. I was at my grandparents' house and had followed my grandad up into the loft when he went up to get the Christmas decorations. While he was sorting out what he was looking for, I went exploring and found, tucked away at the very back, an old toy of my mum's. It was a stuffed dog on wheels – I don't know if you've ever seen them but the dog looks like an Airedale Terrier and it's set on wheels allowing it to be pushed along. Anyway, I dragged this moth-eaten, threadbare thing over to my grandad and insisted I wanted it. He tried to talk me out of it – which was probably a mistake because that would've made me even more determined to have it – but to no avail. He brought it down from the loft and we compromised that if he took the dog off the wheelie-trolley thing, I could have it. Well, allegedly, my mother just about died when she came to pick me up and found me clinging on to this monstrosity for dear life. No amount of persuasion would make me give it up and, one snotty tantrum later, it came home with me. To add insult to injury, when Christmas Day arrived two weeks later, I dutifully opened my presents, said my thank-yous, pushed them to one side, and spent the rest of the day playing with Toby.'

'Toby?'

'Yup, that's what I named the dog. Don't ask me where it came from but it certainly suited him. With hindsight, I can understand why my mother was mortified because he really was a worn-out old rag of a thing but it didn't stop me loving him and taking him with me everywhere.'

'Do you still have him?'

'Sadly, no. He "mysteriously" disappeared when I went off to university. I reckon my mum saw an opportunity to finally get rid of him which is a shame as I told him all my secrets while growing up and I would have liked to have kept him.'

Jools looked melancholily at her glass of wine before taking a large slug and emptying it.

Sally refilled both glasses with the rest of the bottle before clearing the empty bowls from the table.

'Do you know what I find to be a good cure for lonely walks down memory lane?'

Jools looked up at her.

'No, what?'

'Large slices of warm lemon meringue pie accompanied with equally large, hefty dollops of thick cream. What do you say?'

The radiant smile which came back said it all.

'I think that sounds like an excellent cure!'

Jools passed the remaining crockery from the table over the breakfast bar while Sally took the pie out of the oven, the warm sweet and tangy smells assaulting her as she did so.

'Oh my, Sally, that smells delish! And it looks amazing. Did you make that?'

Sally felt herself blushing at the compliment.

'Yeah. I like to bake and cook although I don't do it as much as I used to.'

'Why not? Blimey, if I could create something as yummy as this, I'd be baking and cooking every day.'

'I used to, when my husband was alive but when he died… well…'

'No fun cooking for one?'

Sally gave Jools a small smile.

'Pretty much, yeah. It was easier to throw beans and toast together than to cook proper meals.'

'Do you plan to do evening meals for the B&B? I mean, if what I've tasted tonight is anything to go by, you'd be daft not to.'

'No, it would be too much work for me on my own, especially with having the rescue to look after too. I have been pondering on offering an afternoon tea for any guests who arrive early but, again, it's a lot for one person and I don't want to employ anyone as that would eat up any profit I would stand to gain.'

'You could put out a small buffet, along with coffee and tea-making facilities, and folks could help themselves. You know, maybe some scones and a couple of cakes. Perhaps get some of those gorgeous big glass bell-jars which you could place over them to keep everything fresh.'

Sally looked at Jools and smiled.

'That is a fabulous idea. It would provide the warm

welcome I want our guests to receive without tying me down to the house. I can be here to greet them, show them to their rooms and inform them of the facility. That's genius, Jools. You are clever.'

'Oh, not at all. Just glad it's a suggestion you can run with.'

'Oh, I definitely can.' Sally's head was already running full of things she could make which would be quick, easy, and tasty.

'Well, on that happy note, I'm going to love you and leave you. I don't think Peggy will forgive me if she has to go a second night without her dolly.'

'Thank you for coming over, it's been lovely to have company.'

'No, thank you for giving me a decent meal and letting me off cooking. I really appreciate it.'

Sally walked Jools to the kitchen door and watched as she made her way over the courtyard. She waited until the light went on in the lounge of the cottage before closing the door and locking it. Sure, it was only a small walk over the courtyard but that's what women do for each other – make sure they're always home safe.

As she pulled the heavy, winter curtains together across the large, patio doors, Sally thought back over the evening and found she'd really enjoyed Jools' company which served to reinforce to her that she'd definitely made the right choice for her vet.

'Did you enjoy having some company tonight, Herbie?' she asked, as she plonked herself down beside him on the sofa and pulled her laptop over.

Herbert gave her a look that told her he'd been less

than impressed with having a dog in his home but she knew he wasn't as fussed as he was trying to make out – after all, if he had been, he would have headed upstairs to sleep on her bed and not remained curled up on the sofa, less than two feet from where Peggy had been lying.

She smiled as she typed "Glass Bell Jars" into the search engine and gave a warm sigh of contentment as she began scrolling through the results.

FORTY-TWO

Flora, once again, drove carefully up the lane towards the B&B while this time cursing the frequent road humps Sally had installed to ensure no one drove faster than the five miles per hour she desired. She appreciated the sentiment behind them – after all, Sally cared about the animals first and people second – but when she was in a hurry to get to her destination, they were a right pain in the derriere! The heavy rain pounding on the car roof did nothing to appease her frustration.

When she finally reached the parking area, she jumped out the car, slammed the door shut and ran up the porch steps, stopping only to give herself a small shake before bouncing through the front door.

'SALLY? ARE YOU HERE?' she yelled. 'SALLY?'

She stuck her head through the door of the lounge, hoping Sally was somewhere in the building as she didn't want to go back out in that rain. Maybe she should suggest to Sal and her father that a covered corridor between the main house and the cat barn would be beneficial. She was just pulling her phone out of her pocket when she heard footsteps on the stairs and walking over, she looked up to see Sally's head peering over the banister.

'Oh great, you are here. I really didn't want to go outside again.'

'Hi, Flora, lovely to see you. Come on up, your Uncle Craig is here. Did we have an appointment today?'

'No, we didn't but something amazing has come up and I wanted to share it with you as soon as possible.'

'Oh, that sounds interesting. Go up to the office while I sort out some drinks. I'll be with you in a few minutes.'

Flora went up as Sally walked down and they grabbed a quick hug on the middle landing where they passed. She ran up the next flight to the upper floor and turned right towards the office.

'Hey, Uncks, how you doing?'

'Flora, my favourite niece! Hello.'

She embraced her uncle tightly before standing back and saying cheekily, 'Favourite niece? ONLY niece, mate! You don't get any choice in the matter.'

They both chuckled as she sat down across the desk from him. She looked around the room before commenting, 'I thought Sal was planning to put the desk under the window so she could look out while working?'

'That was the problem – too much looking out, not enough working so it was moved. Anyway, what brings you here?'

Flora smiled before tapping the side of her nose.

'I have some fantastic information but I'm not sharing it until Sally gets back.'

'Oh, don't I get favourite uncle privileges?'

'Nope. You don't even get ONLY uncle privileges.'

'Well, that's you disinherited!'

Flora burst out laughing. She did adore her uncle and since he'd hooked up with Essie Walton, he'd become a different person. The shy, diffident chap had morphed into a funny, witty, charismatic man with a wicked sense of humour. From someone who'd rarely laughed in the past, he never seemed to stop these days. She was happy that he was happy. She was also happy her dad had mellowed towards Craig and her grandfather again. She understood that thinking of her grandmother caused him pain but it wasn't right to rail at Craig for re-establishing his relationship with his mum. That was his prerogative and not for her father to pass judgement. Thankfully, Sally seemed to have got through to him on this where she herself had failed.

'Your grandmother was asking after you on the phone last night.'

Flora's head whipped up. Had Craig taken up mind-reading?

'Oh!'

'Yes. She mentioned she'd written to you, extending an invitation to visit but hadn't received a reply.'

'Maybe because I haven't received her letter…' Flora frowned as she replied.

She knew she could occasionally be a bit scatter-brained, especially when she was working on new contracts, but this was something she'd definitely remember.

'I believe she sent it about six weeks ago, before Christmas.'

'Hmm, maybe it got lost in the post – it's always much busier in December.'

'Perhaps. Well, she'd like you to go up for a visit.'

'Right… I'll need to think that one over and discuss it with my dad – you know how he feels about her.'

'I do, Flora, but this is your life and you have a right to know your only female relative. I'm not going to say anything more, just have a think. If you do want to talk it over, you know I'm always here for you.'

'Thank you. Leave it with me.'

'Here we go,' Sally said, walking into the room, 'As luck would have it, Flora, I made some of those Nutella cookies you like yesterday so I've brought some up.'

'Oh, lush! Thanks, Sally.'

Once they were all sitting with their drinks and munching away on tasty, chocolatey yumminess, Sally asked, 'So, Flora, are you going to spill? What brought you here in a state of such high excitement? You were practically bouncing when I came down the stairs.'

'Oh, you are not going to believe this. The village

wants to hold a fund-raising fete for the rescue.'

'They WHAT?'

The surprise on Sally's face was even greater than she'd imagined it would be and this made her even happier.

'You heard – they want to do a fete with all profits going to the rescue.'

'But… why? How?'

'I was in the café earlier and when I was leaving through the book shop, I overheard Saffy and Jenny talking about how much fun they'd had arranging and doing the Christmas Fayre a couple of months back. Anyway, the three of us got to talking about when we could arrange another when Jenny suggested Easter Monday. With it being later this year, the weather should be better which would attract more people. At that point, Saffy piped up with the suggestion that we could make it an animal themed fete and the profits, or a percentage of them, could be donated to the rescue. As soon as she'd finished speaking, Jenny was all over it. You know how much she loves cats. Anyway, ten minutes later, she's been on the phone to Sukie and Essie and they've already planned their committee meeting. I said I'd give you the heads up so you can let them know a good date for everyone to get together as you'll need to be involved.'

'Oh, I see.'

It was now Flora's turn to look surprised.

'You don't seem all that thrilled, Sally. I expected you to be happier about this.'

'I'm sorry, Flora, I'm just shocked. I never expected, or even considered, that the village would ever want to help out in this way.'

'Hey, the villagers are thrilled with what you're doing here. You already know they're working on putting together rotas to come and help with looking after the cats? Jenny was also saying that several of the retirees over in the retirement village want to come and help – they say it'll give some purpose to their days.'

'Wow! I… I don't know what to say. Thank you, obviously, but… well… wow!'

Flora looked at her watch and stood, placing her mug back on the desk.

'Look, I have to go. I've got a client to visit in an hour and it'll take me half that time to get back down that sodding lane. I told Jenny you'd give her a phone call to arrange a date – I hope that's okay?'

'Of course it's okay. It's more than okay, Flora. Sorry if my enthusiasm has been more muted than you'd hoped for – I'm just dazed from the surprise. I'm sure it's going to be a wonderful event and I've already got a million ideas beginning to brew in my head.'

'Well, I suggest you write them down as Sukie and Essie will also have some and you want to ensure they take on board your thoughts too. They are two very determined ladies when they're working on a project. Aren't they, Uncle Craig?'

'I don't want to speak ill of my lovely partner,' Craig laughed, 'but when she's got the bit between her teeth, the safest course of action is to stand aside and let her get on with it.'

'In that case, maybe I should get this committee

meeting sorted out sooner rather than later?'

Flora smiled brightly as she replied, 'NOW you're getting the hang of village life. Right, I'm gone. Sally, would you think me rude if I took some of these cookies with me?'

'I'd think you rude if you didn't!'

Flora wrapped a couple of biscuits in a napkin, gave Craig and Sally a hug goodbye and literally skipped down the stairs.

She was so excited about the fete and glad that Sally, once she'd recovered from the shock, now seemed to be on board with the idea and, furthermore, from a small selfish standpoint, she'd be doing all the graphics for the flyers and banners which would be great advertising for her business.

This time, Flora barely noticed the rain while running back to her car as her creative brain had sprung into action and was already thinking on what she could do.

FORTY-THREE

Sally waited until she heard the front door slam closed behind Flora before turning to look at Craig.

'Shit! Shit, shit, shit, shit, shit!'

'Not happy with that news?'

'Can you tell?'

'Why not?'

'I never thought for a moment that anyone would think of doing fundraisers.'

'But... you've worked in rescues before this, surely they must have had a few?'

'They did. They were always asking for donations, urging people to leave food in the supermarket drop-boxes or trying to get folks to run car-boots, stalls, and fetes for them – I simply forgot all about that side of things because of the funds I have to put into the rescue. It never occurred to me that people would come up with the idea themselves without any kind of prompting.'

'Essie runs the local W.I. – they're always looking for good causes to champion. Having one on their doorstep is going to be a godsend for them.'

'But I can't take their money. I don't want to take their money.'

'Once again, why not?'

'Because I don't need it. There are so many other rescues who do, I'd feel guilty accepting it.'

'You could pay it forward. You know, donate it to another charity. Or rather, accept the donation for your rescue but then feed it out to others which you know require it.'

'Do you think we could get away with doing that?'

'Who's going to know? It's not illegal and as I'm the only person who sees your finances, there's no reason for anyone else to find out.'

'Well, if you think that's possible, I'd be a lot happier with going along with this event.'

'Look, come and sit here, let me show you how I've decided to arrange your finances.'

For the next forty minutes, Craig went through how he felt it would be better to create three separate accounts – one for each part of the business – and that she could draw an amount from the original funds which could then be "investment capital". This would keep her own bank account as a separate entity from the business.

It was all a bit over her head, numbers had never really been her thing, but she trusted Craig implicitly and was happy to go along with what he thought best. She watched as he transferred the values over and typed in the extra security details required to do so.

'Do yourself a favour, Sally, change the answers to these questions after this. By rights, I shouldn't know them and I don't want to know them. In the event of anything untoward happening, God forbid, I want to ensure that I'm in the clear. This is for both our benefits.'

'Of course. I'll do it once we're done here.'

'Great. Now, if you'll excuse me a moment, I need to visit the facilities.'

'And why don't I make us another cup of tea? All this numbers malarky is thirsty work.'

'It'll improve once we've got the accounts up and running. The start-up phase is always the most tedious. If you think this was bad, give it an hour and we'll see how you're doing after signing all the paperwork!'

He grinned at her as they walked towards the office door. She replied with a grimace before heading off down the stairs where she met Jools halfway up.

'Hi, Sally, I was just on my way to see you.'

'Hey, is everything okay?'

'Yeah, I'm just dropping off some invoices which I've cleared for payment.' Jools raised her hand to show Sally the folder she was holding. 'I've also created a cost-code system, as per Craig's request, so he can sort each item into its correct grouping.'

'Oh, well that's good timing as Craig's here at the moment, so if you head up, you can go through it with him. I'm making drinks – would you like one?'

'Oh, I would kill for a coffee. It feels like an eternity since I had one this morning.'

'Busy early session, was it?'

'I would say so. I think I'm still being checked out by the locals and then I had a few procedural operations after that.'

'It takes a little while for the novelty factor to wear off around here. And, talking about the locals, wait till you hear the news…'

'Oh, what's that?'

'Let me get the drinks and I'll fill you in.'

When Sally returned to the office, bearing another tray of drinks and biscuits, Craig and Jools were sitting side by side, discussing the cost-codes.

'So, if I put this in here, it'll be logged under "Sundries" and so on. Does that work for you?'

Reaching for the mug Sally was holding out, Jools nodded to Craig that she was on board with the system they were creating.

'Right, what's this news then, Sally?'

'Oh, it's a cracker, Jools!'

Sally sat down across the desk from Craig and Jools moved round beside her which cleared her view out of the window and she looked at the rain pelting down outside. She was heading over the courtyard to the cat barn once her meeting with Craig was over and was really hoping it would have eased off by then.

'Before you ladies get into this, I'm going to say my goodbyes and get going. Sally, do you want me to close the computer down?'

'No, leave it be, Craig. I'll do it after I've sorted out that task you've left me with. I may forget if I don't do it immediately.'

'Okay. And, thanks to Jools' timely visit, you're getting off doing the paperwork I mentioned earlier, as some of the authorisations take longer to go through and I'd rather wait until we can do it together.'

'Sure, that's no problem. Just pop over when you need to.'

'I will. Lovely to see you, Jools, and thanks for putting those details together.'

'You're welcome, Craig.'

'See you, Sally.'

'Bye, Craig, oh… would you mind letting Essie know I'll give her a call this evening?'

'Not at all, I know she'll be looking forward to it.'

With a smile and a wave, he left the room and Sally had barely had the chance to take a sip of her tea before Jools was leaning forward in her face and asking, 'Well? What's this news?'

'The villagers have decided they want to hold a fundraising fete for the rescue on Easter Monday.'

Jools sat back in her chair and a large smile lit up her face.

'Oh, how wonderful! That's a fantastic idea. And how very generous of them to think of the rescue. You must be thrilled. Usually, or certainly with any rescues I've worked with in the past, fund-raising is seen as a necessary evil and yet, here you are, with a whole village willing to do their bit to help.'

'Tell me about it! I also found out today that they're putting together more volunteer rotas to come and help with looking after the cats which will include the residents over in the retirement village. I'm beginning to worry we'll end up with more volunteers than we'll have four-legged felines!'

'Hey, don't knock it, Sally. Having the local community behind you is worth more than you can begin to imagine. If anyone was to ever try and cause trouble, their support could be the thing that prevents your rescue being closed down.'

'Oh, don't get me wrong, Jools, I genuinely am happy that they're so keen to be a part of this, I just need to tread carefully as lots of different people coming and going could upset some of our more sensitive and wary furry residents and I don't want to risk offending people if we end up with too many wanting to help.'

'That's a good point. We are trying to give the cats some stability after all.'

'Mind you,' Sally gave a small, wicked smile, 'I suspect more than a few may be under the illusion that they'll just come along and play with cute fluffy kittens. A couple of days on litter-tray duty may help to weed out the ones who are more in love with the *idea* of helping rather than *actually* helping…'

Jools let out a loud, throaty laugh.

'Sally Edwards, you have got a very naughty mind! And I love it! Yes, washing out pens and picking up poop will certainly sort out the men from the boys, or women from the girls – whatever the case may be!'

'Indeed, it will! Now, as the resident vet, would you like to join me when I attend the committee meeting to discuss the fete and would you also mind having a think on some things we can do to contribute to the day.'

'Yes, I will and yes, I can.'

Sally let out a sigh of relief.

'I was hoping you'd say that. Thank you.'

'Hey, no worries. We're in this together.' Jools picked up her mug and chinked it against Sally's. 'Girlfriend, we've got this!'

FORTY-FOUR

Matt sat staring at the drawings in front of him. He had an idea of what he wanted to create, he just had to assess if it was possible. The slam of the front door made him raise his head and his voice.

'Flora, how many times do I need to tell you not to let the door bang closed? I don't have time to be redoing the plaster work again!'

'Well, take off that damn spring you've fitted to it and then, when my hands are wet from the pouring rain, I don't need to worry about them not being able to grip the handle and it slipping from my grasp!'

His daughter stuck her head around the door as she reprimanded him back.

'I don't know why you feel the need to keep the automatic closer on it – I've kind of grown out of the stage where I kept forgetting to close it behind me.'

'Okay! Fine! I'll take it off this weekend. Make sure you remind me.'

Flora walked over and kissed him on the top of his head.

'Are you getting so old now I have to remind you to do stuff?'

'Cheeky girl! I'm just busy and there's only so much I can keep in my brain at one time.'

'Like I said, getting old!' She grinned at him and he couldn't help but grin back at her.

'So, what are you looking at? What's this?' She flicked the pad on the desk and he returned his gaze to it.

'You remember those workers' huts Sally asked me to take a look at?'

'Yeah, the ones she's considering turning into writer's retreats?'

'That's them. I've been up to have a look and they're not very big. I suspect they were probably just shelters from the elements rather than actual living abodes.'

'Does this mean they can't be used as Sally hopes?'

'That's what I'm trying to work out. I'll need to add some sort of extension if Sally intends for them to be self-contained units with full amenities and sleeping facilities. Alternatively, if she's thinking of day-use only with the guest sleeping inside the B&B, then it's simply making the space more attractive with minimal amenities. I'll discuss it with her but thought it might be easier if I have some visuals on hand when I do so.'

'Well, I have to say that what you've got there is very pretty.'

'Thank you. I had a sort of Swiss chalet idea in my head which I thought would fit well with the meadow environment they're both located within.'

'Ah, that explains the enclosed porch on this one. I love the colours you're considering. Very fresh.'

'They're only a thought which Sally may or may not like. The windows on the porch could fold away to give the feeling of more open space but still makes the huts usable in bad weather. If they're to make money, they need to be versatile.'

'Will they require planning permission?'

'It depends which option Sally goes for. As sleeping accommodation, yes, they will, but for day-use only, no they won't. All things which have to be considered and discussed.'

'Which means you'll be spending more time with Sally…'

Flora gave him a sidelong look which held a bucketload of suggestion.

'Yes, I will. Are you trying to imply something within your comment?'

Matt knew what she was getting at but wasn't going to give her the satisfaction of providing the details she was fishing for. Yes, he and Sally were becoming more involved but they'd mutually agreed that nice and slow suited them for now.

'Oh, nothing. Just happy that you both seem to enjoy each other's company given how much time you need to spend together.'

The innocent look on Flora's face didn't fool him for a second, however, as she hadn't come out with a direct question, he was going to continue with evasive manoeuvres until she did.

'Right, I'm starving. Are you ready for dinner?'

He stood and lifted the drawing pad off the desk to close it. As he did so, a letter lifted in the small swirl of air and floated down to the floor. Flora bent to retrieve it and read it as she straightened up.

'Darren Connors? Wasn't he the bloke giving Sally grief last year?'

Matt took the letter from her and looked down at it.

'Yes, that's him. This is a request for a work reference – it's the third one we've had since I let him go.'

'Fired him, you mean.'

'Yes, fired him but I don't tell these people that. I don't want to be the cause of him not getting another job.'

'But you're okay with him being in a position to harass other women?'

'Flora, Darren worked for me for over three years. In all that time, his behaviour, attitude, and work ethic were exemplary. I don't know why that changed when Sally came along but I genuinely don't believe he's a bad person.'

'Well, it looks like you don't need to worry about him being unemployed; if that's the third reference letter you've had, then he's doing that just fine by himself.'

She looked pointedly at the piece of notepaper in his hand before spinning round and walking out of the study.

'I've already peeled some potatoes,' he called after

her, 'I didn't know how you fancied them tonight so left them intact until you came home.'

He threw the letter back onto the desk and walked out of the study after her.

'That was tasty. I can't remember the last time I had simple boiled potatoes. These days, it seems to be that they must be mashed, chipped, crushed or something else other than what they are.'

Matt placed his cutlery on the empty plate in front of him and took a drink of water.

'Hey, not "simple" boiled potatoes, Dad, boiled potatoes gently tossed in melted butter and lightly seasoned with the best Maldon Sea salt flakes and crushed Indian black pepper.'

Flora laughed as she spoke her words in the tone of the famous Marks & Spencer's television adverts.

'When you put it like that, yes, simply the best boiled potatoes…'

He stood, gathered up their plates and was rinsing them in the sink, ready to go in the dishwasher when Flora uttered a sentence which made his blood run cold.

'Dad, I saw Uncle Craig today and he mentioned something about my grandmother having sent me a letter before Christmas. I didn't receive it – did you see anything come in the post?'

He looked out of the window and his reflection looked back at him against the dark sky beyond. He searched his face to see if any sign of the panic within him was showing on it.

'Dad, did you hear me?'

'Oh, sorry, Flora, I was miles away. Hang on, let me turn off the tap.'

He placed the crockery in the dishwasher, closed the door and slowly dried his hands before turning and walking back towards the table where Flora was still sitting.

'You were saying?'

'I saw Uncle Craig earlier and he said his mum, my grandmother – although it feels strange calling her that when I've never met the woman – sent me a letter before Christmas but I've never received it. I was wondering if you had seen it, put it somewhere and forgot to tell me…'

'Erm… I don't recall seeing anything for you. You know I always leave your post on the table by the door. Maybe it got stuck onto another letter or something? Or, you know what the post is like in December – maybe it got lost.'

'That's what I said to Uncle Craig. It's a pity although probably for the best.'

'What do you mean, Flora?'

'I know how you feel about her, Dad, and that you don't want me to have any contact with her. I think I would've felt rather uncomfortable and it might have put me in the position of having to make a choice. This way is easier for me. It might not be right but it's easier.'

Rising from her seat, Flora gave him a smile as she pushed it under the table, picked up her glass and walked towards the door.

'Flora?'

'Yeah?'

Matt looked at her, standing there so tall and straight and gazing at him with those hypnotic silver eyes, just as his own Flora had done all those years ago. His heart clenched tightly with love and from fear.

'If you had to pick between seeing your grandmother or respecting my feelings, which do you think you'd choose?'

She looked at him for a few seconds before she replied, 'I don't know, Dad, I really don't know.'

He listened to her footsteps running up the stairs and when he heard her bedroom door close, he got up and walked into the lounge, heading straight to the cupboard where the brandy lived. He poured himself a generous slug and downed it in one after which he poured a second glass and carried it over to the table in front of the sofa. He sat down and let out a sigh as he rubbed his hands over his face and pangs of guilt rushed through him because upstairs, hidden in a box tucked away behind a false panel in his bedroom, was the letter from Flora's grandmother. He'd recognised it when it had arrived – the lavender ink and Scottish postmark both gave away who it was from. He'd removed it from the pile of post and placed it in the box along with all the other letters and cards which had been sent over the last twenty years, all written in lavender ink and bearing a Scottish postmark.

FORTY-FIVE

Sally drove Frida slowly up the lane, the wipers swishing furiously in the torrential rain. Despite the high hedging on either side, she could feel the wind buffeting against her little car. The full-beam headlights picked out the huge raindrops as they fell in front of her, giving them the appearance of little fat diamonds for the briefest of seconds. She pulled into her reserved parking spot by the side of the house and let out a sigh of relief at having arrived there safely. Matt had had the idea to leave some of the overgrowth in place when it had been cleared away last year in order to provide a distinct boundary between her private space and the guest parking on the other side of it. He'd also put the promised covered trellis in place on the verandah which would hide her from the view of any guests who happened to be sitting outside once the weather grew warmer. There had also been a promise for a hanging swing seat to be put up, just like the ones she'd seen on the American television shows, and she couldn't wait for that. She'd always had a fancy for one and when she happened to mention this to Matt, he'd said he could sort it out for her once he'd finished the renovation of the new writing retreats.

A frisson of excitement ran through her at the thought of her latest venture. She genuinely hadn't thought it would be possible to do much with the old huts when she and Matt had taken a closer look. They were both rather dilapidated when viewed up close and although they had stand taps outside for water, neither had gas or electricity connected and she'd been disappointed by how small they were inside. Matt, however, always the voice of optimism, had assured her that it wasn't too big a job to get them connected to the electric power supply of the main house. He had a small ripper and pipe-laying machine which would be just the right size for the job. Apparently, it could lay a cable underground in seconds while barely disturbing the land around it although Sally was doubtful and said she'd believe *that* when she saw it.

Before all of this, however, they still had to discuss how best to proceed with the renovation and Matt was due to come round the following night for dinner after which he'd show her the drawings he'd done.

'Oh, yes? Is that your play on the expression, "Would you like to see my etchings?" by any chance?' she'd laughed. She laughed even harder when Matt had coughed and sputtered his innocence on the other end of the phone.

Thinking of Matt, she decided to call him to let him

know she was home. Normally she'd wait until she was indoors but the rain was pounding down so hard, she didn't fancy getting out of the warm, dry confines of the car just yet and hoped it might ease off in the few minutes she'd spend talking to him.

As she leant over to retrieve her handbag from the passenger footwell, she thought back on the evening she'd spent at Sukie's where they'd all convened to discuss the Easter fete. This was their second meeting and it had been a good night, full of friendly discussions and she was beginning to feel like she was becoming a member of the community.

The first meet-up, two weeks earlier, had been fairly brief and had mostly consisted of agreeing the date and whether to ask the Victorian fun-fair, who had attended the previous fairs, if they wanted to make an appearance at this one. A couple of the ladies had expressed a concern that people could be bored with the same rides being there and maybe they should look for something else while others thought the fun-fair helped to bring punters in, especially the children, and often it was the pleading of children which led to a pet becoming a new member of their household.

Sally had forced herself to stay quiet when the latter comment was made as her firm opinion was that animals should only be brought into a home after a thorough and well-discussed decision had been taken and not one made on the whim of a five-year-old. She'd understood that the ladies meant well, however, and didn't feel it was the right time to lecture them on it.

Juliet had come along on both occasions, as she'd promised, and her presence had given Sally the confidence to veto some of the more outlandish suggestions which had been put forward. She really couldn't condone the idea of pig-racing, no matter how popular it might be in other areas of the country, and she'd put the kybosh on donkey rides too. Anything that involved animals being around crowds of people was a non-starter as far as she was concerned. When Sukie had asked how they were supposed to promote the residents of the rescue who were looking for homes, Sally had informed her that photographs would be taken of each cat available for adoption and these would be pinned up on a board along with a list of the cat's personality traits and any special requirements it may have. Interested parties could then leave their names and contact details for the rescue to get in touch with them after the event. Thankfully, this approach had been accepted by the ladies of the committee otherwise Sally would have been walking out because there was no way she'd have accepted having cats and kittens on display in pens where folks could poke their fingers in at them and get in their faces.

As it was, Sukie and Essie had spoken with her afterwards and said they'd admired the way she'd stood up against some of the more vocal, but not-quite-so-bright members. She'd had a good laugh with Jools about it on the way home afterwards but she'd been gobsmacked to find that some people had thought exploiting animals for the benefit of other animals was acceptable!

Tonight, however, had been a better and more positive meeting. A compromise had been reached on the funfair with Sukie having found a modern, travelling fair who were happy to share the space with the Victorian fair thus offering a wider range of rides. Jools had offered a few great ideas and her suggestion of a first-aid stall for animals had been met with enthusiasm and had been the first stall to make its way onto the list.

Sally had to concur that it had been a great idea. They were going to put together some "Animal First-Aid" boxes – containing a number of safe, animal-friendly lotions for small injuries, a selection of bandages and a soft-style buster collar – along with pamphlets of what steps to take for their pets in the event of various, common, everyday accidents.

Jenny had then suggested that her book stall have an animal-focused theme and could include books by James Herriot, who'd recently had a second bite at the best-selling author cherry thanks to the revamped TV show, along with other books where animals featured strongly, such as the detective series, Pet Whisperer, P.I., which had a talking cat.

They'd just been getting into the swing of things when the storm arrived and Jools had had to leave because she didn't want Peggy to be alone. After she'd gone, it had cheered Sally no end to hear the other ladies speak so kindly of her. They'd all commented on her lovely warm nature and her soft, kind approach to their pets. As she'd been spending quite a bit of time with Jools since she'd moved in, Sally could only agree with all the positive compliments. Jools really was one of the nicest people she'd met and she was happy to call her a friend.

She let out a happy sigh as she pulled her bag onto her lap, reaching up to switch on the interior light to help her locate her phone which always slipped down to the bottom. As she pulled it out. Sally switched the light off again and swiped the screen to call Matt.

'Hey, how are you?'

He'd answered on the first ring and she couldn't stop the smile which stretched across her lips as she replied, 'I'm fine, thank you. Just calling to confirm we're still good for tomorrow night.'

'Oh, yes? Is that the only reason you're calling?'

'I can't think of anything else, can you?' she flirted back, while her tummy made little butterfly swoops beneath her jacket.

'Well, I am bringing those etchings with me…'

'Really, Mr O'Brien, you do know how to woo a girl, don't you?'

'I'm trying. Still quite a bit out of practise, you know.'

'You're doing just fine.'

'Good to hear. How did the meeting go?'

'That was a sudden change of subject…' she chuckled.

'Yes, it was,' he growled, 'and a necessary one otherwise this is going to be a considerably shorter conversation. So, how did the meeting go?'

'Quite well, I think. That's the impression I got anyway.'

'I'm sure it was, then. Anything more said on the pig-racing?'

'Thankfully, no! I was— Oh, hang on…'

'What is it?'

'Oh, nothing. I'm calling from the car because it's raining so heavily and I was hoping it would ease off while we spoke so I don't get drenched. It doesn't sound as heavy now so I think this might be the best time to make a run for it and get indoors.'

'You're not inside yet? Sally, you'll catch a cold, it's freezing out there.'

'I'm fine, I've had the engine running and the heater on. Not environmentally friendly, I know but I think I can excuse it on this one occasion.'

With her free hand, she moved her handbag over onto the passenger seat before turning off the engine, opening the car door and stepping out into the rain.

'I promise not to tell the Green warriors but my silence could come at a price.'

'Is that so? And what might that price be?'

Sally grimaced as a large wet drip landed on the back of her neck when she turned and bent down to retrieve her bag.

'I don't know yet, I'll have to get back to you on that.'

'Matt O'Brien, you had better not be using this as an opportunity for me to view those etch—'

The pain on the back of her head saw the phone fall from her fingers and land on the tarmac just before she did. The last thing Sally heard was Matt calling her name before a crunching sound brought silence and everything went black.

FORTY-SIX

'Sally? Hello, Sally… are you there? Sally?'

Matt looked at his phone and then put it back to his ear.

'Sally?'

Suddenly the call ended. He swiped the screen and tried to call her back. He wasn't surprised the call had cut out – the signal out at the B&B could occasionally be hit-and-miss in good weather so, in the pouring rain, it would be next to abysmal. He'd give her a few minutes to get indoors and dried off before calling her back on the landline.

He wandered through to the kitchen, switched on the kettle and looked out of the window as he waited for it to boil. The rain was bouncing off the glass and he could hear the wind whistling around the corner as it flew towards the trees at the bottom of the garden, making them dance a furious, swirling, jig.

The kettle popped off and after dropping a teabag

in a mug, he absentmindedly poured the boiling water, while his mind played over the drop-out of his call with Sally. He felt an unease in his stomach which he was trying to explain away by reminding himself that dropped calls were not unusual on mobile phones.

He finished making his drink and dialled the landline for the B&B as he walked into the lounge. The phone was ringing by the time he sat down.

It was still ringing when he took his first sip of the hot liquid and had clicked over to voicemail when he took his second. He terminated the call and tried again when three minutes had passed. Voicemail again. He stood up as his earlier feeling of concern returned even stronger. There were three landline handsets located throughout the B&B – there was no way Sally could miss the call.

Just then, the front door slammed and he rushed out into the hallway to find Flora peeling off her wet Barbour jacket before looking in the mirror and running her fingers through her damp pixie crop.

'Hey, Dad, what a night! Was this predicted in the weather reports? I know they mentioned rain but…'

Her voice trailed off when she turned to look at him.

'Dad, what's wrong?'

'Sally. I can't get a hold of Sally on the phone. We were talking, she was on her mobile when there was a noise and then the line went dead. I've tried calling her back but there's no reply.'

'Dad, you know how rubbish the signal can be over there. Try her on the landline.'

'It's the landline I've been calling.'

'Oh!'

'I don't know what to do. Do you think I should go over?'

'How long ago was this?'

Matt grabbed his phone and swiped through to see what the time had been when they'd been talking.

'Just over twenty minutes.'

'Maybe she decided to have a shower to warm up and she didn't hear the phone ringing. Give it ten minutes and try again.'

'Hmm, yes, maybe she did…'

'Dad,' Flora came over and laid her hand on his arm, 'you don't need to worry about everyone, you know. It's lovely that you do but you need to give yourself a break.'

'I'm just concerned because she's out there on her own.'

'But, she's not alone, is she? Jools is only just across the courtyard. She's closer in proximity to Sally than we are to Lynn and Joe Sleight and they're our nearest neighbours. I'm sure she's fine.'

'Hmm…'

Matt could see the logic in Flora's argument but he just couldn't shake off the feeling of foreboding that was pressing down on him.

'Look, give it another twenty minutes. Let me get out of these wet clothes and grab a shower. If she's still not picking up after that, then we can take a drive over to check everything is okay. Yeah?'

He thought for a few seconds before nodding.

'Okay. I'll try again in a bit, just in case she is in the shower. You go and get yours, Flora, before you catch a chill. Put something warm on afterwards in case we do need to go out.'

When Flora came back downstairs a short time later, Matt was pacing up and down the length of the lounge.

'Come on, answer, damn it!'

He was looking at his phone again as Flora walked in the door.

'Still no joy?'

'No! It's still going to voicemail every time I call.' He turned to look at Flora. 'I'm really worried now. Something just doesn't feel right. My gut is telling me something's wrong.'

'Then let's get over there and see what's going on.'

'Look, you don't need to come with me, Flora, there's no point in dragging you back out again when you've just dried yourself off.'

'Dad, we're going together. End of discussion. Now, come on. The sooner we go, the sooner we can put your mind at rest.'

Five minutes later, as Flora plugged his phone into the car charger, Matt reversed out of the garage, spun the Land Rover sharply around, spewing gravel in its wake, and drove out of the gates as though all the demons of hell were on his heels.

'Keep your eyes peeled for fallen trees, Flora, or any that look unsafe.'

'Weren't they all checked when you did the thinning out last year?'

'Yes, but this wind could have weakened some of

the older ones.'

Matt had just turned into the lane towards the B&B and the vibration of the wind rocking the Landy from side to side was doing nothing to help alleviate the sense of doom that was sitting like a brick in the pit of his stomach.

His sixth sense was screaming at him that something was wrong and he was dreading what he may, or may not, find at the end of the lane. He wanted to get to the house as quickly as possible yet, at the same time, he didn't want to arrive because all his fears could become a reality.

A couple of minutes later, he bypassed the first turning which would take them into the guest car park at the front of the house and took the second turn which brought him to Sally's private parking area. Her little red Focus was sitting neatly parked in its usual spot over beside the hedge and he could see the rescue van underneath the car port next to the quarantine building.

'Well, that's the first question answered, Dad, she's definitely still here. Now we need to find out why she's not been answering her phone.'

He got out of the Land Rover and was relieved to find the wind less forceful in this sheltered spot beside the house and the tall hedging.

'Should we go to the side porch door or the back kitchen door?'

'Hang on, Flora. Stay there and let me just have a look around her car first.'

Matt went to walk towards the Focus but then stopped still.

'That's strange,' he muttered.

He turned and walked back to the Landy, opening the door at the back when he got there.

'What's up, Dad? Have you found something?' Flora twisted around in her seat towards him.

'No, Flora, I haven't found anything yet because the security light hasn't come on. I'm getting a torch to help me see. It's pitch black out here.'

With a large torch now lighting his way, he walked back towards Sally's car. He peered in through the passenger side window and saw Sally's handbag lying on the driver's seat with the contents spilling out onto the floor. He tried the handle of the door and it opened with ease. Matt stopped and closed it again. Finding the car unlocked now had his "something-is-very-wrong-ometer" rocketing sky-high.

He was about to step around to the driver's side, his heart thudding in his chest, when Flora arrived back at his side.

'I can't see anything through the downstairs windows, Dad. The only light on is the one in the far corner which I know she keeps on a timer. I've tried knocking on both doors but there's no reply.'

'Stay behind me, Flora.'

'Why?'

'Just do as I ask.'

Holding his breath, he slowly moved around to the driver's side of the car and dreading what he might see, pointed his torch towards the ground.

FORTY-SEVEN

Sally felt a thick heaviness in her head as she slowly came to. She sat still, with her head down and her chin resting against her collar bones, and hoped the feeling would soon lift and fade along with the throbbing sensation that was pounding through her skull.

When she tried to raise her head, she made a small moan and realised her mouth was taped up. An attempt to open her eyes was useless when she became aware of something tied over them.

She sat for a moment, allowing this information to sink in.

An initial burst of fear ran through her but she quickly worked on quelling it. She'd watched plenty of Hollywood action movies over the years and while she was fully aware of how false they were when compared to real life, they still provided some useful details she could use such as, and most importantly, not panicking until she knew there was something to panic about.

She quietly drew in a breath and began assessing the exact nature of her situation.

She was sitting on a chair. It was an upright chair, something akin to a dining chair or a kitchen table chair.

Her hands were bound on each side to the outside struts of the chair back.

She didn't know what the binding was.

Her ankles were also securely tied – one to each front leg.

Wherever she was, it wasn't warm but it wasn't cold. It was also dry but she could hear the rain outside.

At that moment, she sensed a presence behind her.

'**Do not move! Do not make a sound or you die.**'

And then something cold and metallic was pushed against the base of her skull.

FORTY-EIGHT

Matt slumped against the side of the car as relief washed through him. For some reason, he thought he was going to find Sally's cold, dead body lying there in the rain. The feeling, however, was brief because if she wasn't there, and she didn't appear to be in the house, then where the blazes was she?

He swept the beam of the torch over the ground and saw something glinting just underneath the car. He bent down for a closer look and saw it was Sally's phone, the glass front and casing all smashed. He resisted the temptation to lift it for a closer look and instead straightened up, looked back at Flora who was still standing by the boot of the Focus and said, 'We need to call the police.'

'Right, Mr O'Brien, if I could ask you to just clarify some points again, please.'

Matt tried to refrain from sighing. This was now the third time he'd given the boys in blue the pertinent details of Sally's mysterious disappearance and they didn't appear to be making any kind of moves towards finding her.

'We were chatting on the phone when suddenly Sally stopped talking mid-sentence, it all went silent and a few seconds later, the call cut off. I tried calling back but kept getting her voicemail. I then tried calling the landline several times, but still got no reply. Due to the remote location of the B&B, I decided to come out to check everything was okay. That's when I found the handbag still in the car and the phone underneath.'

'And you haven't touched anything?'

'Only the handle on the passenger side door when I was checking if the car had been locked.'

'Why did you feel the need to do that, Mr O'Brien?'

'To eliminate the possibility that Sally may have locked her bag inside by accident. It was one of those "hunch" things that you guys normally get.'

'Are you being sarcastic, Mr O'Brien?'

'No,' he replied, in a weary tone, 'I'm just tired of repeating myself and feeling that no one is taking this seriously.'

'Oh, we are taking it seriously, sir, we just need to process all the information we have. You may think we're being troublesome by asking you to repeat what you've already provided but sometimes, going over it all again can help bring forth small details you may have previously missed.'

'I see. Well, I really do think I've told you all I know.'

'Thank you. Now, is there any chance that Mrs Edwards could have decided to walk somewhere rather than take the car?'

Matt stared at the police officer and it took all of his best efforts to keep the look of incredulity off his face. Was this guy really that stupid?

'Sergeant—'

'Detective.'

'Sorry, *detective*... the weather conditions hardly lent themselves to going out for a nice, leisurely, stroll. At the time of losing contact, it was blowing a gale and the rain was thundering down. I appreciate this has now eased off but it was wild two hours ago, and the only place Sally was planning to go was indoors.'

'Is there anyone else living close by? Where are the nearest neighbours?'

'Err, there's Jools, I mean, Juliet, who lives in the cottage on the far side of the courtyard.'

'Is it possible Mrs Edwards may be with her?'

Matt suddenly felt like a prize idiot. He hadn't even thought to speak with Jools to see if Sally was with her. He'd immediately drawn up the worst conclusion and had called in the cavalry.

'Yes, now that I come to think of it, there is every chance she could be with Jools. They've become good friends and hang out regularly.'

'Right. And you say she lives just over the courtyard there?'

'That's correct.'

Matt groaned inwardly as his stupidity – why hadn't he thought of that first?

'Okay, I'll get one of the boys to go over and check. In the meantime, can you think of anyone who may have had cause to harm Mrs Edwards?'

'No,' he shook his head, 'I can't.'

'Err, Dad, what about that Darren Connors bloke who used to work for you? Is it possible he could have come for Sally?'

'What's this?'

Matt turned to the detective.

'In the summer, when Sally first moved here, she lived in a motorhome in the barn while the house was being renovated. One of my employees took an interest in her and it went a bit too far. When I informed him he was being moved to another site, he didn't take the news well and took his anger out on Sally. I ended up sacking him.'

'I see. Do you have the details of this person – just so we can check and hopefully eliminate him as a person of interest?'

'Erm, I do, but his personnel details are back at my house. I'll have to go and get them.'

'No, you don't, Dad. Remember I nagged you to save all your files onto the Cloud so they wouldn't be lost if anything went wrong on your PC?'

'I do. Why?'

'You can access them now from your phone. Give it here, I'll get the info for you.'

Matt pulled his mobile from his pocket and handed it over. Within a couple of minutes, Flora was passing it back with the information they needed on the screen. He showed it to the detective who noted down what he required.

'Right, sir, miss, if you can just wait here, we'll look into this.'

'Can we go up onto the porch, out of the rain?'

He pointed behind him.

'Sure, that'll be fine. I'll come and find you there.'

He grabbed a couple of blankets from the Land Rover and led Flora under cover.

'Wrap that around you, love, to keep you warm. And tell me, is anyone looking in this direction?'

'No, why?'

Matt walked over to the security light which was situated at the edge of the porch roof. He still couldn't figure out why it wasn't coming on and as he could reach it easily enough from here, it was a mystery he planned to solve.

He reached up and carefully unclipped the clear plastic cover which he handed over to Flora. He then gently ran his fingers over the bulb. It was intact and not broken as he'd suspected it might be. It did, however, wobble under his touch and when he gave it a small twist, the parking area was suddenly ablaze with light.

'Here, what do you think you're doing?'

The detective ran over and glared up at him.

'Helping you out I would think, now that you have some light to see with.'

'That could have been evidence you've tampered with.'

'The bulb was only slightly loose – it may have been jolted by the wind.'

The detective gave him a hard stare for another few seconds before he was called away by a colleague.

To Matt's dismay, he wasn't out of sight for long and he was soon back, clumping noisily up the wooden stairs of the porch.

'Right, first up, we've checked on the neighbour across the yard. There's no reply but we did hear her dog barking. The curtains are closed so we're unable to tell if there's anyone in.'

'She's the local vet – it's possible she may have had a call-out, especially in this bad weather.'

'Fair enough. Now, the other bit of news I need to ask is, how much do you know about Mrs Edwards' husband?'

Matt frowned as he looked first at Flora and then back to the detective.

'Not much. Only that he died in a road traffic accident.'

'I see. Then you don't know that it was Darren Connors' brother who killed him!'

For a moment, Matt's head spun and he had to grip the balustrade to keep himself upright.

'I'm sorry, detective, come again…'

'Billy Connors, Darren's kid brother, is doing a ten-year stint for killing Steve Edwards. Mr Edwards had just bought a swanky sports car and young Connors thought he'd try and do some kind of drag racing up the dual carriageway of the A38 near Burton. Mr Edwards was having none of it but Connors lost control of his vehicle, tapped Edwards whose car hit the central reservation, causing it to flip over the barrier directly into the path of a lorry coming the other way. Mr Edwards was killed at the scene.'

'Oh, my goodness…' Flora gasped as her hand flew up to her mouth. 'Poor Sally, she's never mentioned a word of this. I'm guessing she didn't say anything to you, Dad.'

'I knew the bare bones of what happened but she never went into any great detail and it didn't feel right to ask.'

'There was a court case, obviously, and it's very likely that big brother was in the courtroom when Mrs Edwards was there. If he saw her then, and recognised her now, it's not inconceivable that he could be planning something untoward.'

'But, why now? After all this time?'

'You say you sacked him?'

'I did.'

'Well, if he's struggling to find new employment, then he could perceive her as being to blame and if he's already holding a grudge because of his brother…'

The detective let his words tail off and Matt didn't need to be a genius to know what he was insinuating.

He looked at Flora who was looking back at him in horror. He knew they were both thinking of the same thing…

The third job reference request that had recently been sitting on his desk.

FORTY-NINE

Sally remained rigid until the person behind her walked softly away and was surprised to find she wasn't as frightened as she'd expect to be in such a situation. Steve had ribbed her many times on her ability to keep a clear head in stressful situations and this surely had to be the most stressful by far. But here she was, calculating her options and observing her surroundings as best she could.

Thanks to the thin-soled fashion boots she was wearing, she'd already assessed she was seated on soft flooring. Some gentle pressure with her toes had met with a small degree of give which suggested a rug or carpeting was under her feet. When the robotic voice had spoken, there had been no echo, leading her to believe she wasn't in a warehouse or barn. She could still hear the rain falling outside although it was muted and the room temperature was ambient. From this she surmised she was very likely being held somewhere small; possibly a house or a flat.

There was also an odour in the air, but not an unpleasant or damp one, which made her think her location was one which was generally occupied. It lacked the atmosphere she'd expect to feel in somewhere derelict or empty. In fact – she sniffed again – the smell was vaguely familiar. She was busy trying to place it when there was a tapping sound and the robotic voice spoke again.

'**As long as you do as you are told, you will not be hurt. Nod if you understand.**'

She dipped her head downwards gently as it was still throbbing painfully. It hurt at the back of her skull and just above her left eye. The first one being where she was walloped, no doubt, and the second, she guessed, from when she'd landed on the tarmac.

'**I'm going to take the gag off your mouth, but if you make any noise louder than a whisper, you will pay. Nod again if you understand.**'

For the second time, Sally dipped her head slowly.

A few seconds later, she sensed someone standing beside her and the tape across her mouth was carefully removed. As soon as it was off, she gasped and drew in several deep breaths.

Cold metal was placed against the top of her neck again.

'**Just reminding you of the outcome if you make anything more than a whisper.**'

With the voice being so close behind her and the cotton-wool sensation in her head beginning to clear, Sally realised what was going on. Her captor was communicating using the text-to-speech facility on a computer thus ensuring she didn't hear their voice. They would only do that if they had a distinctly memorable voice or… if it was someone she knew!

When the latter thought popped into her head, she felt herself straighten up slightly in the seat.

Could it possibly be someone she'd already met? But who?

'**Are you ready to negotiate?**'

'Yes,' she whispered quietly. Whoever it was, they were still standing behind her so they could hear her clearly.

'**When I ask, you will give me your log-on information for your bank account.**'

'Why would I do that?'

'**Because you will regret it if you don't.**'

Sally racked her brain, trying to think who on earth could possibly know the contents of her bank account. Apart from Craig, she hadn't told another soul. And, no matter how much she stretched her imagination, she couldn't see Craig doing this. Although, if he had mentioned it to someone else…

'How much do you want?'

Keep talking, she told herself. That's what they always do in those movies – keep the bad guys talking. Although what good it was going to do her was anyone's guess!

'**I need three-hundred-thousand pounds.**'

Huh?

Her head shot up and a small groan slipped from her lips with the pain.

'**I told you, nothing louder than a whisper.**'

'Sorry. My head is sore.'

Three hundred thousand? Was that all? Why would anyone go to all this trouble for such a small value? Maybe they didn't know just how much was in her bank account although, they soon would when they logged on. She was prepared to hear her "ransom value" increase substantially when they saw her actual worth.

Suddenly, there was the sound of a door being knocked and a dog began to bark.

A bark that sounded exactly like Peggy's.

Or rather, a bark that *was* Peggy's!

In that moment, Sally knew why the scent in the air was familiar – it was the candles Jools favoured to stop her home smelling of dog.

She was in Juliet's cottage.

The knocking sound came again.

'Hello? Police. Is there anyone in?'

Peggy continued to bark.

A thousand thoughts ran through her head at a speed so fast, she could barely catch hold of them but one came to a standstill and held fast.

Jools must also be in danger.

It was the only reason she could think of for her friend to be doing this. Did she have a boyfriend or someone who was forcing her to do this?

She heard a noise behind her and she turned her head towards it.

'Jools? Is that you?' she whispered.

'Oh, shit!'

This time, the voice belonged to her friend.

'It's over. Let me just get a hold of Peggy and—'

'No! Don't. Stay here and let her keep barking.'

'But—'

'Shhhh. They'll hear you.'

Sally felt Jools come to her side and gently remove the blindfold from her eyes. She blinked a few times and then looked about her while her hands and feet were released.

She rubbed her wrists and ankles but could barely see a thing as all the curtains had been closed across the windows, including the ones on the patio doors which led into the small garden. The only light in the room was from the laptop screen which Jools had placed on the coffee table to enable her to see to undo the bindings.

Jools went to stand up but Sally placed a hand on her shoulder.

'Wait…'

The two women sat in situ for several minutes after Peggy had stopped barking.

'Right, go and check they've gone.'

Jools walked over to the window and carefully moved the thick curtain a fraction to the side. The outside security light had gone off. There was no one there.

'They've gone.'

'Good! Now you can tell me what the FUCK is going on!'

The joint intensity of both anger and relief flooding her body had Sally trembling from head to toe and the desire to slap six shades of Sunday out of Jools was so severe, she had to force herself to walk over to the kitchen and stand on the other side of the breakfast bar. Right now, she could easily commit murder herself.

'Why, Jools? Just…why?'

'I was desperate. I'm so sorry.'

In the bluey-silver glow from the laptop screen, Sally could just make out Jools sitting on the edge of the sofa, her face buried in her hands.

'YOU were desperate? YOU? No boyfriend forcing you to do this?'

'Huh? Sorry?' Jools looked up at her in confusion.

'You did this off your own back? No one was forcing you to do it?'

'Erm, no. It was just me.'

Sally placed her hands on the edge of the worktop, dropping her head down between her arms, while taking in deep breaths as she tried to rein in her fury.

After a few minutes, she turned towards the fridge and took out two bottles of water. Walking over to Jools, she thrust one at her and then sat down on the seat opposite.

'Right, lady, start talking. And don't stop until you have told me everything.'

'In a nutshell, I'm in serious debt and I was… am… desperate.'

'How much and how did it happen?' Sally spat the words across the table.

'Just under three hundred thousand pounds.'

As she said this, Sally recalled the comment from earlier. "I need three hundred thousand…"

"I *need*…"

'I'm afraid I lied to you and Nick when I came for my job interview. The gap in my CV wasn't down to me working overseas – I was at home caring for my dying mother. I *had* been overseas but I'd barely been there three months when she called to tell me she'd been diagnosed with a terminal illness. Naturally, I was on the first plane back home.

'When I returned, we went to see her doctor who told us there was nothing he could do. The treatment my mother needed, the treatment that could possibly give her some extra time, wasn't funded on the NHS. The benefits of it weren't conclusive and so it hadn't been signed off. The only way we could hope to get it for her was to go private.

'So, that's what we did. I dragged her off to Harley Street in London where we met a very nice doctor who felt my mum would benefit from the treatment and he started her on it within a week. And it worked. It slowed down the progression of the disease and we got eighteen months more than we would otherwise have had.

'Unfortunately, private healthcare and Harley Street doctors don't come cheap and the bills began to mount up. At first, I was able to hold them at bay with doing locum work. The pay for that is generally better. However, as time went on, and Mum began to deteriorate, I had to stay at home with her. The job I do is not known for its sociable hours so I had to stop work and become her full-time carer. I did this for her last five months.'

Sally sipped her water and leant forward, listening closely. 'How did you manage to keep paying the medical bills?' she asked.

'Credit cards. I had a load of them which I'd never cancelled. You know that way, when you get an offer to transfer balances for a lower, or zero, interest rate? I always took advantage of such offers and in doing so, acquired several cards which were then at my disposal. They had high credit limits meaning I was able to spread the fees over them and get away with paying the minimum sum each month. I wasn't worried about the increasing balances, I knew Mum had a good life insurance policy – she'd mentioned it several years before – and I figured that would clear, if not all the debt, then certainly most of it.'

'So, what went wrong?'

'The policy falling through is what went wrong. Or rather, Mum missed one of the payments and the policy got cancelled.'

'Oh no! Surely the company could have worked around one missed payment. After all, how much was it? Thirty, forty pounds?'

'Ah, that's where my mum came into her own. She always paid everything off in one hit. She didn't like the idea of being in debt and never held with direct debits or standing orders. Therefore, if the yearly payment for an insurance policy was one hundred and fifty pounds, she would pay the full one hundred and fifty pounds.'

'Oh, crap!'

'Yeah, oh crap indeed!'

'And is there no one else in your family who could help with the bills? You haven't mentioned your father.'

'He died when I was a teenager. I do have a brother but he's an arse. Never once helped me with Mum, barely came to visit her and refuses to put anything towards the debt. He made his feelings perfectly clear after the funeral and we haven't spoken since.'

'Oh, Jools.'

Sally felt her sympathy placate the last remnants of her anger. What a terrible position to be in.

'The worst of it is, I haven't been able to mourn her loss because I've been so angry with her for letting the policy slip but then I feel guilty because I knew it was a result of her illness that she forgot and it wasn't intentional. The truth is, I know she'd be utterly horrified that she's left me in this position.'

'I'm guessing that, with only paying off the minimum over the years, the interest has clobbered you?'

'You guess correctly. The interest is now more than the initial debt. Even if I work 'till I'm a hundred, I'm never going to be able to pay it off.'

'Could you declare yourself bankrupt?'

'I could but that could have an impact on my job because good veterinary practices like their vets to be solvent so that partnerships – and cash injections – can be offered.'

'Ah! So, you thought thumping me on the head, kidnapping me, threatening me with a gun—'

'Err, not a gun. A glass test tube…'

'Say again! NOT a gun?'

'No. A glass test tube. If it's cold enough, it can feel like a gun. And, if held the right way, the imagination sort of fills in the blanks…'

Juliet's explanation tailed off and her head dropped down again in shame.

'It just gets worse!' Sally shook her head in

disbelief and immediately wished she hadn't when it began throbbing again.

'What on earth did you hit me with?' Her fingers touched the back of her head where a big lump was now residing although there was nothing to suggest any bleeding which was one small mercy.

'A junior cricket bat. I kept my brother's one from when he was a kid, for security purposes. I didn't want to hurt you, truly, I really didn't but when I saw all that money in your bank account—'

'Whoa! How did you see that? WHEN did you see that?'

'The day Flora came to tell you about the fete. We met on the stairs when I was going up to the office with the invoices? The office was empty when I walked in and I placed the folder on the desk where Craig would see it. As I put it down, it knocked the mouse which caused the blank screen to come back to life and there was the information, in plain sight. I'll be honest, I nearly keeled over when I saw it. It was that night when the idea first came to me to try and get some of it from you. I didn't want loads, just enough to clear the debts. That was all. I tried to ignore the thought but it continued to grow and fester until it felt like it was taking me over. I couldn't sleep and I certainly couldn't think straight. A small voice kept telling me it was a splash in the ocean to you. As you now know, eventually all reason flew out the window, I succumbed to the stupidity and now I've completely ruined everything. I'm going to end up in prison, my career is over and I have nothing left. I'll even lose Peggy. And all because I wanted to give my mum some extra time to live. It doesn't seem fair that by trying to do something good, I end up coming out of it all so badly.'

By this time, Jools was sobbing hard and the tears were pouring down her face. Peggy sat beside her, nudging her with her head, trying to give her some comfort.

Sally felt her own heart break for Jools. In that instant, she became aware of just how fortunate she'd been. Sure, she'd lost her husband in the most awful way but she'd had the luxury of worry-free grief. She hadn't had the stress of trying to care for children or family while not knowing how they were going to manage now that one of the wage-earners in the home was gone. She'd had the security of knowing the roof over her head wasn't going to be taken from her and had been able to dive right into her mourning without any financial distractions and she was only now realising that this made her one of the few lucky ones. Not every family could afford life insurance when it was a toss-up of paying the policy or a new pair of school shoes.

She was still annoyed with Jools for what she'd done to her but she was also deeply sorry that an otherwise decent, kind person had been pushed so far down the path of desperation that she'd go to such lengths to get off it.

'Jools,' Sally moved over to sit beside her and put her arms around her. 'You're not going to prison; I'm not telling the police and you're not going to lose Peggy. We'll sort this. It's okay. It's over now. I promise.'

As Jools clung onto her and cried out all the pain she'd held in for so long, Sally realised that there was something else she could do with her money. And Jools was just the person to help her.

FIFTY

Matt stood on the porch and looked out over the front meadows. The sky was no longer the darkest shade of black and was slowly moving into the hazy grey of dawn. Flora was curled up asleep on a chair in the lounge of the B&B. One of the two guests currently residing there this week had let her in when he'd returned from the conference centre the night before and after feeding Herbie, she'd kept the door on the latch so she could come and go throughout the night. Matt had told her to take the bed in the spare guest room but she said she'd waken quicker if she remained in an upright position.

'Mr O'Brien…'

He turned to see the detective walking across the tarmac so he stepped down off the porch to meet him.

'Any news?'

'Some but none that really helps us. We can rule Conners out of the equation. He was over the other side of Oxford getting a caution for causing a disturbance in a pub at the same time as you were talking to Mrs Edwards on the phone. Unless he can do time travel, I think it's fair to say he had nothing to do with this incident.'

'So, are there any other leads? Is that it?'

'No, not at all. But it does mean we're back to square one—'

Just then there was a shout and one of the police constables was pointing towards the courtyard. He ran around the side of the building, the detective beside him, and saw the surprising sight of Sally and Jools walking slowly over the old cobbles.

'Sally! Oh, my goodness…'

He pushed past the policewoman and dashed over to Sally, gathering her up in his arms and holding her tightly to him. He rained kisses upon her head until she let out a yelp of pain and he quickly released her, only then noticing the large bruised graze on the left side of her face and around her eye.

'What's wrong? Are you hurt? Where the hell have you been? Why didn't you call me back? I've been worried sick about you—' His voice grew louder with each question.

'Okay, Mr O'Brien, let's take it down a notch.' The detective placed a firm hand on his arm before putting his other hand out towards Sally.

'Mrs Sally Edwards, I presume? I'm Detective Allenson, Thames Valley Police. Is there somewhere we can talk? I think we need to clear things up here.'

'Err, certainly. Please, come with me.'

Matt just stood there until the detective looked

back and said, 'Well, aren't you going to join us, Mr O'Brien? I'm sure you're as interested to find out where Mrs Edwards has been all night as I am.'

'Oh, yes, sure.'

He followed Sally, Jools, and Allenson through the back door into her apartment. He was just pulling the door closed behind him when he saw Flora come around the corner. He waved to get her attention and waited for her to join them.

Sally pointed everyone to the lounge area and told them to take a seat.

'Can I get anyone a tea or coffee?' she asked.

Before anyone could respond, Jools took her gently by the arm and led her to one of the chairs.

'YOU will sit yourself down. I'll sort out the drinks.'

Matt watched Sally give her a tiny sheepish smile of thanks and sit down as she'd been instructed. She looked over and caught his eye, wincing as she gave him a quick smile before Allenson gave a small cough to gain her attention.

'Mrs Edwards, can you please tell us where you've been since approximately ten p.m. last night?'

'I've been over at the cottage with Jools. And, if I may ask a question, why are the police crawling all over my property?'

'Because I was talking to you on the phone one minute and then the next, you were gone! I came over here and you were nowhere to be found. I was worried and called the police.'

Matt spoke more sharply than he'd intended but he currently felt like a fool for panicking and was now worrying that he'd get done for wasting police time.

He saw from Sally's eyes that her temper was beginning to flare but before she could reply, Allenson said in a gentle tone, 'Mrs Edwards, would you mind filling me in on your movements from when you spoke to Mr O'Brien on the phone last night until we saw you walking across your yard? Everyone has been very concerned for your safety so please forgive us if we appear to still be on edge.'

He looked at Matt as he made this last comment and Matt felt himself bristle under his gaze. Sally also threw him a look which he couldn't quite decipher but he let it go as she began talking.

'Matt, I was talking to you on the phone and as you are aware, I was getting ready to make a dash for the house because the rain had let up slightly. Unfortunately, when I leant over the front seats of the car to get my handbag from the footwell on the passenger side, in my haste, I straightened up too quickly and thumped the back of my head on the top-sill of the car, just above the door. And when I say I thumped it, I mean I THUMPED it! There was a brief moment of seeing stars and then everything went dark. The next thing I know, Peggy's snout is pushing on my face and Jools was trying to bring me round and pick me up off the tarmac.'

Allenson turned to Jools with a questioning look.

'I was giving Peggy her last walk of the night,' she answered. 'Because of the rain, I took a much shorter, quicker route – around the back of the barn, up the side of the quarantine bay and then it would have been through the private car park and across the yard.

Except, when we reached the car park, Peggy began barking and ran over to Sally's car. The door was open and, with the aid of the interior light, I saw Sally lying on the ground. She was just coming round, moaning and groaning. Naturally, my first thought was to get her up off the wet ground into the dry and the most obvious option was to take her to my cottage.'

'Why?'

'Why what?' Jools looked flummoxed at the detective's question.

'Why go to your place? Why not bring Sally into her own apartment, especially as it was closer?'

'I didn't know where her door keys were and had no desire to waste time looking for them. Time was of the essence to assess why she'd blacked out and how badly she may be injured.'

'I see.' Allenson nodded. 'Carry on.'

'By the time we got inside, Sally was speaking coherently but saying her head was really painful. She was still a bit confused as to what had happened and with her hair being wet, I couldn't feel if she had a bleeding wound. I gave her some dry clothing and while she changed, I dried Peggy off. Once she'd done that, we went up to the surgery so I could properly inspect her injuries.'

'Why did you go to the surgery? And what time would this have been?'

'We went up to the surgery as it has an operating theatre which has excellent lighting for inspecting wounds. Trying to check a wound that is surrounded by fur or, in this instance, hair requires good light. Also, as you can see from Sally's face, she had an open wound which required cleaning. Again, good light is needed and I had the tools there to ensure it was properly cleaned.'

'Tools? Such as?'

'Extra fine tweezers for removing small particles of grit…'

'I see. And what time was this?'

'I don't know, I didn't check. Maybe about eleven-ish? A bit later?'

Allenson got up, walked over to the kitchen door, and stuck his head out. He called over one of the PC's and said a few words. Matt saw the PC take his notebook from his pocket and then show it to the senior officer. Allenson nodded, then turned round and walked back to his previous spot.

'My officers came to your cottage at eleven-forty-five last night but there was no reply. They knocked twice and your dog barked but no one answered.'

Jools and Sally looked at each other before Sally answered, 'So, that's what Peggy was barking at. We heard her but as Jools was in the process of stinging my face off with antiseptic, we weren't in a position to check. We returned to the cottage about ten minutes later and she had settled down again so I didn't give it any more thought.'

'Neither did I. I was too busy sorting out blankets for us to cosy up on the sofas in my lounge.'

'Are you telling me you didn't notice the lights or the police cars or the action going on around here?'

Jools and Sally looked at each other again before Jools replied this time, 'No, detective, we didn't. There's a high, closed, fence between the wall of the barn and the wall of the cottage – for the benefit of my dog – so we didn't see or hear anything when we returned to the cottage and I had earlier closed all the curtains inside to prevent Peggy being disturbed by the rotten weather. They're thick winter curtains so nothing penetrates through them, I'm afraid.'

'Why didn't you come home, Mrs Edwards, after Ms…' He turned to Jools with a questioning look.

'Turner,' she replied.

'… after Ms Turner had attended to you?'

'Because I'd suffered a head injury and she wasn't prepared to let me be alone in case anything happened.'

'Yet you were walking home at six in the morning?'

Sally sighed. 'Detective, I run a bed and breakfast facility and currently have guests who need to be seen to. As I'm in no fit state to do it, Jools has kindly offered to step in and help out.'

'So, you can assure me that nothing untoward occurred to you last night, Mrs Edwards, and that you merely suffered an accident with your friend here coming to your rescue.'

When Sally and Jools exchanged glances again, Matt saw a tiny flicker cross Sally's face. It was so brief you would only have noticed it if you knew Sally well. And he liked to think he knew her pretty well.

'Yes, detective, that's it in a nutshell.'

'Why didn't you call me to let me know you were safe? Surely you must have realised I would be worried?'

'I'm sorry, Matt, I never even thought.'

'Well, Sally, let's be honest,' Jools glared at him, 'you weren't really in a state to be thinking about other people. You'd just knocked yourself unconscious!'

'Right,' Allenson stood up, 'It would appear I'm no longer required here so we'll pack up and be on our way. Mrs Edwards, at the risk of sounding patronising, please take more care when exiting your vehicle in future. We don't want a repeat of this if we can help it.'

'I think I can manage that, detective. It's not something I intend to make a habit of!'

Despite the anger still simmering in his chest, Matt couldn't help but grin at Sally's feisty response to Allenson. He appreciated all the bloke had done through the night but he was still a bit of an asshole.

Once he'd left, Jools turned to Sally.

'Right, gorgeous, I'm off up to try and feed those two guests of yours. I hope they like charcoal toast and rubber eggs because my cooking skills ain't the best.'

'I'll come and give you a hand.' Flora stood up with a smile. 'Dad says my breakfasts are quite something so I'm sure between us, we'll be able to send them off without poisoning them.'

They giggled as they went out the door and when it closed behind them, the silence hung heavy in the air.

'So, how about you tell me the truth now that the police have gone.'

Sally looked at him. 'What do you mean?'

'Don't lie or fob me off, Sal. I've spent enough

time with you over the last year to know when you're not being truthful. Usually, it's to do with one of my suggestions that you don't like but this is more than disagreeing with the colour of tiles in the bathroom. I saw the looks between you and Jools and I'd appreciate it if you didn't treat me like a fool.'

He watched a range of expressions flit across her face until finally she looked at him and said, very simply, 'Okay. I'll tell you everything.'

An hour later, Matt sat back and rubbed his hands over his face. He couldn't believe what he'd just heard.

'So, you're telling me that Jools assaulted you, kidnapped you, tried to extort money from you and you *didn't* turn her in? Seriously? Are you mad?'

'No, Matt, I'm not mad. I've just explained to you why she did it. I'm showing compassion.'

'You're showing stupidity, you mean.'

'I beg your pardon?'

He got up off the sofa and began to pace around the room.

'How... how can you just let it go? She shouldn't be allowed to get away with that!'

'Matt, she made a mistake in a moment of desperation. Jools is not a bad person; she was just a desperate one.'

'You say that now – what if she comes back for more money? What then? You won't be able to go to the police...'

'She's not going to ask for more money.'

'How do you know that?'

'Because she didn't ask for more in the first place. All I keep hearing are her words "I need…" She never said, "I want…" she just said, "I need…" and that's enough to make me believe her. Not once did she ask for more than she needed. And she could easily have done so, there's plenty of money there after all.'

Matt drew in a deep breath at the reference to her bank account. Oh, yes, Sally had told him everything and he honestly didn't know which of her revelations had floored him more – the fact she was richer than the Bank of England, that Jools had kidnapped her for money, or that she'd lied to the police and was not only letting Jools get away with it but that she was also intending to give her the money! All of it beggared belief!

'Well, I think you're a fool to let her off and an even bigger fool to give her the money.'

'Yes, Matt, you're making that very damn clear but as it's my money, I can do with it what I like. Jools made me see how fortunate I was to be able to grieve for my husband without worrying about how I was going to pay the bills. Not many families get that luxury. So, with that in mind, I'll be looking into setting up a charity – only small and local – which helps people when they're left high and dry after a bereavement. I don't know all the ins and outs yet but I'm sure Craig can help me.'

'Oh, I'm sure he'll love that!'

'Matt, do you have a problem with the fact I have all this money? Because I'm certainly getting that feeling from you!'

He stopped pacing and turned to look at her. He'd

thought he was falling in love with this woman but now he felt he didn't know her at all. How could anyone have a bank balance of those proportions and be happy to be with a mere builder. Okay, sure, he was comfortably off from a financial perspective but he now felt like a Dickensian pauper compared to what Sally was sitting on.

Finally, he replied. 'I don't know what I feel right now, Sally, apart from right bloody stupid for calling the police and for worrying myself silly. You're not the woman I thought you were and yes, I have a problem with that. You're planning this fete to raise funds when you don't need to, you have all the money you need. People are volunteering their time when you could easily pay them. You've set this thing up under false pretences, I… I…'

He stopped. He didn't know what else to say. He didn't know what else he could say.

'Look, I'm going home. I'm exhausted. I've been up all night, *in the freezing wet cold*,' he couldn't stop himself from making the dig, knowing as the words left his mouth, how pathetic he sounded, 'worrying about you when clearly I needn't have bothered, so now I'm going home for a hot bath and some sleep.'

He was almost at the back door when her voice quietly followed him across the room.

'Will you call me later?'

He hesitated for a moment.

'I'll see.'

He let himself out, knowing as he closed the door behind him, that he wouldn't be calling her later.

Or anytime soon.

FIFTY-ONE

Sally slowly opened her eyes and squinted against the sunbeam which had slid between the gap in the curtains. South facing aspects were all very well and good, she thought, but she was definitely putting up a blackout blind for the summer.

She rolled over onto her back, stared up at the ceiling and gently prodded the new feeling of relief sitting inside her which had come about from finally sharing the news of her lottery win and her new venture with her family. She hadn't told them the full value of the win – there were limits, after all, to just how much they could handle – but had "awarded" herself just enough to justify her new businesses.

She'd invited her parents, along with her brother and his fiancée, down for Easter. They'd arrived early yesterday morning and after showing them to their bedrooms and giving them time to refresh themselves, she'd sat them down in the B&B lounge and told them everything before taking them out to show them around. They'd taken the news far better than she'd anticipated although the later response from her mother had left her more than a little astonished.

All through growing up and beyond, Sally had known that Chris was the apple of her mother's eye and it was the reason why praise seldom came in Sally's direction. She knew her mother loved her, of that there was no question, but she'd always felt second best. So, when her mother had pulled her back for a talk, as they'd all headed out for a tramp over the fields, she couldn't have been more surprised at what she'd said.

'Sally, I am so very, very, proud of you. Well done!'

'You're not annoyed with me for not sharing everything with you sooner?'

'No, not in the least. You explained why you kept your secrets for this long and, believe it or not, I do understand.'

'You do?'

Her mother stopped walking at this point and had turned to look into her eyes.

'I do. People don't need to know every part of your life, it's important to keep some of yourself back for you. You *needed* to go through with this new venture on your own and I will be the first to admit that had your father and I known of your plans, we most likely would have interfered in some way or another because we're your parents and it's one of the conditions. You were proving, first to yourself and then to the rest of the world, that you could do this and you could do it without anybody else.'

'I suppose…'

'Sally, don't sell yourself short. I know you believe I was harder on you growing up than I was with Chris but it was because I knew how much potential you had within you. You were so brilliant in many ways but you lacked direction. You never seemed to know what you really wanted from life and as much as your father and I wanted to push you down certain paths, we couldn't. You would only be happy from the choices you made yourself, not the ones we made for you. Unfortunately, you never really seemed to make any choices, you just floated along, letting life take you wherever it wanted. It was frustrating for me and I think I let that show more than I should have done.'

As Sally had had this same realisation herself just a few months previously, she couldn't argue with her mother on this point. At the same time, however, she wasn't about to let on that she agreed because she'd never hear the end of it in years to come if she did.

'You could say I got lucky with the lottery win. It wasn't all my own doing.'

'But, darling, look what you have chosen to do with that luck. You're paying it forward to help those less fortunate. Sweetheart, the tragedy which brought you here will never be forgotten and I would never have wished for you to go through something that painful but to see you so glowing and radiant now… well, it's all a mother could ever wish for her child.'

Darling *and* sweetheart in one breath? Sally was all set to phone Jools to come and check her mum hadn't received a bump to *her* head!

Her mother's final words, however, were the ones she would remember for a long time to come.

'My dearest girl, now that you've finally learnt to make your own decisions, don't ever stop. Trust your gut, and trust your instincts, because if all this proves anything, it's that you can do whatever you want, when you put your mind to it.'

Sally let out a little sigh of contentment, rolled back onto her side and curled her body around Herbert, happy to lie in her bed a little longer and just enjoy the moment.

Unfortunately, the moment was short-lived as thoughts of Matt barged in where they weren't welcome. She hadn't heard from him since the day after the storm – both literal and metaphorical – and she hadn't contacted him. Nor did she plan to. He'd walked out on her; it was up to him to make his way back. She'd done nothing wrong and therefore had nothing to apologise for.

Her mother had told her to trust her instincts but she was in a right quandary over Matt. Her instincts were telling her not to give up on him yet, he wasn't a terrible person, but her brain was screaming at her to kick him to the kerb and move on. The fact that she wasn't interested in moving on didn't seem to come into the equation.

A bigger sigh escaped through her lips and with a small growl of annoyance, she dropped a kiss upon Herbie's head before throwing back the quilt and getting up. The moment of peacefulness was now lost so she may as well get dressed and feed her family before they all headed down to the village to get on with the final preparations for the fete. As she walked over to open the curtains, she thought, well the upside of a late Easter is that at least the sun is shining!

'I now declare this fete, in aid of The Bramblebush Cat Rescue, open!'

Sally cheered and clapped along with the rest of the villagers as Ken Bartleby cut the purple ribbon with a pair of garden shears and then stepped aside as the crowd swarmed past him, anxious to visit their favourite stalls or be first in the queues for the funfair rides.

'Thank you, Pete, for arranging this with Ken. It really is something to have him here doing this.'

And she wasn't joking either. Ken Bartleby, the best-known newscaster in the country, and even more so after winning a certain, highly-popular, celebrity dancing competition on the television, was the name on everyone's lips at the moment and his presence here today had given the rescue a massive shot of publicity.

'I was happy to help, as was Ken.'

'How did you do it? Are you friends?'

'We are now. We met about eighteen months ago at some bash and he was telling me about his daughter. She has a disability and he asked me for an autograph for her as she was a huge fan but also if I could donate a couple of items for a charity auction he was putting together to raise funds for research and stuff. I offered myself as a date for the night, met his lovely daughter and family and we became friends.

When I asked him if he'd mind doing this, he jumped at the opportunity.'

'Hi, Pete, Sally, I hope that was all okay for you. I didn't waffle on too long, did I?'

Ken shook her hand again and thumped Pete on the back.

'Not at all, Ken, thank you so much again. This means a lot to me and for the charity.'

'It's no problem, I'm happy to help.'

'I was about to say, Sally,' Pete gave Ken a sidelong look before a cheeky grin rocked across his face, 'that Ken's wife and children are here today. Make sure you get them to your stall to make a few purchases. Ken has never been able to say no to either of his daughters.'

Ken grinned back. 'He's right you know, they have me wrapped around their little fingers, I admit it. So, what are you selling on your stall, Sally?'

'I'm in charge of signing people up for the cat adoptions…'

Pete burst out laughing at the look of dread which suddenly appeared on Ken's face and Sally couldn't help but join in.

'Er… right. I'm just off now to locate my ladies before we find ourselves with half-a-dozen new family members.'

'Good luck with that one, mate, they'll need to fight off Sukie first.'

The two men walked away, laughing and joking and Sally took the opportunity to quietly walk round and take in all that the wonderful ladies of the WI had pulled off. She checked the time – Essie was manning the adoption stall for the first couple of hours so Sally could do whatever meet-and-greet duties came her way and as she strolled by the stalls, she thanked the stallholders for being there and joining in.

The sun was high in the sky and the day was pleasantly warm. All around her people were laughing, smiling, and chattering. Some of the stallholders were calling out their wares and adding their voices to the general happy hubbub.

She caught Flora's eye as she passed the cake stand she was helping with. Both she and Sally had spent the last week baking in the big kitchen of the B&B. It turned out that Flora had quite a knack for it and her sponge cakes were as light as anything. Between them, they'd provided about seventy-five percent of the goods on offer; Sam from the Victorian tearoom had provided the rest in the shape of her home-baked artisan bread loaves.

Spending so much time together had also allowed Flora to have a good old moan about her father and his over-the-top stubbornness! She didn't know the ins-and-outs of their falling out and Sally didn't provide any information, but she knew something had gone down because her father had gone from dropping Sally's name into almost every conversation to now not mentioning her at all.

'I know he's had plenty of opportunities to come and speak with you but all of a sudden, he's decided he prefers to send emails. This is the man who thinks technology is the spawn of the devil but he'd rather do that than see you and apologise.'

'What makes you think he needs to apologise?'

'Because I know my father, Sally, and he's a stubborn, pig-headed old goat. I'm still arguing with him about visiting my grandmother in Scotland.'

'You could just go, you know, you're old enough.'

'I know I could but now that I've decided I would like to visit, after what happened with my mum, I'd prefer to go with his blessing. I wouldn't feel right in myself if I didn't have that.'

Sally had replied that she understood.

She walked past the last stall in the row and saw Jools speaking with a family while demonstrating the items in her first-aid kits. She exchanged a smile with the vet but felt a small stab of pain that the trust had gone from their friendship. Sally genuinely hoped that time would help to repair the damage caused by Juliet's actions because she was missing the easy friendship they'd been developing. As she turned onto the path that led towards the funfair, she saw Matt walking in her direction.

Her breath caught in her throat and the ache of seeing him for the first time in over two months slammed into her chest. His hair was slightly longer and she could tell from the golden tone of his skin that he'd been working outside. His blue eyes seemed even brighter against the slight tan which was enhanced by the brilliant whiteness of his shirt. Jeans and boots finished off his casual ensemble and Sally didn't think he'd ever looked as handsome as he did now. She normally wasn't one for having her photograph taken but she was glad now that today was a day of cameras being pointed her way because she'd taken care over her appearance and her favourite long, summery dress, with its little capped sleeves and large red poppies, gave her a confidence she didn't always feel. And right now, she needed every ounce of confidence she could muster.

'Matt.'

She inclined her head and made to walk past him but he put out his arm to stop her.

'Sally…'

She raised her head to look at him and hoped he couldn't hear the thumping of her heart. She waited for him to speak and used the moment to drink in the nearness of him.

'I…'

'Yes?' She cocked her head to one side. As her own pride kicked in, she realised how much she'd missed him and how much he'd hurt her with his silent treatment and overblown obstinance. Whatever he was about to say, she sure as hell wasn't going to make it easy for him.

'I…' His shoulders sagged and he ran his hand through his hair. 'You look lovely. That dress is very pretty, it looks good on you.'

'Thank you. With all the photographers around, I thought I should make some kind of an effort.'

He looked around them and then turned his gaze back to her.

'You've got a good turnout. You should make quite a bit of money from this.'

'I won't but other animal rescues will.'

'What do you mean?'

'I never thought the village would take the rescue to its heart in the way it has and I certainly didn't think they'd go all out on fund-raising for it. Therefore, on paper, the profits from today will come to the Bramblebush Cat Rescue but then donations adding up to the same value will be sent to other animal charities, from me.'

'You never told me you planned to do that.'

'Matt, you didn't give me the opportunity. Besides, I don't need to explain myself to you – you should have trusted me. If you cared for me at all, even if only as a friend, you should've known me well enough to know the kind of person I am.'

'I do know, I really do. It's the kind of person I am that I'm struggling to deal with.'

'Meaning?'

'I'm far too stubborn for my own good. I take the moral high ground far too easily and once up there, I'm pretty crap at finding my way down again.'

'I wouldn't disagree with that.'

'Would it help if I told you that I've missed you every single day, thought of you every single minute and was regretting my stupid actions even as I drove away that day?'

She gave a small shrug. He still hadn't said he was sorry and until he did, she was going to prove just how stubborn *she* could be.

'Sally, you forgave Jools for bashing you on the head, kidnapping you and trying to extort money from you. I've not even done a fraction of that.'

'No, but you have managed to think I'm an unscrupulous person who would happily take advantage of other people's good intentions. Jools has only ever held me in high esteem – can you honestly say the same?'

She saw a flash of pain cross his face before he lowered his head to stare down at his feet. A moment of silence passed and she was thinking that maybe she should just walk away when he looked up at her again.

'No, I can't,' he whispered. 'I can't say that and it makes me ashamed to know it. I am so sorry. Deeply, deeply, sorry. I shouldn't have doubted you. I know you're a good, kind person. I've seen it over the months and I just…'

He paused… and she waited.

'I think…' he stopped again and drew in a deep breath, 'No, I KNOW, that I was falling in love with you and I'm now fully aware that it was scaring the crap out of me. Despite all the years since Flora's death, I can still feel the pain of how it felt to lose her. I didn't want to feel that pain again and getting close to you meant I left myself open to it happening once more. I used that morning and your revelations as the excuse I *thought* I needed to step away. But it was already too late. I've been in pain since that day but this time it was worse because it was a pain of my own making. You were still here and I had pushed you away. I have no one to blame but myself.'

He looked away again and she barely heard his next words above the happy, piped music which suddenly started up from the nearby carousel.

'I'm so sorry, can you forgive me? Can we try again?'

She stepped forward and closed the gap between them. He'd said what she wanted to hear. It was time to let him off the hook.

'We can. But this time, we're all in, yeah? No more taking it slowly. Let's just go for it, jump in at the deep end and see where it takes us!'

His smile lit up his face along with the joy in her heart when he took her in his arms. As he held her close, he whispered, 'I can do that!' before giving her a kiss which told her in no uncertain terms, just how much he'd missed her.

The joy rapidly spread from her heart into every part of her being and she thought of how they'd both loved and they'd both lost.

And that they had almost lost again.

But they'd found their way back to each other and this time she wouldn't let him go so easily.

When he eventually released his hold on her, Sally stepped back and gave him a big grin.

'You know what I said about jumping in at the deep end?'

'Yes.'

She looked over his shoulder and smiled at the couple walking towards them.

'Well, you're about to meet my parents…'

AUTHOR NOTE

Some readers might feel that I have been somewhat 'preachy' in my descriptions of the suffering faced by those who work in animal rescues and I make no apology for this. The details I have given are barely the tip of the iceberg of what rescues centres see most days.

The saddest thing of all, and every rescue centre in the land will agree with this, is that much of the suffering could be prevented by the simple act of neutering. This is not cruel; cats do NOT need to have "just one litter" and it is as important for boys to be done as well as girls. It's not just about controlling the cat population; it is also better for their health – both short and long term. At the time of writing this, I recently had to say goodbye to one of Moggy Towers long-term residents. She'd fallen pregnant when only six months old – a mere kitten herself – and given birth to a litter of four. She came to us aged ten months. Unfortunately, she fell ill with kidney disease in her early teens and, most likely due to the nutrients taken from her body in her pregnancy, she succumbed very quickly to the disease despite our best efforts to bring it under control.

At this time, small home rescues are crying out for funds. These are the rescues who don't have fancy headquarters and advertise on the television – these are the people who work around the clock trying to give cats, dogs, and all other animals a better life after we humans have let them down. If you have been touched by what you have read here and wish to help, please look for a small, local, rescue who will appreciate anything you do.

Alternatively, if you would like to know more about Sally and her rescue, you can find her on Facebook under The ARC – the Ashmore Rescue for Cats.

ABOUT THE AUTHOR

Kiltie Jackson spent her childhood years growing up in Scotland. Most of these early years were spent in and around Glasgow although for a short period of time, she wreaked havoc at a boarding school in the Highlands.

By the age of seventeen, she had her own flat which she shared with a couple of cats for a few years while working as a waitress in a cocktail bar (she's sure there's a song in there somewhere!) and serving customers in a fashionable clothing outlet before moving down to London to chalk up a plethora of experience which is now finding its way into her writing.

Once she'd wrung the last bit of fun out of the smoky capital, she moved up to the Midlands and now lives in Staffordshire with one grumpy husband and another six feisty felines.

Her little home is known as Moggy Towers even though, despite having plenty of moggies, there are no towers! The cats kindly allow her and Mr Mogs to share their home as long as the mortgage continues to be paid.

Since the age of three, Kiltie has been an avid reader although it was many years later before she decided to put pen to paper – or fingers to keyboard – to begin giving life to the stories in her head. Her debut novel was released in September 2017 and her fourth book was a US Amazon bestseller in Time Travel Romance.

Kiltie loves to write fiery and feisty female characters and puts the blame for this firmly on the doorsteps of Anne Shirley from Anne of Green Gables and George Kirrin from The Famous Five.

When asked what her best memories are, Kiltie will tell you:

1. Queuing up overnight outside the Glasgow Apollo to buy her Live-Aid ticket.
2. Being at Live-Aid.
3. Winning an MTV competition to meet Bon Jovi in Sweden.

(Although, if Mr Mogs is in earshot, the latter is changed to her wedding day.)

Her main motto in life used to be "Old enough to know better, young enough not to care!" but that has since been replaced with "Too many stories, not a fast enough typist!"

You can follow Kiltie on the following platforms:

www.kiltiejackson.com

www.facebook.com/kiltiejackson

www.instagram.com/kiltiejackson